"If you think you know how a superhero novel is supposed to read, then you'll find *Playing For Keeps* a revelation. Part satire, part thrill ride, this saga of a ragtag band of superheroes with a most unlikely assortment of abilities starts at a gallop and then accelerates. Now the world knows Mur Lafferty's superpower: she can astonish us!"

—James Patrick Kelly, Hugo and Nebula Award-Winning Author

"Mur Lafferty's *Playing for Keeps* brings the super-hero novel down to street level: your street, populated by the everyday heroes you know, laugh with, and drink with. You'll raise a glass to characters with third-rate powers and first-class heart. This book made me cheer out loud!"

—Matthew Wayne Selznick, author of *Brave Men Run*

PLAYING FOR KEEPS

A Superhero Novel By
MUR LAFFERTY

MARTYN -
Thanks for everything -

[signature]

SWARM PRESS

WWW.SWARMPRESS.COM

PLAYING FOR KEEPS

A **SWARM PRESS** book
published by arrangement with the author

ISBN10: 1-934861-16-2
ISBN13: 978-1-934861-16-5
Library of Congress Control Number: 2008932545

Swarm Press is an imprint of Permuted Press (permutedpress.com).

Cover art by Christian Dovel.
Copy edited by Leah Clarke.

10 9 8 7 6 5 4 3 2 1

For Jim.

1

The supervillain attacked at the most inconvenient place and time: right on Keepsie's walk to work. She looked into the sky at the costumed combatants and groaned.

"Why did they have to do this on a Thursday?"

Crowds gathered on the sidewalk to stare up at the battle, clearly ignorant of the danger. Not to mention ignorant that they were making her late.

"Oh my God, it's White Lightning!" screamed a woman directly in Keepsie's way, pointing at the sky.

Despite herself, Keepsie looked up. She'd heard of the Academy's newest hero, but hadn't seen him yet.

The sinister laugh of some villain and the deep voice of the hero rang out above the excited crowd. A loud crunch of breaking glass and bending metal sounded above them as someone was thrown through a building. Keepsie guiltily hoped it was one of those damn holier-than-thou superheroes from the Academy hitting a skyscraper.

She held up her hand to block the sun. "Another building to repair."

Another crunch, and several people screamed. Keepsie stumbled as people slammed into her, desperate to get out of the way.

Keepsie had been watching to see if the hero would get out of the building. She grunted in alarm when a massive object ran into her. Her breath whooshed out and instead of falling underneath whatever had hit her; she was airborne, wedged painfully in a strong grip. She winced when she realized she was now five feet from one of the more prominent supervillains.

Up close, her abductor's commanding presence was even more frightening than on television; he was seven feet tall, bald, and handsome in a Harley-Davidson riding kind of way. He had a monocle implanted where his right eye should have been, and circuitry glowed under the skin around his neck and jaw line. She had seen pictures, but had never seen him up close: Doodad, Master of Machines. Although he looked as if he could punch out an elephant, she had never heard of Doodad participating in a physical fight. His power was in his brain, and his skill to bend machines to his will.

Doodad's flying crab machine had plucked Keepsie painfully from the sidewalk. When the news had shown pictures of the machine, Keepsie had giggled, reminded of the Jetsons' little hover car. Now, flying above Seventh City wedged in its one claw, it didn't seem so cute. Although the claw pinched her bruised ribs, she clung to it and forced herself not to look down. It wasn't as if she could fly.

On the whole, the villains didn't scare Keepsie, but heights terrified her. Doodad wouldn't drop her; he wasn't into blind terrorist acts like dropping innocents to watch them splatter. He always had a reason for his actions unlike some of the more homicidal villains like Seismic Stan. The wind pulled tears from her eyes and she gulped. At least, he'd always had reasons for his actions in the past.

Keepsie screwed her eyes shut as they gained altitude. Where the hell were the heroes that he'd been fighting? Her stomach turned at the unfamiliar wish for a hero. Or maybe that was the altitude.

Almost as an answer to her question, a booming voice said, "Put her down!"

And then he came; his glorious blonde hair perfectly styled and unruffled by the wind. He had apparently had time to restyle after freeing himself from the building Doodad had thrown him into. The hero filled out a black leotard and tights, his costume completed with a black cape with white lightning bolts covering it. A black mask covered his eyes, but allowed his blonde hair and chiseled jaw to show in true superhero glory. This must be the rookie, White Lightning. He flew, tall and proud, over the rooftops, straight for Keepsie and Doodad.

Keepsie gritted her teeth. *Be careful what you wish for. Why did it have to be the rookie?* She could have stomached being rescued by the veteran heroine, Pallas.

"Let her go, Doodad! You'll get nothing this way!" White Lightning said, his booming voice hurting Keepsie's ears.

"Tell them at the Academy, tell *her*, that if you want to see this woman alive, you'll send me Timson by midnight!" Doodad shouted back.

Midnight? Who would open the bar?

"You'd never drop her, you have too much to lose!" shouted the newcomer. He hovered about thirty feet from the flying crab machine. Keepsie's feet kicked in the breeze and she was thankful she'd worn boots today.

"Lose? What do I have to lose? Family? Job? People that I love? I had none of those to begin with," Doodad said.

The hero scowled at him, and something caught Keepsie's eye over the skyline. A news helicopter buzzed toward them, camera pointing right at Keepsie and her captor.

"Shit," she said.

"We don't negotiate with villains!" White Lightning said.

Good. Go for the textbook response. That'll convince him. This guy was an idiot. Was every other hero busy at the moment?

As the shouting match continued, a low whirring sound caught Keepsie's attention. The claw gripped her somewhat tighter, and she squirmed.

The hero raised his hands to the cloudless October sky and Keepsie realized too late what was about to happen. The lightning bolt snaked down and slammed into the machine, filling Keepsie's nostrils with ozone and her eyes with blinding light. The deafening crack came a millisecond later and Doodad's machine faltered in midair.

The rubber-padded claw squeezed tighter and tighter, causing Keepsie to cry out in pain and struggle against it, despite their altitude. Then it opened.

She fell.

2

Keepsie had always hoped that she would be heroic in a situation such as this, but her hopes that she would at least act dignified died when she screamed and didn't stop. She screwed her eyes shut as her stomach dropped away from her. In the abject terror that flooded her body, she still wondered in a moment of clarity whether her will was in order.

She stopped falling with a jolt, and a loud cheer rose from the street. Shamefully she clutched the hero's heavily muscled arms, but her fingers slipped over the spandex. They flew higher, to Keepsie's dismay, and circled the Jameson building, the tallest building in the city.

"Please let me down," she said, but the wind whisked her words away.

White Lightning waved at the news helicopter. Keepsie hoped it wouldn't see her. She clutched the hero's one arm and shuddered. Her mouth filled with nauseated bile. She hadn't been this close to a hero since she'd applied at the Academy ten years ago. She had never been in a damsel-in-distress situation before. She didn't think she liked it.

The hero turned toward the street and they finally started their descent.

This couldn't be over fast enough. He finally deposited her lightly on the sidewalk, and she looked up at her disgustingly glorious savior.

"Thank you," she managed to say.

A frown creased his blemish-free forehead. "Are you all right, miss? Did he hurt you?"

She shook her head and brushed her messy brown hair from her face. "I'm fine. You're new, aren't you?"

"White Lightning, Seventh City's newest hero." He smiled widely, reminding Keepsie of the high school quarterback who tried to get her into the backseat of his car.

"Flight and lightning control. Neat. No wonder they're happy to have you," she said.

He beamed. "I would like to hope so."

An awkward pause hung in the air between them, Keepsie realizing too late that he was hoping for another thanks. The crowd pushed closer, eager to touch his cape, get a picture, anything.

"Well, thanks again, and—"

"You're welcome, ma'am," he said, speaking loudly for the benefit of the crowd. "Incidentally," he added, "what's your name?"

"Keepsie."

"That's an interesting name. Is it Indian?"

Keepsie fought the desire to look pointedly at her very white skin. "Uh, no, it was a nickname given to me when I got my power when I was fourteen. I'm Third Wave."

His eyes narrowed. "Third Wave pseudonyms. Hero names are illegal, ma'am. Only registered heroes may have them," he whispered, and leaped into the air, flying toward Doodad's retreating vehicle, which was floundering through the sky and belching black smoke.

People cheered and waved at White Lightning, some women screaming that they loved him. Keepsie's adrenaline left her. She was cold with shame and anger. The news crew would be here soon; she pushed her way through the crowd and actually snarled when a starry-eyed woman asked her what White Lightning was *really* like.

The short walk to the bar failed to calm her down. "'Hero names are illegal,'" she said, imitating White Lightning's deep

5

voice. "Fuck you." Her voice sounded muffled to her own ears. She hoped the hero hadn't damaged her hearing.

Keepsie thrust her hands into her jacket pockets and sped up, hoping her deliveryman would wait on her. Her breath caught in her throat when her hand closed around an unfamiliar object.

It was a heavy metal sphere, about the size of a golf ball. Realizing that Doodad had slipped it into her pocket, she stuffed it back. She'd examine it later.

Her legs still shook with reaction as she approached the delivery truck waiting outside the stairs to her basement bar. Carl stood at the bottom of the stairs and peered through the window.

"Sorry I'm late, Carl," Keepsie called down to him.

He looked up and waved at her. "Oh don't worry nothing about it, I just got here myself 'cause traffic wasn't moving hardly at all," He climbed the stairs. "I think it was another one of those hero battles slowed things down." He handed her the clipboard and slid the door up on his truck.

"Yeah, I know. I got caught up in it myself. I had to get…" she made herself say the word, "rescued." She scanned the purchase order and didn't look at Carl.

"You shitting me?" Carl said, wheeling his loaded hand truck to the stairs. "You OK?"

"Of course," she said, sniffing. "The city's newest egotistical hero, White Lightning, personally rescued me from certain death and insulted me in the process." She slid past him on the stairs and opened the unlocked door.

Carl stopped the hand truck midway down the steps to stare at her. "Did you say 'White Lightning'?"

She grinned up at him. "Yep. He flew away so fast I didn't have a chance to tell him he named himself after mountain corn squeezins."

Keepsie went inside and turned on the lights, Carl's laughter still booming on the stairs.

\#

Unlike most bars, which depended on a Saturday rush, Thursday's were Keepsie's busiest night of the week. Her bar was popular with the locals; although it didn't have the usual hero memorabilia covering the walls like a lot of Seventh City's bars did, it did have the best bar food in the city. It was also the cleanest, with the best service in town. These made it a hopping place of business normally, but tonight was special. It was Third Wave Thursday.

Keepsie didn't put up any banners and she didn't have any specials, but it was an unspoken truth that the third generation of people with strange superhuman powers, named the Third Wave, gathered to drink together on Thursday. It was their night of solidarity.

Her staff had closed the bar in perfect condition, as always, the night before. The various little victories Third Wave citizens could claim were precious, and she appreciated each of her staff's talents. Keepsie's talent was not one that she could get paid for, which had always bugged her, but she was happy to hire a chef with super-cooking ability and a waitress with the inability to drop a bar tray.

She had little to do to open except check Carl's delivery and sign his invoice. She readied the kitchen for the chef and then checked the clock: good. Michelle, her assistant manager and closest friend, wouldn't be there for another five minutes at least, and the rest of the staff wouldn't get there for fifteen minutes after that.

She didn't relish telling Michelle about the afternoon.

She sat at the bar and pulled the ball out of her pocket. It was made of a dull metal and was seamless, like a large ball bearing. She rolled it around in her hands, listening for any noises inside. She heard nothing.

Why had Doodad dropped an oversized BB into her pocket?

The front door opened and Michelle walked in. Effortlessly beautiful as always, Michelle exuded the passion of her Jamaican father and the temper of her Irish mother.

"Hey lady, did you hear the news?" Michelle said, her dark eyes shining with excitement. She brushed past Keepsie and hung her coat and purse on a hook behind the bar.

Talking to Carl about the attack had been easy; he wasn't her friend, someone she saw daily, someone who knew the same people she did. He also wasn't someone who saw the villains as rock stars. Michelle's interest bordered on illegal, but a bill that Third Wavers had called the "Hero Worship Bill," which would make villain sympathizing a crime, had yet to get out of committee.

Keepsie bit her lip and slipped the ball into her pocket. She followed Michelle into the kitchen.

"I didn't hear the news," Keepsie said truthfully. "But—"

"Doodad fought this new hero guy, even grabbed a hostage!" Michelle could hardly contain her glee. "Then the hero rescued her and made Doodad crash."

"Do you think Doodad's hurt?" Keepsie said, knowing which part of the story Michelle wanted to focus on.

"There's no word yet, but they took him away in an Academy ambulance, so I think he's still alive. They usually take them away in a regular ambulance if they're dead."

The villain Seismic Stan had died five years before in a battle with Pallas, the city's oldest hero. But Keepsie didn't remember an ambulance.

"Guess you didn't get my message?" Michelle asked.

"No, what was it?"

"I left it on your cell's voice mail, telling you to take another way into work because the news was all about the reindeer games going on with Doodad," she said, tying an apron around her waist. "You must have been on the phone."

Keepsie gritted her teeth. "No, my cell phone just sucks. Thanks, though. Listen, I—"

"So did you see any action?"

"Yes, actually, Doodad—"

"Oh man, you saw him?"

"Michelle!"

Her friend finally stopped talking. Michelle was not someone who was offended when you told her to lower her voice or stop interrupting. She smiled expectantly.

Keepsie suddenly found it difficult to talk. "I was the hostage."

"Holy shit! Are you OK?"

Keepsie busied herself with stocking the already-stocked pint-glass tray. "Yeah. I mean, I got the shit scared out of me, I was nearly electrocuted, the hero humiliated me, I think my hearing is damaged and I may have cracked a rib." She lifted her shirt to view the blossoming bruises on her torso. "The good news is that Carl got caught in traffic too, so I wasn't too late to meet him."

"Jesus. Why you?"

Keepsie lowered her shirt and sighed. "He planted something on me. I don't know what it is." She pulled the ball out of her pocket and showed it to Michelle.

"Why would he—oh," Michelle said, her eyes growing wide. "He wants you to keep it."

Keepsie nodded. "My thought too. But who does he want me to keep it from? And does he really think I'll give it back to him after this afternoon?"

"I guess he does," Michelle said thoughtfully. "He's hot, but he's also smart. He probably wants it back at some point. And he probably thinks he can get it."

"Well, he's in the Academy jails now, so he's not coming for it any time soon. That's a relief."

"Poor guy," Michelle said.

Keepsie glared at her. "Can I get some sympathy for at least a second before you go all Stockholm Syndrome on me and are sorrier for the villain than his hostage?"

Michelle hugged her gently, mindful of her ribs. "I do love you, lady. But I still wouldn't kick Doodad out of bed for eating crackers."

Keepsie laughed at last. "Fine, fine. This guy wants to screw up the city, scare people, take hostages, and you want to reward him with sex."

"Someone needs to reward him for giving the heroes hell," Michelle said. "And I volunteer to take one for the team. Two, if he's up for it."

The door opened and other staff began to arrive, and Keepsie composed herself. She slipped into the kitchen and dropped the ball into the Lost and Found box that sat beside the supply closet. It would be out of the way there. And safe.

Keepsie didn't have a power that would help her tend bar, or cook, or fight crime. Her power was quite passive, but it serve to be useful to her. Anything she owned, she kept. It was that simple. No one could take anything she owned away from her. And if they tried, they quickly abandoned their desire to steal.

She had never considered it might be useful to someone else. She had been unable to get a job in security because no one trusted her enough to give her all of their belongings. The items in question had to belong to *her*, and no one would trust her without her official hero license. Doodad had given her his metal golf ball, clearly for her to protect from anyone else.

Why did he think she was going to give it back to him?

#

When the bar opened at five o'clock, it filled quickly. She greeted the regulars by name.

Her patrons talked about Doodad's attack. People had heard about it but apparently no one had seen the televised news. Keepsie said a quiet prayer of thanks.

As she tended bar, Keepsie kept out of the discussions.

"The heroes are a menace to the city. Hell, arson doesn't even do as much damage to property as one of those hero battles," said Geoffrey, a florist.

Vincent, Keepsie's busboy, dishwasher, cleaning crew—and anything else that had to do with dirt—bussed a table and nodded to him, his black hair falling into his eyes.

"What are our cops doing these days, anyway? Unemployment is up because the police don't have anything to do," said Stella, a human resources director. "And the damn villains can't be that hard to catch. Hell, heroes do it."

"What you do when a villain shows up is wait for the damn hero to save your ass," Barry said. He was First Wave, a generation ahead of most of Keepsie's patrons. He'd come into his strange power late in life after an accident had severed his legs; only then had he realized he could regrow his limbs. He stared into his daiquiri. "Face it, no one has powers to match the villains except for the heroes."

"And no one talks about this, but I remember. Did anyone notice how we never had villains until we had heroes? If the goddamn government hadn't messed with that drug, we wouldn't be living in a city where you can get a building dropped on you," said Len "Goddamn Government" Wise.

The bell above the door tinkled, and Keepsie looked up. She smiled and waved as her two favorite regulars, Peter Ross and Ian Smith, walked in.

Peter was a tall man in his thirties and dressed in a way that hinted that he still got his fashion tips from his mother. He took a seat at the bar beside Samantha, a newcomer to Third Wave

Thursdays. Ian, a pudgy man with stringy blond hair, loved arguing with Samantha more than he loved poking fun at stuffy Peter. He eagerly grabbed the seat on her left.

Samantha was older, Keepsie guessed around 45, and had gray streaks in her red hair. She and Ian launched immediately into a heated discussion about whether the Academy should have to pay for property damage. Keepsie grinned; they hadn't even said hello to each other.

Peter motioned to Keepsie, who finished pouring a beer for a man who looked uncomfortably out of place. "What can I get you, Peter?"

"Tanqueray and tonic, please." Peter said. He lowered his voice. "Are you all right, Keepsie?"

Keepsie blanched. "What are you talking about?"

"I went home early today because of the hero battle; my company's building was damaged. I saw the news."

"I'm fine. Can we talk about it later?" Keepsie said, and went to make his drink. She avoided his concerned gaze as she poured the gin. Ian and Samantha were arguing loud enough to distract her from her embarrassment.

"I'm telling you, Sam," Ian said, slapping his hand on the bar. "They're flying around, busting up buildings and shit, hurting civilians, and then they have the audacity to expect us to give them our tax money so they can go on and do it again tomorrow!"

Samantha remained calm. "I'm not saying that they deserve worship, but the recent villain attacks are far and above anyone's ability to deal with except for the Academy. No one knows where they came from, but they are definitely a force to be reckoned with." She took a sip of her beer.

"Ian's right, Samantha," Peter said. "I had one of the heroes thrown into my building today. He took out one wall of windows and injured ten of my coworkers. You won't see that on the news."

"Holy shit, man, are you OK?" Ian asked.

Peter smiled thinly. "I don't rank a window office." He cleared his throat and glanced at Keepsie.

"The Academy will make sure the injured are taken care of, and they also cover the building repairs," Samantha said.

"And what if someone dies, can they bring them back to life?" Ian said. "Can they regrow someone's severed arm?" He raised his

11

beer to Barry, a couple of seats down, who grinned and toasted him back.

Samantha raised her hands, giving up the argument. "You've got me. I don't think they have any heroes that can do that yet."

"And what about that hostage Doodad took?" Ian said. He grinned as Michelle walked by with a tray of empty pint glasses. "I'll bet you wish it was you up there, huh?"

Michelle laughed. "No, sadly. But man I'd give anything to meet Doodad."

Peter stared at Michelle for a moment, his jaw slack. He recovered quickly. "Doodad snapped her up off the street and carried her away, but, as the news tells it, White Lightning saved her." Keepsie glanced up; he wasn't looking at her. "I don't think she was hurt."

Ian, not catching on, groaned. "White Lightning? Who the fuck is that? A new one?"

"So it seems. But from my office, it more looked like White Lightning attacked Doodad while he held the hostage, causing the villain to drop her. She nearly hit the ground before he caught her."

Michelle handed Keepsie a check and a credit card. "She's a little bruised but she's OK, right Keepsie?"

Ian gaped. "You?"

Keepsie glared at Michelle. "Thanks a lot."

"Whoops, I figured you'd told them."

"You OK?" Ian asked.

"Do I look hurt?" Keepsie said.

"That's not what I meant," he said.

Keepsie grimaced. "I'm... fine. A little bruised, and I'll probably never fly again, but," her voice took on a sarcastic edge, "I got to meet a *real hero*!"

Samantha smiled, but most of the others looked concerned.

Michelle finished the credit card transaction for Keepsie. "Well, they were bound to find out anyway. And they would have been pissed if you hadn't told them." She took the slip and card and headed back to her customers. Keepsie sighed and watched her go.

Ian snickered. "What, is Michelle mad you got to meet Doodad and she didn't?"

Keepsie forced a grin. "Actually, I think she is."

Peter still looked concerned. "Keepsie, did anything else happen?"

Keepsie dropped her head and fiddled with the bar rag. "He was a real bastard. The hero, I mean. I mentioned to him—well, he figured out I was Third Wave. And after he let me down he pretty much treated me like crap."

"Fucking heroes, think they're better than all of us." Ian clenched and unclenched his fists rhythmically. He took a deep breath and relaxed. "He's just an asshole, man. A flying asshole."

The image of White Lightning, buff and ripped in his tight costume, with a sphincter sitting atop his shoulders, made Keepsie laugh.

The night wore on and Keepsie kept busy, trying not to relive her afternoon's adventure any more than necessary. She gave a few more details to Peter, Ian, and Samantha, but left out the bit about Doodad planting something on her.

"So I said that the villains clearly come from Washington DC," Barry's companion said as Keepsie handed Barry another banana daiquiri. She didn't recognize the man, and she eavesdropped as she made change for Barry's ten.

"What makes you think that?" asked Barry.

The man's voice slurred slightly, but his eyes were bright. "They're making them in Washington to battle the terrorists, and the experiment went wrong!"

Barry shook his head. "So, why do the villains come here where the heroes are? Wouldn't it be easier to go somewhere that doesn't have heroes?"

His companion lapsed into a brief silence. "They're from Washington, I tell you," he said, and dug into the burger Michelle set in front of him.

"What do you think, Keepsie?" asked Barry as she set the man's beer down.

Keepsie opened her mouth to answer, but froze when something on the staircase outside caught her eye. Barry followed her gaze and swore loudly.

All conversation in the bar ceased as every eye turned to stare at the tall, glorious visitors. The heroes stopped as they got inside the door and looked around, frowning.

White Lightning (*Corn Squeezins*, Keepsie thought, and smiled slightly) lead the group inside and stared at Keepsie. The Crane joined him. He was a man around forty years old with white wings and the power to stretch any part of his body. He had been the dreamboat of the Academy, but Keepsie guessed that would end as soon as White Lightning became more popular. The other was an Academy scientist; shorter and older, she wore slacks and a lab coat with the Academy insignia on the breast pocket. Her short brown hair neither flowed nor gleamed.

"Dr. Timson, it's been a long time," Keepsie said, after a moment of silence.

"Laura, we're here to make sure you're all right. The Academy is obligated to pay the medical bills of anyone hurt during a powered altercation."

They didn't look like they were there to check on her. Why would she need muscle for that?

"Took you long enough," Keepsie said. She checked the clock on the wall. "The attack was at least six hours ago."

"We were just concerned, Laura. White Lightning had to file his report; he didn't have your full name. It took some time to find you."

Keepsie laughed. "The Academy is right across the street from here. The sign for my bar, 'Keepsie's Bar,' is right outside."

"Yes, you are called Keepsie now, aren't you?"

"You knew that when I applied at the Academy, Doctor."

"Secret identities are for heroes, Laura."

An annoyed rumble passed through the bar. Keepsie chewed on her lower lip a moment, then said, "I guess you'll have to go arresting every Christopher called Chris and every Michelle called Shelley. I didn't know that nicknames were illegal."

"Very well, *Keepsie*," Timson said, "We came for another reason; we need to talk. Do you have an office?" She looked around.

"This is a bar."

Dr. Timson sighed and stepped forward to close the distance. The patrons of the bar made no pretence of their eavesdropping. "We need your help. The villain Doodad has stolen an object of some importance from the Academy. After hearing about his attack earlier today, I think that Doodad targeted you specifically. We think he planted the device on you for, ah, safe keeping, so to speak. We need it back."

Keepsie grinned, delighted. "You want the help of a Third Wave power? I never thought I'd see the day. That's awesome!"

Dr. Timson smiled back, looking relieved. She took a step forward, "Yes, very much so, your talent would be of great help right now."

Keepsie leaned forward, still smiling. "No."

Tension in the bar increased. Keepsie squirmed inwardly, there was no backing down now. Not in front of her customers and friends.

The heroes glanced at each other, but only the doctor spoke. "White Lightning said you might react this way."

White Lightning met Keepsie's eyes without flinching.

"He's smarter than I gave him credit for. What did you think my reaction would be, doctor?"

"Well, I expected you to want to serve your city. You seemed quite dedicated to that, once."

"You know, you people just don't get it. You say you want to educate people with powers, to teach them to use their power for good, to help people. Maybe the Third Wavers can't fly or shoot laser beams, but we've still got powers no one else has. And you wanted us to register those powers so you could track them."

Timson opened her mouth, but Keepsie continued. "You gave us hope that we'd be heroes once we registered. That one day we'd put on a costume, serve the public, be worshiped. But Third Wavers are just not powerful enough for you. No hero license for us. But when you realize you need us, you come asking for help in the name of goodness, or God, or country."

She paused, enjoying the looks on the heroes' faces. "Well screw that. You have people who can talk to animals or run faster than cheetahs or call lightning to hit people and deafen their hostages. You don't need me."

"Hell yeah!" shouted Ian, pounding his empty glass on the bar. Everyone took up his cheer.

Timson stood impassively.

When the noise had died down, Timson spoke in a tight voice. "Keepsie, I don't think you understand. We need you. We need that piece you're protecting."

"Hey Ian," Keepsie said. He grinned. "Suddenly they need me. Would you come if they ever needed you?"

Ian made a face. "Maybe to keep the city's janitors busy."

"What did they say when you applied at the Academy to obtain a hero's license?" she asked.

Ian didn't meet her eyes, the shame apparent on his face, but he spoke clearly. "After they tested my power they told me that I was disgusting and unsanitary and clearly couldn't fight for the city, simply on the basis that the clean-up costs would be monumental. They said they would never need something so foul. But they gave me my very own hero name. 'Feculent Boy.'"

"Wonderful. Flattering," Keepsie said, facing Timson. "And you, yourself, told me my power was so weak it could never be of any use to anyone. You need to be careful what you tell the young and impressionable, doctor, it may come back to bite you."

White Lightning's face reddened and Keepsie felt giddy at the risk she'd taken. Years of bitterness, pouring out of her. It felt good. She didn't think he would attack her, but lightning in a basement bar would be bad for business.

Timson looked at Ian. Her lip curled and she swallowed, saying, "Not everyone has what it takes to be a hero." She tried to continue, but boos and hisses from the bar patrons drowned her out.

"You are extremely lucky that you just ended up with a bitter man instead of someone truly evil, Timson," Keepsie dropped the honorific purposefully. "Ian is a good man. And he's the most powerful Third Waver I know. And you guys dumped him in the gutter.

"So let's get down to business." Keepsie leaned forward on the bar. "What will you give me for doing this favor for you? My own license? Money? The respect *they* get?" She waved her hand at the heroes.

Timson cleared her throat. "There is the greater good to think about—" she began, and the bar booed her loudly again.

Keepsie laughed. "Does White Lightning use his powers for the greater good, or does he get money from my taxes so he can protect everyone?"

"Including you!" White Lightning said. "I saved your sorry life today!"

Keepsie snorted. "And now I owe you? Does everyone in Seventh City owe you? No. We pay our taxes and that pays your salary. And really," she added, looking his perfectly shaped body up and down, "I really can't respect anyone who names himself after moonshine."

Her audience laughed and White Lightning clenched his fists.

"I offered you my services once," Keepsie said to Timson. "You said no. I moved on. No takebacks. Now, are you going to order a drink or am I going to have to ask you to leave?"

"Keepsie, the object belongs to us," Timson said. "You can't keep it."

Keepsie slammed her hand flat on the bar. "That is where you are one hundred percent wrong, Dr. Timson. You said it yourself, keeping something safe is the only thing I do well, and if keeping it makes life tough for you, then I will be proud to keep it. Thanks to my 'useless' talent, there is no way you can take it."

The heroes stood uncomfortably as she stepped out from behind the bar, walked over the door, and put the CLOSED sign in the window. She opened the door and waited.

"There are ways we can make you give it to us," White Lightning growled.

"No, there aren't."

"Kinda losing your 'hero' routine there, aren't you, dude?" Ian said. He got off his bar stool and started rolling up his sleeves. Peter put his hand on Ian's arm as White Lightning stepped forward.

"Try it, little man," he said.

"Don't," Peter said. After a pause, Ian sat down again. Dr. Timson put her hand out as well to stop White Lightning. She gave Keepsie a long look and then motioned the heroes to leave.

Keepsie had only heard such applause in her dreams.

3

Peter watched Keepsie down drink after drink, at first celebrating with her, and then, as she got drunker, becoming more concerned.

Peter, Ian, Keepsie, Michelle, and Samantha sat at the bar in relative quiet. Most of the customers had left, each pounding Keepsie on the back or hugging her. "Give 'em hell, girl!" said Barry as he left.

Hell indeed. While it had been quite cathartic to watch Keepsie use her minor talent (that of allowing no one to take what she owned) to confound the pompous heroes, it seemed to be a bad idea to make enemies of the strongest people in the city, possibly the world. Peter didn't like the look that the heroes had given Keepsie on their way out.

Peter hoped Keepsie was done drinking; Patricia, the waitress with the power to sober people up, had the night off. Peter had assumed he'd left his dragging-drunken-friends-home days back in college.

Ian and Samantha were no help. They had kept up with their host, matching her drink for drink. Michelle had slowed down after a few drinks.

"This feels so weird," Keepsie said. "It's not like I'm evil. I never wanted to be evil. It's like we've always been told that heroes are good and the people that fight the heroes are bad. Am I evil? Do I need a laugh now? An evil laugh?"

18

Ian snickered. "I don't think so, Keepsie. Not letting the heroes fuck you like a drunk prom date isn't a bad thing."

"So what were they after, anyway?" Samantha asked.

Keepsie didn't respond. "It was just so cool to see them grovel. They've been so—" she groped for a word, screwing up her face with effort, "superior for so long."

Samantha didn't pursue her question. "Well, they are stronger than us. Do you really hate them so much?"

"I didn't have high hopes for the Academy," Keepsie said, pouring more vodka into her glass and spilling a bit on the bar. "My talent is passive, after all. But sheesh, what Third Waver didn't dream of joining the Academy on the off chance they say, 'Why yes, we do have a large stash of doubloons to guard, here's your costume, welcome to the Academy!'"

They all nodded.

"When Michelle and I talked about opening this bar," Keepsie said, frowning, "we just wanted a place to go where we could get away from them. I was really pissed off, guess I still am, but I didn't figure I'd end up evil."

"I had a hunch," Michelle said, grinning at Keepsie. "You have those dark thick eyebrows, you clearly cheat your customers, and you're just a hair above eating babies. When we got kicked out of the Academy, I knew you'd head toward villainy. Why do you think I stuck around so long? I'm protecting the world from Keepsie the villain!"

Peter was familiar with this story. Keepsie and Michelle had met when they applied at the Academy on the same day ten years earlier. They had been rejected immediately after a quick test each, and had gone looking for a drink together. The closest bar had been two blocks away and was a hero-worship area, signed pictures all over the walls, an old costume of Pallas's, and other memorabilia. They had decided then to start their own bar, close to the Academy, to cater to First and Third Wavers.

Ian picked at a spot on his chin. "It's a gray area. We're not good or bad. It's not like hoping the good guys lose means you hope the bad guys win."

"Exactly!" shouted Keepsie, banging her hand on the bar and making them all jump. "That's what I'm saying! Do I want this city run by Doodad and his little spidery things and smoke bombs and shit? No. But do I want these freaks to screw up the city and take all the credit and get a salary from my tax dollars? They can't even give themselves reasonable hero names! I mean, White fucking Lightning? Come on!"

"However," Samantha said quietly, fixing her brown eyes calmly on Keepsie, "who says we can't work apart from them? We can't work with them as heroes, but why can't we work for the same goals? And if we happen to trip them up in the meantime, well, then...." She grinned.

"Who says we can't do it?" Michelle said, staring at her. "Are you nuts? The government, that's who. The cops do their jobs, the heroes do their jobs, and us proles go about our daily business and kiss their asses. Without a badge or a license, we're vigilantes and rogues setting ourselves up to be arrested by people stronger than us. Everyone knows that, where the hell have you been?"

Samantha's cheeks colored. "I wasn't sure. I never registered with the Academy."

"Hey, really?" Ian asked.

"Never."

"You know, I don't think I know what your talent is," Ian said, leaning unsteadily towards her.

Samantha didn't look up. Her hair obscured her face, and she muttered something low.

"Sorry, I didn't hear that," Ian said. Samantha remained silent. "Look, Sam, I probably have the worst talent ever. You saw them when they looked at me. I make people sick when they see what I can do. What kind of talent is that for a good guy? Yours can't be worse than mine."

"How old would you guys say I am?" Samantha asked, looking up and brushing her hair back. Gray streaks stood out against her curly brown hair and fine lines marked the soft skin around her eyes.

"Oh, no, I'm not going there," said Ian. "That's up there with, 'do I look fat?'"

"All right, I'll ask it another way. Do I look twenty-two?"

Ian glanced at Peter who shook his head. "Um, no?" Ian said.

"I'll be twenty-two next week. My particular power comes with a rather strong curse. I can know anything, I'm fairly sure. But each piece of information costs me, I figure about a year off my life. When I was going to apply to the Academy, I decided it was worth it to use one of those years. I found out that if they had taken me, I would be dead of old age within a year. My information would be so useful that the cost to me would be acceptable in their eyes. I discovered my power when I was twelve, and I used it several times for stupid stuff—I won a lot of bets on sports games and elections—until I woke up one morning and discovered that my joints ached and my hair was gray.

"No one else knows about my power except my parents. I just came here because it was a bar where the heroes didn't hang out. Once I discovered what they would have done to me, I cancelled my plans to apply and have been living off the money I made with my bets." She raised her glass to her lips and sucked at an ice cube.

No one spoke. Keepsie screwed her eyes shut, apparently trying to focus. "Shit. That really sucks."

Peter smiled. "Succinctly put. Would you mind if I got you some water?"

She shook her head.

Ian hopped off his stool. "I'll get it, I gotta whiz anyway." He staggered toward the bathroom.

"It's brave of you to tell us this," Peter said. "Who's to say one of us isn't an Academy agent? Or someone working with Doodad? There are a lot of people who would love to get their hands on your particular talent."

"Oh, there's no Academy agent hanging out at Keepsie's," Samantha said, grinning. "What do we have to hide? Patricia's sobering power is not in danger of taking over the city. And Peter, are you planning on smelling your way to villain-hood anytime soon?"

Peter smiled thinly. He didn't like to talk about his power very much; the power to determine private information about someone by smelling them had always felt shifty and perverted to him. He tried to avoid using it at all costs.

Ian came out of the bathroom and headed into the kitchen.

More somberly, Samantha said, "I got tired of keeping the secret, I guess. I don't have any friends besides you guys, and I got tired of lying to you."

"That's beautiful, Sam," Keepsie said, hugging her.

"Dear Lord," Peter mumbled. "Ian, where is that water?"

Ian didn't respond. Peter and Michelle exchanged glances and slid off their stools, leaving Keepsie and Samantha to proclaim their undying friendship to each other.

Ian came out from the kitchen just as they reached the door. His mouth was set in a flat line and he had lost all pretense of drunkenness. "Did you know what Keepsie can do? I mean, like how powerful her talent is?"

Peter shook his head. "All I know is people can't steal from her. I've never seen it in action."

"I have," said Michelle. "Who was dumb enough to steal from her?"

Ian grimaced. "You're about to find out. And she's no help right now. Let's just hope her talent works when she's bombed off her ass."

Keepsie had passed out on the bar, Samantha making a messy pillow for her with bar napkins. Peter sighed.

Ian motioned for them to follow into the kitchen. "I was getting her water when I saw this." He pointed at the floor beside the supply closet.

A large cardboard box sat to the right. "Lost and Found" was written in black marker on the side, and various books, backpacks, umbrellas and other discards lay inside waiting for their owners. Everyone knew Keepsie's lost and found was safe, because anything lost in the bar became the property of Keepsie, and therefore stayed there until she allowed it to leave.

The man sitting in front of the box apparently did not know this. He was the most plain and nondescript man Peter had ever seen, the everyman, the perfect spy. Or the perfect villain.

His brown hair was just a little too long, with enough dirty blond in it to make it look sad and forgettable. His hazel eyes seemed to switch between green and blue as he looked at them with a steady gaze. His age hovered around thirty, but Peter could see him looking younger or older with little effort.

The man sat on the floor with one arm reaching inside the box.

"Dude. It's Clever Jack," Ian whispered.

The most notorious villain since Seismic Stan grinned up at them and waved with his free hand. "Hi there. Can someone go get Keepsie for me? I'm kind of stuck here."

#

Ian and Peter made small talk about Keepsie's afternoon while they waited for the very irritated Patricia to arrive. Michelle had found the waitress's cell number on a phone list in Keepsie's small office.

"Huh. So she did have an office in the bar," Ian said.

They had called Patricia, apparently interrupting her on a date. After they impressed the importance to her, she finally said she'd come, but she had better be able to clock in overtime, and she was owed a day off.

"Sure thing, whatever you like," Michelle said.

Samantha made her apologies and said good night, begging drunken tiredness. "Tell me everything that happens tomorrow night, right?" she asked. Peter nodded.

Patricia arrived twenty minutes later, looking as if she had been drinking about as much as Keepsie had and did not appreciate being summoned. She stumbled a bit on her high heels and accepted Peter's steadying hand with bad grace.

"You're going to make this up to me, right?" she asked.

"Yes. We wouldn't ask you to—"

"I know," Patricia said, "You told me on the phone. It's 'really important.' Incidentally, my date with Marc Sneed, an *executive* with Seventh City Bank and Trust, was kind of important too!"

Ian scowled at her. He grabbed her by the elbow and dragged her, protesting, to the kitchen door. "If your date with Moneypants is more important than a villain who is currently stuck in Keepsie's kitchen, with Keepsie passed out and unable to free him, then you just go right on back to him. Why don't you let the Academy know about this on the way, and maybe you'll get a better job there than you will have lost here!"

Patricia's eyes got wide. She peeked into the kitchen, the color draining from her cheeks. She walked over to Keepsie and placed her hand on the back of her head.

A strong whiff of alcohol permeated the air, as if someone had spilled a bottle of vodka on a hot radiator. Keepsie raised her head off the bar, scowling.

She smacked her lips a couple of times. "Isn't it your night off?"

"Hey, don't look at me, I've got a date to get back to," Patricia said, taking her coat from Peter. "Now, before I go, does anyone else need me? I'd like to be left alone for the rest of my evening."

Peter gave Ian a look.

"No, man, I'm cool," Ian said.

Peter raised his eyebrows. "You're prepared to deal with that?" He pointed to the kitchen.

"Fine, Dad, whatever," Ian said.

After sobering Ian up, Patricia headed for the door. "Enjoy your battle with the villain, but don't get into too much trouble. I need this crappy job where my bosses call me in the middle of my night off."

"There goes *her* raise," Michelle said lightly.

Keepsie rubbed her face. "Someone want to tell me what's going on? I mean, I appreciate the lack of hangover tomorrow, but Patricia's not someone we want to lose."

Ian looked at Peter. He took a deep breath.

"Keepsie, that thing that the heroes were trying to get. Where did you put it?"

Keepsie's eyes narrowed. "In the Lost and Found box. It's still there."

"Oh, yes," Peter said. "Only I believe someone has tried to steal it from you. I have to commend your power, Keepsie, I didn't know it was so effective."

Keepsie's eyes widened. "Who would be stupid enough to—"

"Clever Jack," Ian said in a low voice.

Keepsie gave a low whistle. "Whoa. I didn't know he was back in town."

"Peter thinks he's, like, working with Doodad or something," Ian said. "I don't think Doodad told him not to steal from you, though." He grinned.

"He's in there right now? Stuck?" Keepsie asked.

"He's not going anywhere," Peter said. "That's why we had to sober you up. This is all you, Keepsie."

"But we can't fight a villain!" she said. "Then again, I'll be damned if I call the Academy to help. If I set him free, he'll have that thing Doodad gave me. And if I don't, he'll be stuck in the kitchen. Colette won't like that."

Peter smiled at the thought of the boisterous cook having to step over Clever Jack every time she needed to leave the kitchen.

"Well. We could talk to him," Ian said after a pause.

They gaped at him. "You do know who he is, right?" Keepsie asked.

"Yeah. I mean, I've heard the stories. But they can't all be true, can they?" Ian asked, looking uncomfortable as they all started shaking their heads.

"I've seen him in action, he's the real thing," Peter said. He winced at the memory. Clever Jack had a passive power much like Keepsie's. His incredible luck kept him alive in any circumstance, giving him the dexterity to dodge attacks and attempts to capture him. This power also allowed Clever Jack to be impossibly accurate with any weapon. Peter had seen him throw a steak knife and pin two police officer's hands to a wall, one on top of the other. He had escaped handcuffs without incident and gunfights without a scratch.

How had Keepsie's power caught him, then?

"I think," Peter said, "you need to tell us what happened today, and what this mysterious item is."

Keepsie sighed and told them the story of her capture, the drop Doodad had made, and her attempt to figure out what it was.

She held her thumb and forefinger together to make a circle. "It's just a ball bearing about this big; no seams, no obvious use."

"Doodad's mechanical power is probably what drives it, whatever it is," Peter said. "Why did he plant it on you just to have Clever Jack steal it back?"

"Hell if I know," Keepsie said. "Maybe they're not working together after all. Maybe we *should* talk to him."

They groaned.

"I know, but we have to do something," she said. "Besides, he asked for me." She stepped forward and put her hand on the kitchen door.

Her friends remained motionless. Keepsie looked over her shoulder. "Are you coming?"

4

Keepsie took a deep breath. She'd had Patricia's sobering services before, but it was always disorienting to lose a good strong drunk in the span of two seconds. It was rather like a deep-sea diver surfacing too quickly, although there had been no apparent risk of catching the bends with sobering up in an instant.

She had no idea what she would say to Clever Jack, but she pushed on the door and entered the kitchen.

He sat exactly where her power had trapped him. His arm was stuck inside the Lost and Found box, and he looked up at her, smiling.

"Ah, so you're Keepsie. I wasn't sure which one you were," he said. "I'd shake your hand, but you've already got it in a pretty tight grip."

Keepsie didn't laugh. "Yeah, I was the one outside trying to enjoy a little celebration. What do you want?"

"Hey, calm down, I'm not the enemy. My friend Doodad dropped something today, I'm just trying to get it back for him." Damn, but he was friendly.

Keepsie felt her friends' presence behind her and took a deep breath. "I don't think you understand me. I know what you're trying to steal, but what is it? What do you want with it?"

Clever Jack looked at Keepsie as if she were slow. "Oh, that's not important right now. The important thing is that you get me

26

out of this box. I just need to get Doodad's toy back and I'll be on my way."

"So first I'm being used by the heroes, then the villains?" Keepsie frowned.

Clever Jack looked offended. "Now why did you have to go and use that word for? I thought you had no love for those hero-types, and here you are putting down myself and my friend Doodad."

"You're the one trying to steal from her, at least the heroes had the decency to ask first," Michelle said, stepping forward.

Keepsie glared at her. "What?" Michelle whispered, looking wounded.

"This is Keepsie's show," Ian whispered to her. Michelle stepped back, glaring at Ian.

"True, but it was never hers to begin with," Clever Jack said. "It was Doodad's. He loaned it to her."

"Now that's where you're wrong," Keepsie said. "If he gives it to me, it's mine. No take-backs." She thought for a moment. "So how did Doodad know about me, anyway? And how did the heroes find out that I had the—whatever it is?"

"And what the hell is it, anyway?" Ian asked.

Clever Jack smiled, his hair falling into his eyes. "I'll tell you if you free me."

Ian snorted. "Dude, I've heard all sorts of stories about you and your power, you're like a god in some of the small towns around here. Fuckin' Robin Hood without the whole giving to the poor thing. But you've avoided the cops, the heroes and the Academy goons only to get caught by a woman thrown out of the Academy for being too weak!"

Peter nodded slowly. "Yes, I don't think you're really in a position to bargain. Keepsie can keep you there until she decides it's time for you to be free, no sooner. It might be best to tell her what you know."

Keepsie relaxed a little. Her friends' brave words belied her nervousness. It wasn't as if she could *do* anything to him except for keep him where he was.

Clever Jack leaned back against the box, his immobile hand allowing him little wriggle room. "Sit," he said, gesturing with his left hand. "I'll tell you what I can."

Keepsie sat cross-legged. Her friends assembled themselves around her, Peter looking stiff and out of place on her kitchen floor.

"Everyone knows where the First and Third Wavers came from. But no one ever talked about where the heroes came from, much less those of us who, well, aren't terribly heroic," Clever Jack said.

"Well, we asked, they just didn't answer," Michelle said, but got quiet at Clever Jack's look.

"That's because the government didn't want people to know they were experimenting with Zupra," Clever Jack said. "Your parents were born with powers, but too many babies were miscarried because of the drug, so the FDA banned it officially, but they bought up all the company's stock under the table. Then they took poor pregnant women and promised them health care and a future for their babies if they would participate in these studies. They offered it as an alternative to abortion. Even got some small town churches to support their campaign."

Keepsie's mouth dropped open. "That's sick. But what does that have to do with this ball everyone is so uptight about?"

"Getting to it," Clever Jack said. "They didn't make the experiments public. They knew it would take a couple of tries to make the babies they wanted. So Pallas was the first successful baby born. You all know the ones that came after. They let her start fighting crime when she was only fifteen."

"Engineered superheroes," Keepsie said.

Peter frowned. "So, providing the government got all the drugs, it started manufacturing heroes. What does this have to do with you?"

"I was getting to that," Clever Jack began, then cocked his head. "Did you hear something?"

Ian jumped up. "Keepsie, did you lock the door?" he asked.

"No, there's no need—" she began.

"Oh there's need," Ian said, peeking through the kitchen door. "Heroes."

"Patricia, that little shit," Michelle whispered.

Clever Jack leaned forward as far as he could. "Listen to me, Keepsie, I need this, and I need it now."

Keepsie had no time to consider. "You can't take it. But go," she said, and Clever Jack wrenched his hand free. He was up and running through the kitchen door and up the stairs to the alley before any of them could say anything further.

Michelle ran to the box and grabbed a coat, pulling it over the small silver ball that lay where Clever Jack had left it. "What are we going to tell them?"

Keepsie stood up slowly. "We'll tell them that they're trespassing."

#

Timson pushed the door to the kitchen open a second later. Keepsie stumbled into Peter's arms and glared at the intruders.

"Wha' d'you want?" she said.

"We have reason to believe you had a known fugitive captured here. We came to apprehend him," Dr. Timson said. White Lightning and The Crane flanked her. White Lightning looked ever the asshole, but Keepsie had always liked The Crane. He seemed awkward and un-hero-like until he took the air, where he was just as graceful and heroic as the others. But now his regal features contorted to show haughtiness and perfect righteous action. It was clear that Keepsie and her friends were, if not evil-doers, definitely not on the side of Good in his eyes.

"Do ya see an arch-villain here?" Keepsie asked, miming an attempt to stand. Peter gripped her tightly.

White Lightning made a point to check the freezer and storage room for hiding villains. Keepsie watched him while her friends watched her.

"Keepsie, do you want to sit down? I think you've had enough," Peter said.

"M'fine," Keepsie said.

White Lightning walked up to Keepsie and stared at her, towering over her in what he undoubtedly thought was an intimidating fashion. "Where did you put him?"

Keepsie kept herself calm by realizing she could look straight into his nostrils. "'Put' him? Do you think if a villain came in here that I could 'put' him somewhere? You do know that I have a useless talent, right?" This was getting kind of fun.

The Crane put his hand on White Lightning's arm, pulling him back slightly. "Look, ma'am, we know he was here and we know you were ready to negotiate with him. All we need to know is when he left, if he took the device with him, and where he was going."

Keepsie almost felt kindly towards him until she realized he was playing the good cop. She remembered her assumed drunkenness and frowned at him. "I don't know what you're talkin' about. I was drinking. That bitch Pat came by to sober me up, so I got drunk again. Anything else you think you know is pure concepture."

"'Conjecture,'" Peter said.

"Right. Concepture," Keepsie said.

Dr. Timson looked at Keepsie for a long time. "Keepsie. We're not stupid. We have the best powers and the best minds working at the Academy. We know what kind of club you have going here. We know what happened today with Doodad. We know what happened here tonight. Do you really want to go against us?"

Keepsie's heartbeat quickened at the threat. Peter's arms gripped her more tightly and she caught Michelle's eyes—they were wide. What could Timson do to them?

"I don't know nothing," Keepsie said.

Timson pursed her lips and inhaled audibly through her nose. "And I suppose that the device is still... not available to us?"

"Who's to say it's mine to give?" Keepsie asked.

Timson nodded. Without another word, she turned and left, the heroes following her after another long pause.

"Dude," Ian began, but Michelle shushed him.

"Wait," she said.

They waited until the heroes had climbed the stairs to the street. When it was clear the heroes had gone, they relaxed.

Keepsie stood up and smiled at Peter. "Thanks for catching me."

"Of course," he said, not meeting her eyes.

"What the fuck? I mean, seriously?" Ian asked. Everyone stared at him. "First the dude puts an oversized BB in your pocket, then the heroes get their panties in a wad about it, then the villains get their panties in a wad—and tell us a pointless story in the middle—and then the heroes come back with more panty problems! It looks like one of our own tipped them off, and now they're threatening us and that's not cool!"

Peter nodded. "This has gotten much bigger than we had anticipated, Keepsie. Maybe we should just give it to the Academy."

Michelle shook her head. "Huh-uh. No way. If they'd treated us with respect, maybe. As equals, I mean. But no, we're no better than bugs in their eyes, and I don't think we should help them."

"So do we help the villains instead?" Keepsie asked. No one answered. Keepsie had grown up hearing about the horrendous plots of Seismic Stan and later Clever Jack, Doodad and others. These were not nice people.

Keepsie rubbed her face with both hands. "I need to sleep on this. Let's talk in the morning. Meet at the diner for breakfast?"

Peter checked his watch. "It is already morning, Keepsie, it's around three o'clock. Let's shoot for brunch, OK?"

"All right then. Get some sleep, and I'll see you guys at the diner around eleven tomorrow. And," Keepsie added, "don't tell anyone about this. It looks like we can't trust, well, people." She was loath to say "Patricia."

On their way out, Michelle put her hand on Keepsie's arm. "What are we going to do about her?"

Keepsie shook her head, staring at the ground. "I don't know. Fire her, I guess. Let's talk about it tomorrow, OK? My brain hurts."

Together they walked up the stairs to the main street level, Keepsie stopping to lock the door for the first time.

5

Keepsie slept fitfully that night, her body crashing from the multiple adrenaline rushes the day had given her. Whatever wisdom she'd hoped her subconscious would reveal during the night never came, and she awoke with more questions than she'd gone to bed with.

Michelle woke her at ten o'clock. "Hey, I just found out some pretty interesting stuff."

"Did you sleep at all?" Keepsie asked, trying to buy time to clear the cobwebs from her head.

"Not a whole lot. I just kept thinking about everything Clever Jack told us. The media really haven't covered the origins of the heroes, although it feels like they do a human interest story on one of us every time a talent makes itself known."

"I just turn off the news when they start talking about heroes," Keepsie said. "Pallas is, what, forty-five?"

"Something like that, yeah. There was a web site that launched a couple of years ago with conspiracy theories regarding the heroes. It got shut down, but not before it was mirrored at a couple of places. They're not highly-traveled sites, and it seems as if they do all they can to avoid the search engines to keep the heroes off their back, but the conspiracies are pretty intense.

"According to this, the heroes were manufactured by the Academy," Michelle said breathlessly.

Keepsie held her hand up. "Wait. So the Academy wasn't created to train with the heroes, it actually created them?"

"Apparently."

"Does that mean the Academy made the villains as someone the heroes needed to fight?"

"I don't know, it doesn't go into that. But here, it says that Seismic Stan and Pallas made their public debuts around the same time in 2005, and they were around the same age: 15. They both appeared in Seventh City. The Academy was founded—officially—the same year," Michelle said, her voice muffled like she'd taken a bite from something.

Keepsie realized she was hungry. "Listen, I'm starved. Let me get a shower and I'll meet you at the diner. Print out whatever you can and bring it along. I'll see you in an hour."

"Sure thing, see you in a bit," said Michelle, and hung up.

Keepsie put the phone down slowly. This was beyond her capabilities. When she had been a child, she'd watched her mother's talents—the ability to grow plants in impossible ground—and knew her mother was very useful. She'd spent a good deal of time in the Peace Corps before having Keepsie, and Keepsie was proud of her accomplishments, but secretly she had hoped her own powers would be more suited to allowing her to fight crime and defeat the bad guy. Her mother had told her, Mr. Rogers-style, that she could do anything she wanted, even after her passive power revealed itself during an uncomfortable post-prom encounter with a football player.

Her hopes of making a difference had changed when the Academy lobbied for the Vigilante Bill of 2012, stating that only licensed heroes were allowed to use their power to stop criminals. It didn't stop people from using their powers in their everyday life; that would have been difficult for people like Michelle, whose job depended on her power, and Keepsie, who simply couldn't stop using hers. However, if the First and Third Wavers had decided they wanted to pursue a criminal with their paltry powers, they would need to join the Academy or be subject to law enforcement. And the Academy didn't accept many First and Third Wave citizens.

Would Timson try to throw Keepsie in jail for the obstruction of justice or possession of stolen property? Why hadn't she just arrested her? Of course, if she'd done that, Keepsie would have become even less likely to hand over the device. Her power was in effect for all of her possessions; if she were in jail then Timson still wouldn't have been able to get her hands on the device unless Keepsie allowed her.

If only the heroes weren't so damned smug. They always reminded Keepsie of the quarterbacks and cheerleaders from high school. Talented, beautiful, popular, and hated by Keepsie and her friends. Bullies who were loved—and therefore ignored at all the right times—by adults.

Some Third Wave powers manifested at birth, others at puberty, like Keepsie's. She's been starry-eyed in love with a football player, but he'd gotten a little grabby after the prom. She'd protested, and when he tried to forcibly remove her top, he froze.

At first Keepsie thought her shock had slowed things down. Later, as she and some willing subjects tested her power, she realized it was actually her that slowed things. As the jock's hand closed on her lapel, it slowed as if it were moving through water and then stopped.

Fear scrawled across the jock's face. It would have been funny if Keepsie hadn't been so upset. "What did you do? Let me go!" he said. His hand looked shellacked into place, but the rest of his body moved, straining to pull his hand back. Keepsie wrenched herself free and he stayed put, looking comical and frightened.

"I'm not holding you!" she cried, and just like that he was free. He stumbled backwards and landed hard against the car door.

He scrabbled past her to open the car door, shouting, "Get the hell out of here, Third Wave freak!" He shoved her out and drove off.

Then it dawned on Keepsie: that was her power. She had been wondering when it would manifest and when it finally had, she had been too startled to realize it. Sobbing, she got her phone out of her purse and called her mother.

Mom was comforting, and called the football player's parents. She emerged from the conversation with a grim look on her face, saying it was Keepsie's word against the boy's, and she wasn't hurt, which was important. She also reminded Keepsie of the prejudice the general public had against much of the First and Third Wave and hugged her.

The next day, she had told Keepsie to forget about the incident and focus on her power. They went on a shopping trip to celebrate. It was much more fun than the fuss her mother had tried to raise when she'd gotten her first period.

Through careful testing, they tried to identify her powers. They discovered that the best way to go about it was to take Keepsie by surprise, so her mom would try to take her jacket or her backpack when she wasn't prepared. Keepsie felt a frightening rush of power when she realized that her mom would remain immobilized until she let her go, either verbally or mentally.

It was disappointing to the teenaged Keepsie that, although her power seemed to be a strong one, she had no control over it. She felt no different, she couldn't do anything exciting, but her stuff seemed to be protected for a good long while.

Her grandmother was the happiest of them all when she heard the news. Having taken the drug Zupra fifty-five years earlier when pregnant with twins, she lost one to miscarriage and delivered Keepsie's mother, a healthy First Wave baby complete with a very minor power. A prosecuting attorney, she wasted no time in suing the makers of Zupra, Haldor Limited Drug. She took their settlement and invested it. Her family lived well off the money, and when Keepsie's powers manifested, her grandmother lost no time in giving her the money already marked off for inheritance.

She enrolled Keepsie in money management classes, and Keepsie sat with people three times her age and learned as much as she could about how to manage her newfound wealth. She'd have been really bored, but the constant knowledge of her money coupled with her grandmother's promised wrath if she squandered it made her pay attention.

Keepsie realized she had been letting the water run over her shoulders for far too long. She had no idea what time it was. She wondered whether she'd rinsed the shampoo out of her hair and then wondered if she'd already conditioned it. She decided to take the chance that she was done and got out of the shower.

Dressing was a quick affair, pausing only to run a comb through her hair and realizing she had not, in fact, used conditioner. Swearing, she shoved a ball cap on her head and left her apartment.

Outside her door, she paused for a moment. She hadn't locked a door since her powers had manifested, but last night proved that there are more reasons for someone to break in than to steal things. She pulled out her key ring and fumbled around, looking for the right one. Her apartment key was shiny and unused.

Keepsie scanned the sky as she walked. This was her habit, looking intently like a teenager searching for zits to stress about. Today was different, though, as she scanned the sky in slight fear that she would be followed, chased, captured or attacked.

The apartment buildings in Seventh City stretched four and five stories high, blotting out much of the sky. Keepsie was used to seeing the occasional hero on patrol, or even the occasional villain fleeing a heroic pursuit. These things happened every day.

She sidestepped kids playing on the street and people returning from the corner grocery store. Some called a greeting to her, but she only managed to return a tight smile and a wave. She was not in the mood to chat. The sky was gray with clouds that threatened nothing but casting a dour mood on the day. Keepsie scowled at them.

Although the diner was only a three-block walk through residential neighborhoods, Keepsie's hands shook by the end of the walk. She gripped the door tightly, feeling the metal knob slide under her sweaty grip. Pausing to collect herself, she pushed the door open.

Her friends waited for her at a corner booth. The restaurant was crowded with Saturday morning customers lounging with coffee and their papers. The booths flanking her friends' each contained a solitary man immersed in his newspaper.

The perky hostess smiled at her. "M'am, are you waiting on a table or would you like to sit at the counter?"

"My friends are over there," Keepsie said, pointing. Michelle waved.

"Then feel free to join them," she said. Keepsie hated her at that moment. So cheerful, so unafraid.

Peter, Ian and Michelle all looked better rested than she felt. They even managed to smile at her. She hated them too.

Ian slid into the booth to make room for her. "Keepsie, you look like shit." She glared at him.

Michelle kicked him. "Did you sleep at all?" she asked Keepsie.

"Not well," Keepsie said, appropriating Michelle's coffee and taking a swig. She made a face. "God, don't you use any sugar?"

"Not when I'm making it for me," Michelle said, grinning.

Peter signaled for the waitress and ordered Keepsie a large coffee while she stared miserably at the menu. The waitress looked down at her. "The usual, Keepsie?"

Keepsie looked up. "Oh, hi Wanda. Yeah, the usual would be good."

The older woman waited for a moment, her hand on her meaty hip. "You must be in a mood today or something, Keepsie."

"Huh?"

"You're messing it all up. You know, you ask me, 'Hey Wanda, when are you going to come work for me?'" Wanda's voice hit a falsetto that didn't sound like Keepsie at all. "And I say, 'When I divorce the owner of this joint and marry you, Keepsie,' and we all laugh."

Keepsie forced a smile. "Sorry, Wanda, I'm distracted today. But you know, if you ever chose to leave, you have a job waiting for you at Keepsie's Bar."

"Sure, when I divorce the owner of this joint and marry you!" Wanda said, chortling, and took Keepsie's order to the kitchen.

Ian watched Wanda waddle away. "OK, that was weird."

"Wanda's OK," Michelle said. "First Wave, perfect memory for everything, but it makes her a little too attached to rituals. The old jokes are the best ones in her mind."

"Oh. What the hell is she doing waiting tables with a power like that?"

Michelle's voice dropped low. "She's not terribly bright. She can remember anything but she doesn't process well. She fell in love with Larry in high school and wanted to help him run this diner. She's perfectly happy, and it's nice having someone who knows your usual order."

"You should see her when we want to order something different, though," Keepsie said.

Wanda returned with Keepsie's coffee, along with a sugar bowl. Keepsie managed a weak grin that slipped from her face the minute Wanda turned her back.

Peter leaned across the table. "Are you all right?"

Keepsie poured too much sugar into her coffee and regretted it with her first gulp, wincing as she burned her tongue. She put down the coffee cup and slid her hands across her face. "I'm just not ready for this. I didn't sleep well and I have no idea what to do about this whole thing."

Peter nodded. "Yes, I'm at a loss myself for what to do. We are skirting the edge of illegal vigilantism here. We are also skirting the edge of refusing to cooperate with an officer." He drummed his fingers on the table.

Keepsie stared at the table, avoiding their eyes. "You guys aren't in it, you know. This is me, my power. No offense, but none of you could be keeping this thing from them."

Michelle leaned over the table and poked Keepsie's arm. "We're not going to leave you sandwiched between the heroes and bad guys. No way."

That was it. That was what she had feared. Her power alone was working to stymie those who wanted the device, and she was terrified her friends would call it her problem alone and abandon her. The relief that flooded her was palpable, and she smiled.

Keepsie realized that Ian was prattling on. Only the occasional "dude" and "what the fuck" had entered her consciousness.

"—I mean, I know all I can do is give the damned heroes a face full of shit, but you, Keepsie, you're stronger than they know, and you can hold them back until..." Ian's face became almost angelic with the dawning comprehension. "No, I've got it, by God, we're going to take the device to the SCU Stadium and sell tickets to an old fashioned smackdown! Doodad, Clever Jack, whoever else they're working with, and all the heroes! Winner gets the device! We'll make a fortune in ticket sales, the device is out of your hair, and maybe some of them will be so nice as to kill each other off during the fight!"

He looked so pleased with himself that Keepsie laughed. Michelle giggled, and Peter looked as if he would consider it for a moment. He shook his head.

"There's no way we could make that legal," he said.

"Dude, lighten up, I just thought our girl here could use a laugh," Ian said.

"Thanks, Ian," Keepsie said. Wanda had arrived with their food and Keepsie didn't want her to overhear their conversation.

"So," Michelle said, spreading paper on the table in between the plates, syrup and butter. "I came to some conclusions regarding the villains. I think the Academy made them the same time they made the heroes, and I think they made them to grab political power. Throw some villains out there, then throw some heroes after them, deny all knowledge of the villains and make buddy-buddy with the mayor."

She paused to take a bite of pancake while Keepsie looked over the documents in front of her. Most of them were from conspiracy sites, but they did seem to match what Clever Jack had started to tell them the previous evening.

"Since 2012, the laws have equated heroes to law enforcement officers, making them part of the Seventh City Government, eligible for salaries out of our taxes," Michelle said, handing Keepsie a folder of old newspaper articles. "Every mayor Seventh City has had since 2010 has been endorsed by the Academy. They're a political powerhouse."

She lowered her voice and they leaned in to hear her. "This is truly a hero-run town, even moreso than we'd thought."

"You don't know the half of it," said a voice over Keepsie's and Michelle's shoulders.

The man who had been reading his paper when Keepsie had arrived was leaning over the back of the booth, grinning at them.

"Hello, Clever Jack," Keepsie said.

6

There was a pause. Peter's eyes darted around; no one had noticed the wanted man casually sitting in the diner. Clever Jack wore a baseball hat and a denim New York Yankees jacket, blending in with the other customers so that even Peter, Keepsie, Michelle, and Ian hadn't noticed him.

That's real *powers for you.*

"Did you tell the heroes I said hello last night?" Clever Jack asked, grinning.

"No, we were too busy trying to not get arrested, thanks," said Ian.

"Yeah, sorry 'bout that." Clever Jack didn't sound very sorry at all. "Thanks for letting me go, by the way."

"I'm not sure I did the right thing, there," Keepsie said.

"Can I join you?"

Everyone looked at Keepsie, who looked uncomfortable with the leadership thrust onto her shoulders. She paused, and Michelle took up the role.

"Sure. Five minutes, Jack, that's all," she said. "We wanted to enjoy our food."

"Now that's bullshit and you know it," Clever Jack said. He slid out of his booth and snagged a spare chair from a vacant table. He put the chair at the end of their booth and was in it before Peter could blink. *He moves like mercury.* Peter got a distinct feeling that they should not anger this man. Still, no one in the diner seemed to notice Clever Jack.

The villain reached forward with both hands and grabbed a piece of bacon from Ian's plate with his left and Michelle's folder on the Academy with his right. Keepsie looked at him with obvious dislike, but he ignored her as he munched and flipped through the folder.

"Oh yeah, sure, go ahead, take my bacon," Ian said. "And you say you're not a villain."

Clever Jack looked over the folder at Michelle. "You're pretty smart to pull all of this together."

She smiled, tight lipped, at him.

"But you got one major thing wrong, miss. You got it right where I came from, but not why I left the teat of the Academy."

"My mama's from Elk Park, NC. She got knocked up by her prom date," Clever Jack said. "There was nowhere local to have an abortion back then, so she drove to Charlotte to get help. In the Planned Parenthood office, she ran into an Academy official who was stalking the waiting room. This woman offered my mama free health care, free pediatric care, a future for me and even a college education for her, if she would just have me in Seventh City and allow the Academy to adopt me."

"But I thought heroes were the ones with poor mothers getting prenatal care?" Ian asked.

Clever Jack gave him a withering look. "You're not too bright are you? I was raised in the Academy; I was engineered to be a hero."

They looked at each other. "What happened?" Michelle asked finally.

"What happened?" Clever Jack looked at her as if she were an idiot. "I didn't want to be their lapdog. They studied us, tested our powers, trained us, yeah, but they also gave us ethics courses, told us how to think and how to serve and what to do in this or that case.

"We were *bred* for this, like horses. What happens with a thoroughbred decides not to run? They will give it extra attention. Then they will beat it. Then, if it still won't run, they might put it out to pasture for stud duty, if they want to risk continuing the undesirable personality quirk. But what if," Clever Jack leaned forward in his chair, whispering intently, "what if that horse could melt metal with his mind, or influence the tides, or could fly faster than sound? Do you think they would just put it out to pasture?"

Keepsie was very still. "No. They would put it down."

Clever Jack exhaled loudly. "Finally, someone with a brain. Yes. There were some of us who did not embrace our destinies with open arms. From time to time, the best were apprenticed to the heroes. Well, of course White Lightning and the others got their apprenticeship, and the rest of us were treated like second-rate heroes, then like criminals. Being better than any normal human at something was just not enough for them."

Peter stiffened. Michelle and Keepsie exchanged glances, and Ian slammed his fist onto the table. Clever Jack jumped.

"Now you're speaking a language we can understand!" Ian said. "So you were treated like we were? By the Academy that raised you?"

Clever Jack looked in turn at all of them. "I don't know how you were treated. I was in a cell in the lower levels of the Academy for ten years. But if you tried to get acknowledgement for your lesser abilities from the Academy I'm sure it went about as well as farming tobacco at a mile above sea level."

Peter shook his head in amazement at the comparison. "We were all rejected from the Academy for being of insufficient power, yes. If you didn't know this, how did you know we had powers to begin with?"

"Doodad told me," Clever Jack said. "He'd been out of his cell for a lot longer. I broke out several years ago, but headed home to the mountains of North Carolina."

"To find your mother?" asked Michelle.

Clever Jack looked down at the table. "I suppose. She wasn't there. I don't know where she went after the Academy gave her the 'Get Out Of The Mountains Free' card. She could be dead now, for all I know. Internet searches don't help much; the Academy didn't tell us our parents' names."

"Did most of the women leave their babies to be raised by the Academy?" asked Keepsie.

Clever Jack sipped at his coffee. "All of them."

Michelle choked on a bite of scrambled eggs. "You mean they all just abandoned their babies at the Academy, took their checks and ran?"

"Most of these women didn't want their babies anyway," Clever Jack said, his voice dull. "And the Academy didn't do anything to encourage them to have contact with us. Like those surrogate women who don't hold their babies after they have them—no connection."

Peter was moved, but the image of the violence Clever Jack had brought to Seventh City remained with him. "So instead of going on Oprah, you decided to harm innocent people?"

Michelle, Ian and Keepsie looked at him in surprise. "Dude, that's cold," Ian said.

Clever Jack gave Peter an appraising stare. "If you want to look at it that way, yeah, I hurt innocents. I hurt anyone I could in order to escape the cell they threw me in when they realized I couldn't be a hero. I high-tailed it out of town and headed to the only home I could claim."

"And Doodad called you back?" Peter said.

"Yes. He needs that device back, Keepsie," Clever Jack said. He put his hand on hers, and she pulled it back quickly.

"Why did he give it to me in the first place?" she asked, not looking at him.

"He knew you could keep it safe while he had other business to attend to. You were the only one he knew couldn't be forced to give it over to Timson and her lapdogs—and he knew you were unlikely to be convinced to do it."

"Wait, how much do they know about Keepsie?" Ian asked.

"More than you think," Clever Jack said. "They keep track of all First and Third Wavers, watching for vigilantes. Since your bar is right on their doorstep, you're pretty easy to keep an eye on."

"But heroes never come in the bar," Keepsie said.

"Heroes don't, but they're not the only people associated with the Academy," Clever Jack said. "Now, don't ask me who the spy is, cause I don't know, but Doodad says there are some pretty fat files on all of you."

Peter watched Keepsie carefully. She stared at the table and fiddled with an artificial sweetener packet. Instead of seeming upset, she appeared to be thinking something over very hard.

She raised her head and looked at Clever Jack. "I still need some time. Come to my apartment tonight at eight o'clock. I'll have an answer for you then."

With his characteristic liquid grace, Clever Jack stood and slid the chair back under the table. "Done." He pulled his baseball cap low over his eyes and headed out the door.

"What are you going to do, Keepsie?" Michelle asked.

"I don't know," Keepsie admitted, draining her coffee mug and grimacing. "But I'll know tonight. I'll need your help, though."

"You've got it," Peter said at once.

She smiled at him. "Good. Now, where's Wanda with that coffee pot?"

It turned out that Wanda was approaching them as she said this. As she filled each of their mugs, she said, "Your friend didn't pay his bill, Keepsie, are you picking it up?"

#

After grudgingly picking up the tab for Clever Jack's breakfast, they left the diner.

"We can go around and around on the villains versus heroes thing all day. The thing is," Keepsie said, "that the Academy is full of thugs. But we still don't know what this thing is or what Doodad plans on doing with it."

"He's been spreading mischief for weeks," Peter said. "There was no breaking out of his cell and finding a safe place to be like Clever Jack did; Doodad stayed here. He may even have a lair or something by now."

Ian nodded fervently. "Dude just tries to make trouble for the heroes, and we get caught in the crossfire."

"But isn't that what I did last night? Make trouble for the heroes because I could?" Keepsie asked quietly.

Michelle looked at her, stricken. "You're not like them, Keepsie!"

Keepsie kicked a rock into the gutter. "Really? I didn't have any affection for Doodad. He scared the shit out of me yesterday. He kidnapped me and used me; he knew exactly how I'd react when the heroes came calling. And still I didn't help the Academy. White Lightning saved my life and I can't do anything but hate him because of how he treated me."

"Yeah, but he's an asshole, Keepsie. No one can like that guy," Ian said.

They walked on toward the bar. It was not yet time to open, but they figured it was a good place to talk in private and discuss Keepsie's options. Peter had no idea what he would do in her position.

"Pretty day," Michelle said after a while. They made agreeable noises.

"Yeah, real nice, except for the heroes flying around," Ian said. Keepsie snapped her head up.

Peter followed her gaze. White Lightning was flying over them, arms outstretched, cape flapping behind him. He looked as if he was heading for the Academy. The few people on the street called out to him and waved, and a few women blew kisses.

"It's just a hero," Peter said when he saw Keepsie's stricken expression.

"'Just'." Keepsie replied. She stopped in the middle of the sidewalk. "I can't do this, guys. I can't fight them. I'm scared of what the villains will do with the device and I'm scared of what the heroes will do to me."

"It's not like they can take anything from you," said Ian.

"True, but they can arrest me. I can still protect all of my stuff when I'm sitting in jail. I'm going to give it to them."

Michelle put her hand on Keepsie's shoulder. "We're with you, Keepsie, whatever you decide."

"Thanks," Keepsie said.

Peter looked up the street and his heart fell. "Um, Keepsie. You need to see this."

People were collected at the top of the stairs leading down to Keepsie's Bar. Police officers. Three tall men, complete with blue hats, badges, doughnut bellies and guns (and one even sported the handlebar moustache), accompanied by a shorter black man in a suit. They stood expectantly and watched Peter, Keepsie, Ian and Michelle.

"Shit. What do we do now?" Ian asked.

"Go talk to them, I expect. They have guns, we don't," Peter said.

Ian pushed up his sweatshirt sleeves. "The hell we don't."

"Ian, chill," Michelle said. "You'll just get yourself in trouble if you attack cops. Come on."

Keepsie hadn't spoken. She stared at the men. Without looking at her friends, she walked forward with a "welcoming a new customer she didn't know" smile on her face.

"Gentlemen, the bar doesn't open for a couple of hours. But I'll be happy to serve you when it does," she said.

"Ms. Laura Branson?" asked the shorter man, pulling aside his jacket to indicate a silver badge hanging on his belt.

"Please, call me Keepsie," she said, stretching her hand out. "And you are?"

"Michael Orson of the State Alcohol Board." He did not shake her hand. She dropped it after a moment's hesitation, but her smile did not waver. "Ms. Branson, we are here to suspend your alcohol license; your last report to us listed you making fifty-two percent of your net profits from alcohol sales instead of food sales, which violates Statute 756-A stating that every restaurant must make fifty-one percent of profit from food sales or call itself a private club."

Keepsie's smile evaporated as her jaw dropped. "That can't be, I track the books myself before I send to my accountant."

Orson hooked his thumbs through his belt and sighed. "Well, Ms. Branson, if that is indeed true, it will show up in your next audit in sixty days time. Until then, we have to suspend your license and close your bar. We'd appreciate your cooperation with us." The officers at his back puffed themselves up menacingly.

"You can't do that, you can't take anything from her without her permission," Ian said.

"That may be true for Ms. Branson's possessions, but an alcohol license is something that belongs to the state, and can be taken by the state, just like a driver's license," Orson said.

Keepsie eyed him warily. "If you know that, then you must have friends at the Academy."

"Academy officials are acquainted with many other government agencies, ma'am," Orson said. "We do talk on occasion."

Cold comprehension washed over Peter. This was the only thing they could take from her, and possibly the thing that meant the most to her.

Keepsie allowed Orson to lead her mutely down the stairs into the bar. They came out with the alcohol license—Keepsie had removed it from her frame—and Orson instructed her to lock the door. One officer came downstairs with a drill and a padlock and quickly installed another lock in Keepsie's door.

"They can't do this, can they?" Michelle asked.

"They can do anything they want," Peter said. "I'm sure if Keepsie has a change of heart about the device, then the audit will show no such numerical errors."

"But she was going to give it to them anyway!" said Ian. "Hey, Keepsie!" he called down the stairs. "Tell them you were—"

Keepsie looked up at him and shook her head sharply, her eyes cold and dry.

"Oh dude," he said. "She is *pissed.*"

They watched as the officer finished his work and the three came up the stairs. Orson handed Keepsie his card and said, "We'll be in touch. And, if you wish to tell me anything, I'll be available to listen."

"This is bullshit!" Ian cried. "This is utter bullshit! You can't do this to her just cause she pissed off the heroes! She didn't break any laws, you're just Academy puppets!"

"Sir, I'll appreciate it if you keep calm," Orson said, but the officers behind him exchanged nervous looks.

They must have read the files on all of us, Peter thought.

"Ian, don't—" said Keepsie, but it was too late.

Ian raised his fists and his terrible talent spewed forth. Filth and excrement shot from his hands with firehose-like pressure, coating the men in feces and knocking them back.

"Oh no," groaned Michelle.

Ian laughed as he effortlessly kept the scrambling men at bay, slipping and falling again in the shit. He allowed them to get up only to knock them down again with a fresh stream.

Peter held a handkerchief to his nose, gagging. Keepsie lifted her arm to her face. She and Peter exchanged anguished looks, but before they could do anything, they heard a voice behind them.

"Thanks for finally giving me an excuse," said White Lightning, and he punched Ian in the back of the head. Ian fell forward. Peter leaped to try to catch him but he had edged too far away to avoid the stench. Ian was already unconscious as he hit the pavement.

"You're under arrest," White Lightning said to the prone Third Waver. He lifted him into his arms and flew toward the Academy.

7

Dimly aware that Michelle was ranting and Peter was escorting them both down the street, Keepsie walked. The world was a flat image; a picture of the Seventh City Main Street that she walked twice every day, rain, shine, snow, heroes, villains, or, apparently, shit. There was shit on her pants and shoes.

"They took him, Keepsie, they took Ian, what are we going to do?" Michelle said. "They've gone too far this time!"

"Come on, Michelle, calm down, it'll be OK," Peter said, still pulling both women along by their elbows. "Keepsie, I believe you live closest, can we go to your apartment?"

Her apartment. They couldn't go to her apartment; it was locked. Her bar was locked; they couldn't go there either. They couldn't go anywhere. She felt Peter's hold tighten on her elbow.

"Keepsie, you have to hold it together, I can't take care of both of you," Peter said, desperation seeping through cracks in his usually calm voice.

Keepsie shook her head. No one had barricaded her apartment—she'd locked it herself. "Right, sorry, yeah, let's head back to my place. We can, uh, wash up." She lifted one leg and then the other, grimacing at the foul splatters covering her sneakers and her jeans.

Still feeling as if she were acting in a movie, moving stiffly through blocking set by a director, she helped Peter urge the enraged Michelle down the street. Other people on the street were the actors who took their cues and turned their heads to stare at them: a concerned, well-dressed man, a furious tall woman with cornrows and a Keepsie Branson, the star of the show who was horribly miscast, played by a woman who couldn't for the life of her remember her lines.

Michelle had calmed down to grumbling by the fourth block and was only fuming in silence by the time they got to Keepsie's apartment.

Keepsie tried the door and found it locked. She stood there dumbly for a moment, staring at the door, feeling the fear and helplessness well up inside her again.

"Do you have your keys?" Peter asked.

Keys. Of course. Keepsie searched her jacket pockets and found the keys. She tried three before coming to the one that opened her apartment. She led the way inside and looked around. It was her place; it looked like the set where she pretended to live her life, secure in her hubris that the Academy could never hurt her. She was too small, too below the radar, too insignificant. Anyway, they couldn't take anything away from her.

Peter was talking. Why was he always talking? "I mean, you were already going to give it to them, now it seems the way is clear. You can give them the device and get your bar back. They are only doing this to intimidate you. And maybe we can get Ian back if you negotiate right."

Keepsie looked for her cue card. Keepsie the character was supposed to agree with him, take the easy way out. Giving the device back was the obvious choice, as Peter said. And it was what she was going to do anyway. It might get Ian back. Keepsie the character would get her bar back and go back to work, cowed and ready to live in a city run by those who considered her a second-rate citizen. Her lines were on the cue card, and the stage manager in her head had started prompting her with a loud and desperate whisper. The dawning realization came to her that it was time for improvisation.

"No."

"I'm sorry?" Peter said, confused.

"No. I'm not going to give it to the heroes."

"But—why?"

Her words were coming faster and easier now. "They are bullies. Bullies and manipulators and thugs and, as Ian said, assholes." The stage manager gave a horrified gasp and the cue card holder checked the cards, flipping through them to find the right spot in her lines, but Keepsie was beyond them.

"The villains have been straight with me, the heroes haven't. The villains have treated me with respect, something I've never gotten from the heroes."

"Keepsie," Peter said, "they are called villains for a reason. They have hurt people, caused city-wide destruction, I've seen it with my own eyes! Doodad kidnapped you, for God's sake!"

"And still I can't find it in my heart to root for the heroes. The villains have never *hurt* me. The heroes have."

"Awesome," Michelle said, slapping her hands together. "But what about Ian?"

Keepsie felt a smile lift the corners of her mouth, and the sensation was foreign. "I didn't say that I was going to give it to Clever Jack for free."

#

Keepsie paced the apartment, going from living room to kitchen and back again. Michelle and Peter sat on the couch; she relaxed back and he sat stiffly, his gaze flicking from the clock to Keepsie and back again.

It was six-thirty. At seven o'clock, many of the bar's regulars were to arrive at Keepsie's apartment. Between their own memories, and a quick phone call to Wanda the memory-perfect waitress (who, although she refused to work there, had been known to have a drink or three in Keepsie's Bar), Keepsie and the others had figured out most of the regular customers' last names. They looked up phone numbers and called the regulars, explaining to them the short version of the day's happenings. They included the bar's closing and Ian's arrest, but left out dealing with Clever Jack and Doodad. Several were eager to help.

"I'll tell them everything when they get here," Keepsie had said, crossing the last person, Samantha, off the list.

"Keepsie, what about Patricia?" Michelle asked.

Keepsie stopped pacing and bit her lip. "I don't know. We don't want her knowing what we're going to do. She'll tell the heroes. But if she hears about this meeting through someone else, she'll tell the heroes then."

"We could invite her and reveal her as the spy here," Michelle said.

Keepsie frowned. Patricia had a talent that was less power-ful—offensively, at least—than her own, and that was hard to come by. It's not like she could sober them all up and then make a break for it. But Ian was their strongest offensive power, and he was gone.

"I think that might be the safest. Let's see how she reacts when we tell her about what we know."

Michelle nodded and picked up the phone. Keepsie resumed her pacing as she listened to Michelle's side of the conversation.

"Well, I know it's your night off, but it's important... well, no, not as important as last night... but... oh, I'm glad the date wasn't ruined. But I think you should know the bar is closed and we're meeting at Keepsie's apartment to discuss further action... it's closed because of the books... yes, you'll still get your check... well, I think you should be here, we're meeting with some of the regular customers... No, you're not expected to serve everyone..." Michelle rolled her eyes.

As they argued, Keepsie paced. Michelle finally slammed down the phone and said, "There was nothing I could say to entice her to come. She just wants to collect her check, and she wants us to call her when the bar is back in business."

Keepsie shook her head. "Amazing."

"It doesn't sound like she's your spy," Peter said. "If she were, she would want to be here to find out what we're doing. The Academy would love to catch us forming a vigilante group. Look at how fast they came down on Ian."

"What do you think they're doing to him?" Michelle asked.

"I would guess interrogation and incarceration in some sort of cell where he either can't use his powers or it would be very inconvenient to," Peter said. "If what Clever Jack says is true, it seems the Academy has cells that are well-equipped to handle any kind of powers, and Third Wave powers shouldn't be a problem."

"Interrogation? About what?" Michelle asked.

"Whatever secret society they think we're forming, I expect. They want to fill in any holes their spy may have left."

"Whoever the spy is," Keepsie said.

"Is it possible there isn't a spy?" Michelle asked. "I mean, the Academy is full of superheroes for God's sake. They might have people who can read minds or something. Or people who can tell the future. Or locate people or items. Who knows how they knew Clever Jack was in the bar trying to steal the device?"

Keepsie plopped down on the couch and propped her head in her hands. "I don't know. They surpass us in everything. Resources, skills, powers, everything. And then they forced us to fight with them. This is not good."

"That has already been established," Peter said mildly. "What happens next is what's important."

Keepsie turned her head as the doorbell rang. "And here they are."

#

"You're insane," said Jason. "We can't do this." The dark, thin man sat cross-legged on Keepsie's floor, an untouched mug of tea cooling beside him.

"We don't have a choice!" said Michelle. "They have Ian."

"But you don't know that they'll give him back! He broke the law; you can't attack police! That was insane," Jason said.

Keepsie perched on a stool and listened to the argument. She had presented her plan calmly and clearly, and then watched the room erupt around her.

There were the people clearly behind her: Peter, Michelle and Samantha were on her side. The others, Tomas, Barry and Jason were not so sure.

"Keepsie, I understand the need to free Ian. If it happens to him, it can happen to any of us, and that's scary," said Barry.

Jason nodded. "That's an understatement." Jason was one of Keepsie's most bitter customers, hating not only the Academy but also his own powers. Jason had power over elevators; he could summon them, make them skip floors or cause them to stop completely. He only talked about his power during periods of extreme drunkenness, and then only if prodded.

"Jason has a point," Tomas, a tall Norwegian, said. "This is not pulling a prank. This is breaking the law and messing with heroes. This is dangerous." Keepsie's heart sank as he looked at her with level blue eyes. "You will need all the help you can get. I am with you."

She let out a held breath and smiled. Tomas had super-strength, but he could only sustain it in five-second bursts.

Barry cleared his throat and everyone looked at him. "Me too. We're being bullied. My parents always told me to stand up to bullies."

Jason stood up. "You guys are insane. Try not to die, OK?" He handed Keepsie his mug and left. Keepsie shut her eyes and sighed as the door clicked shut.

"Keepsie." Peter's soft voice snapped her out of her despair. He was looking significantly at the clock. It was seven forty-five.

"All right. Does anyone else want to leave?" Keepsie asked, sliding off the kitchen counter and looking around the living room. "I'd prefer anyone who's not on board to leave now. That way you can't be incriminated for knowing too much."

The remaining people seated on the floor and on stools looked around at each other. Her army was small: Michelle, Barry, Tomas, Peter, Samantha, and Keepsie made six. It would have to be enough. She thought fleetingly of the tough cook, Colette, who had been unreachable.

"Fine. Now, in about five minutes—" a knock at the door interrupted her.

She frowned. "He's early." She went to the door, but it opened before she got there. She looked at the figure in the door and stopped cold.

Dr. Timson stood at the door, smiling.

8

Dr. Timson, dressed in street clothes, watched Keepsie attempt to regain her composure. Keepsie stepped into the hall, closing her apartment door behind her.

"What are you doing here?" she asked, hoping to sound cold and bored and not at all terrified.

"I just came to talk," Timson said. "Can I come in?"

Enough Third Wavers were in her apartment to cause suspicion, not to mention that Clever Jack was due to arrive any minute. Which was worse, consorting with a super villain or forming a vigilante hero group? It was best not to find out.

"I don't think so," Keepsie said, frowning. "We can go for a walk, I guess."

"I can't come inside?" Timson asked, her eyebrows raised. "Why not? Something you don't want me to see?"

"No," Keepsie said quickly. "It's because I don't like you very much."

Timson smiled thinly and followed Keepsie down the stairs. Keepsie checked her watch: seven fifty-eight. She had a feeling Clever Jack was the kind of guy to arrive on time. She scanned the street briefly, and no one stood out as a red flag, which of course meant nothing. They walked away from her apartment building.

Keepsie sighed. "What do you want, Dr. Timson?"

"You know what I want," she said. "And now we have something you want."

"You have two somethings I want," Keepsie said.

"Ah," Timson said. "Mr. Jacobsen. Yes, I thought his arrest would have upset you. But that is a matter for the courts to decide, not us."

"No," Keepsie said. "Like you guys don't have your fingers in every bit of politics in this city. You use your heroes to intimidate us and to shut down my bar, you arrested my friend—you, not the police—and you say you can't help me. Well, I can't help you, lady. Sorry." She turned to head back to her apartment, praying Timson would let her go.

Timson grabbed her arm. "Now, Keepsie, be reasonable. Even if we could influence the courts, how would it look if we released a Third Wave man who attacked police officers in public?"

Keepsie faced her, trying to form her features into stone. "That is not my problem."

Timson's face lost all pretense of friendly overtures. "It doesn't have to be this way, Keepsie. You are putting the city in danger by keeping that device. And we can do more to you than close your bar and take your best friend."

The rage pushed the words out before Keepsie could stop them. "I thought we were going to deal, Timson, and yet all you can do is threaten me. You don't seem to understand. I can keep this device safer than anyone else in the world. Safer than you; you let Doodad steal it."

"Doodad invented it," Timson said, and Keepsie thought she looked sad. "He knew exactly how to steal it. Machines are like his children. He knows exactly how the device works."

Keepsie laughed. "So it belongs to him? Doesn't that make you the thief?"

"Don't talk about things that you don't understand," Timson said. "Give me the device, Keepsie."

"No."

She turned and walked back to her apartment. Timson did not follow.

Clever Jack was sitting on her doorstep.

He stood up in one easy movement when he saw her. He wore a battered denim jacket, a blue sweatshirt and a pair of jeans.

Had she and Timson passed him on the street? Keepsie couldn't remember.

He smiled at her. "You're late."

"I was distracted," Keepsie said, and opened the door to her apartment.

"Keepsie, what—" Samantha asked, but stopped when she saw Clever Jack.

Keepsie placed her hand on his shoulder. "This is Clever Jack."

The room was silent as her friends stared at the villain. They had all seen pictures of him, heard about him on the news, but this was the real thing.

"Pull up some floor, Clever Jack. We want to talk," Keepsie said.

A smile flitted across Clever Jack's face, and he sank into a cross-legged position and looked up at Keepsie, who perched on a stool. She propped her elbow on the bar between the kitchen and living room. Pulling the small ball from her pocket, she peered at it.

"You know, I don't even know what this does," Keepsie said. "And I wonder if my decision would be made easier if I did."

Clever Jack said nothing.

"But as it stands, I have no desire to help any of you. Throwing it away won't work though. So I obviously have to choose.

"If I give it to the Academy, I could get my bar back. I could also get Ian released. But I know that wouldn't be the end of it—they'd probably lean on me even harder since I stood up to them. They might even start sending heroes into my bar to drink, driving away customers." She slipped the ball back into her pocket.

"What can you give me?" she asked Clever Jack.

He was silent for a moment. "I don't think we can give you your bar back."

"Oh, I know that," Keepsie said, smiling. "We want you to get us Ian."

Clever Jack stood up. "Done."

"Wait," Keepsie said. "That's it?"

Clever Jack paused with his hand on the door. "You wanted something else?"

"Files. Files on our parents, and files on us. We want to know what the Academy knows about us."

"That will be more difficult," he said.

Keepsie waited.

Clever Jack sighed. "But we can do it."

"Great. We'll help." Keepsie stood, and her friends joined her.

"What?" They had finally thrown Clever Jack off guard. It felt good.

"We're going to help. You don't think we trust you, do you?" she said, pulling on her jacket.

"I can't be responsible for you all. You're on your own."

"Ah, but we're not. We're in this together," Peter said. The others nodded, although some looked scared, others resolute. Samantha looked positively elated.

They followed Clever Jack out the door.

"Keepsie, can I make a quick call before this descent into madness?" Samantha asked.

Keepsie nodded. Her heart hammered. *What have I gotten us into?*

#

Samantha caught up with them outside on the street. She linked arms with Peter, who looked startled. "This is very exciting. Forming a vigilante group, working with a villain to infiltrating the Academy and remove a known criminal. What good ideas you have!

"And, you're all under arrest," Samantha said, pulling an Academy badge out of her purse.

The Third Wavers stared at her. Clever Jack ran.

He disappeared into the dark faster than he should have been able to. But then again, he had super powers, while they had next-to-nothing.

"Run!" cried Michelle, and they scattered. Peter wrenched free of Samantha's arm and grabbed Keepsie's hand.

"You bitch," Keepsie managed to say before Peter pulled her down the road.

Her friends did not disappear under the streetlights as well as Clever Jack had. Keepsie and Peter ran in the direction of her bar, dashing past startled people on the street. Keepsie heard a rumble of thunder and swore.

White Lightning and the Crane flew over an apartment building and right toward them. Having been plucked off the street once that week, Keepsie had the mindset to duck as they came close. The Crane swept Peter up in his arms, but White Lightning missed, passing close enough that his cape stung her face.

Keepsie had never seen so many heroes working together at once. The heavily muscled and tattooed hero who went by the questionable name Tattoo Devil pulled up on his motorcycle and hopped off, his sidekick, Cage, climbing out of the sidecar. Heretic, the powerful hero with fire elemental powers, flew high above them, pitching fireballs in front of fleeing Third Wavers, herding them. She laughed as she did so, and Keepsie realized why she wasn't used for crime fighting that often—she was batshit insane.

Her friends screamed around her, and Samantha shouted loudly for the heroes to round up the vigilante group. *Otherwise it looks like the heroes are attacking innocent folks,* Keepsie realized. Michelle struggled inside a cage of glowing ropes, to little effect, and Barry hopped on one of his legs, leaving Tattoo Devil holding the other one with a bemused look on his face. He tossed it aside and tackled the older man. Barry's head hit the sidewalk with a smack.

Keepsie struggled to her feet and tried to find Peter in the sky. White Lightning hovered a few feet above her and she readied herself for another attack. But he didn't swoop down on her again. He raised his arms to the sky and she felt her skin prickle.

"I bet your power doesn't work so well when you're dead," he said. "I don't know why they didn't let me just do this before."

Keepsie ran for it, even though she knew she couldn't win. The flash lit up the street around her, but Keepsie never heard the thunder.

9

Peter had heard Keepsie's story of her abduction, and had, at the time, admired her wisdom in not struggling against Doodad as she soared above the city. Now that he was in a similar situation, he felt no such peace of mind. He batted at the Crane's arms, knowing it would do no good—and if it did do any good, he'd fall to serious injury or death. The Crane wrapped his extended arms around Peter like ropes.

"Stop that, you don't want me to drop you, do you? Cause I can. I can let you fall and fall and then catch you at the last minute," The Crane whispered into his ear. Peter turned his head and recoiled at the sight of The Crane's lips elongating to meet his ear. They smiled at him and then snapped back into place.

Peter forced himself to be calm. He looked down. Previously, he hadn't had a fear of heights, but there was something about putting his trust completely in a stranger who wished him harm— or at least incarceration—that made him suddenly fear the street below. His friends struggled with heroes, most of them being pacified almost immediately. Clever Jack had gotten away, he was sure of it. That's what Clever Jack did. Used his unbelievable luck to simply slip away when the heroes came around, and anyone with him got caught.

When Peter's eardrums bulged with the deafening crack of thunder, he whipped his head around in time to see Keepsie crumple to the pavement.

His struggles began again with renewed strength. "No, no, let me go, take me back."

"She should have given it to us," The Crane said, flying farther and farther away from Keepsie's body.

"You're a murderer," Peter said. The Crane's right ear had stretched to his mouth to hear him.

"That device is more important than any one life. If we have to kill one Third Waver to save the population of Seventh City, we will. She was breaking the law by forming an illegal vigilante group and she avoided capture, we followed the proper procedure."

"Deadly force on an escaping Third Waver is proper procedure?"

The Crane withdrew his ear. His hold on Peter tightened. "I would recommend coming quietly; you saw what happened to your friend."

Peter subsided. The Academy loomed in front of him, and it felt as if The Crane picked up speed as they approached the starchy white building.

The other heroes, the ones with travel powers anyway, were arriving at the same time. Michelle and Barry trailed along behind Tattoo Devil and Cage, trapped in a net of the girl's energy as Peter and The Crane descended. Samantha pulled up at the same time as a silver van. She ran around to the side and began directing Academy stooges to unload the unconscious Tomas. Peter hoped he was unconscious, anyway.

White Lightning and Timson had not yet arrived. Peter wondered what they were going to do with Keepsie's body. The realization of the situation hit him, and he shuddered uncontrollably. The Crane deposited him on the front steps of the Academy and he stumbled and fell.

The concrete bit into his cheek. Hands grabbed his shoulders and forced him to his feet. He looked around him. Michelle bled from a cut on her forehead, and Peter hoped it looked worse than it was. She was crying, and that scared him. This was *real*.

Peter's legs wobbled. Michelle propped her shoulder under his arm and helped him walk as the heroes herded them inside.

"Keepsie—" Peter choked.

"I know," Michelle whispered, squeezing him a little. "She's gone."

They were separated and shuttled into elevators. The Crane pulled Michelle out from under Peter, and when he stumbled again, said, "Come on, be a man," with a derisive tone. Michelle shot him one final look before entering the elevator with Cage, Barry, and Tattoo Devil.

Peter leaned against the wall of his elevator and stared at the buttons. The two upper floors that could be seen from the outside were indicated above the Ground Floor button, but the array of buttons indicating floors below the main floor was impressive. There had never been any outward sign that the Academy had floors stretching that deep under Seventh City, and the vastness of the organization frightened him.

"Samantha," Peter said, surprising himself. "Where is she?"

The Crane pushed the button marked B7. "Why, are you going to exact your revenge? You don't need to know where she is. She's done her job."

"Her job as a hero? Heroic to infiltrate a group of friends and betray them, ending in the death of one?" Peter's voice failed to carry the anger he felt—it sounded flat and weak.

The Crane looked at him with obvious distaste. "Ghostheart found a rat's nest of vigilante wanna-bes and uncovered it before any innocents got hurt. Yes, she's a hero."

"But Keepsie—"

The Crane's arm snaked across the elevator and his hand covered Peter's mouth. "You don't get it, do you? You guys aren't innocents. You're criminals. You broke the law simply by forming the group. And when we find out what you were planning to do as that vigilante group, I'm sure we'll be able to accuse you of conspiracy to commit several other crimes. So shut the hell up about Laura Branson. I'm tired of your whining."

Peter considered biting his hand, but he had nowhere to run and The Crane had already proven to be more than strong enough to overwhelm him. He inhaled and his head swam with information-

The Crane sat a desk in what looked to be a windowless schoolroom. He checked the answers on his test and smiled, confident that he had answered all the questions correctly. He put his pen at the top of the page to sign his name when his desk rumbled and tipped. He toppled from his desk and sprawled on the ground, his left wing twisting painfully. He looked up.

Seismic Stan grinned at him, braces flashing, and said, "Oops, sorry Frank, I burped."

The rest of the class, all ten of them, laughed. The Crane flushed and righted his desk, gingerly flexing his wing. He picked up his test paper and saw with horror that his pen had scrawled across the top in an indistinguishable glyph. The perfect white space had been marred and he didn't have time to redo the test. Stan would make him look bad—look messy—in front of the teacher, and he would get him, he would get all of them who laughed.

The Crane removed his hand from Peter's mouth, and Peter returned to reality. "So do you get it?"

Peter nodded, distracted by the revelation. Clever Jack had been right. The first super villain, Seismic Stan, had come from inside the Academy, had been trained beside the heroes. Had he really just been a prankster who had gone bad? Or had he been trained to be evil, to give the heroes something to fight against, someone for the city to fear so the heroes would seem more impressive?

Peter remained silent as The Crane manhandled him down the dark, echoing hallway of the seventh basement floor. None of his friends had arrived on that floor, and he felt very alone.

The Crane sneered. "Prison level 2. Like it?"

"Lovely," said Peter. He went without a fight into the room that The Crane unlocked for him. It was lit by one light bulb sticking out of the wall and furnished with one wooden table and two wooden chairs. The door slammed behind him and Peter collapsed into the nearest chair, relieved to be free of the insufferable hero.

There was too much to consider. What was going to happen to him? Could he get a lawyer to stand up against the Academy? Or were crimes against the heroes considered above the jurisdiction of the judicial branch? Peter couldn't remember whether he'd ever heard of a trial for Doodad or any of the other villains. Clever Jack had never been caught, once he had escaped from his assumed imprisonment.

And then there was Keepsie. Peter's mind swam with the image of her slight body collapsing, jerking slightly, onto the street. She was their strength. She had been the one who believed that they could use their paltry powers to go against the heroes.

Peter had stifled his powers since childhood. He hadn't liked knowing things, secret things, about other people. He had learned through a hug that his father was cheating on his mother. He had learned while doing laundry in the college dorm that his posturing, macho bully of a football player roommate was gay. He felt as if he were an unwilling therapist who received everyone else's secrets. He kept a polite distance from people. He knew people—especially Ian—thought he was gay since he was never seen with a woman, but he was too afraid of finding out something horrific about someone if he got close enough to smell her.

Ian. Ian was also held here, they had all assumed. Ian's power, one of foul violence, had been unable to help them. Peter had never considered his own power to be of any use at all.

He stared at his hands. Usually they were clean, but now they had blood on them-probably from Michelle's cut. His throat felt very tight as he swallowed and sniffed gingerly at his palm.

Darkness and fear. They'd locked her away, then. No pain, though. Peter got up and stood by the door. The hall was silent; he had some time. He closed his eyes and sniffed deeply. The room smelled stale-no one had been in it in some time. The chair he had been sitting in smelled like nothing. Peter walked around the room, breathing deeply until he got light-headed. He leaned on the table, panting shallowly, when he caught a whiff near the other chair.

Of course. Ian would have had the strongest and most lingering scent of anyone, especially after his adventure that afternoon. Peter leaned closer to the chair and closed his eyes.

Ian was in considerable pain, but he gave them no information. The pain stopped. A tall woman with red hair said to take him to the eighth floor. Two men carried him away.

That was all. Peter sat down again, exhausted. What good did it do him to know where or how Ian was? It's not like he could get out of the room to save him or anything.

He'd had enough. Arrest, betrayal, murder, incarceration. He was sure he'd have enough strength to deal with this if only he could get a little sleep.

He rested his head on the table and closed his eyes.

10

Someone slapped Peter on the back of the head.

"Wha?" he said, sitting up with a jolt.

The Crane sat across the table from him, withdrawing an extended arm. His blonde hair was tousled and he looked annoyed, almost frightened.

"You're clearly not too concerned about your situation," The Crane said.

"Oh, but I am," Peter said. "I just needed a rest. It takes a lot out of you, getting abducted and abused by heroes."

The Crane slapped him hard, open handed. Peter's lip split and blood welled up inside his mouth. The harsh copper taste bought him back to reality. *This is actually happening.*

"How long have you been a part of an illegal vigilante group?" The Crane asked.

Peter stared at him. "You are aware of my power, right?"

"How long have you been a part of an illegal vigilante group?" The Crane's voice was louder.

"I'm not part of a group," Peter said. "I can tell things about people by smelling them. That's not terribly useful for crime fighting."

The Crane slapped him again.

"Look, what do you want from me?" Peter said, dabbing his lip with the heel of his hand to keep blood from getting on his shirt. "You're clearly the more powerful person in this room. I could tell you where you've been by smelling you. You can fly and stretch your limbs out. The right person is fighting crime here. I can do no more than a mundane police officer."

"Then why were you with a group of confirmed vigilante Third Wave and First Wave citizens?" The Crane said, slamming his fists on the table.

Peter forced a grin. "You mean my friends from the bar? We were hanging out at Keepsie's to watch the game." *God let there have been some sort of sports game on tonight...*

"What game?" The Crane asked, his watery blue eyes narrowing.

"I don't know. I'm not into sports. I was just there to be with my friends."

"I'm getting tired of this," the Crane said, and both of his arms snaked out to wrap around Peter's chest.

"Hey, I—" Peter's words were cut off as The Crane's arms constricted slowly, pushing all of the air out of his lungs.

"Feel like telling me now?" asked The Crane.

Peter fought for breath but his lungs wouldn't comply. His face burned and his mouth opened as he tried to speak. Black flashes bloomed in his vision and his heartbeat thundered in his ears.

Just as he felt consciousness begin leave him, the arms relaxed and he gasped, filling his chest with what felt like gallons of air. Without the arms around him he fell forward onto the table, arms splayed, content to merely breathe beautiful air for a moment.

"The next time I'll hold on longer," said The Crane.

Peter nodded, still too busy gasping to answer him. There was a clink on the table, and he raised his head with some effort.

The Crane had placed two ice picks in front of him. "Now, my bosses would really like their information soon so that they can go home to their families. I may have to get mean."

Peter eyed the ice picks. "Yeah, you've been a real *saint* so far, Frank."

The Crane picked up an ice pick and touched its tip, testing its sharpness. Peter felt reasonably sure it was a bluff, but in a flash the ice pick came down and impaled his left hand.

Peter threw his head back and howled. Instinct warred within him; it demanded he pull his hand away from the hell that was penetrating it, but logic begged him to keep the hand as still as possible, else it will hurt more if he moved it.

"It's illegal to reveal a superhero's secret identity," The Crane said. "How did you know my name?"

Peter gritted his teeth against a whimper. He barely heard the hero's words. He couldn't think past his hand. He moved his right hand gingerly toward the left. The Crane watched him, sweat beading his brow. Peter tried to remember something. Something important about The Crane. Something to distract his mind from what his right hand was trying to do.

As his right hand grasped the ice pick, he remembered. He pulled the ice pick from his hand with a cry and cradled his hand to his chest. Blood poured from the wound and he slipped out of his sports coat and then clumsily out of his shirt, scrabbling at the buttons with his right hand.

He wrapped the shirt around his bleeding hand and stood up from the table. The Crane still watched him. *How does this guy manage to fight crime?*

"I need to go to a hospital," Peter said through clenched teeth.

"Sit down, Peter," The Crane said.

"No. I need to go to a hospital," Peter said, mind focused only on his small rebellion, his ruse. He really did need to go to a hospital, but focusing on that instead of The Crane's torture and questions that would be too easy to answer was his only defense. And if he could get close enough for another whiff of the hero... The Crane was sweating enough, but his scent felt just out of Peter's reach.

The Crane picked up the ice pick and his arm elongated quickly and stabbed Peter's left arm, going deep enough to cause pain but not going through his arm. He withdrew it quickly. Peter hissed and took a step back. The ice pick then pierced his abdomen.

"What is the vigilante group's plans? How can we get the device from your friend Laura Branson? When was the last time you had contact with the known villain Clever Jack?" The Crane punctured Peter in a new place with each question. He shrank back, trying to protect himself. Blood ran freely from his chest and arms.

Peter collapsed and mumbled, "Hospital."

The Crane got up and approached Peter's fetal body. "This is getting us nowhere." As he bent down, his wings brushed Peter's face, and the pain receded as The Crane's life filled his mind.

"Goddammit, Crane, you're completely useless if you get a speck of dirt on you," Pallas was saying, her face twisted into a look of disdain. Blood coated her white uniform, some her own, some belonging to someone else. From the Crane's viewpoint he saw a wing outstretched and desperate hands scrubbing blood from the feathers.

"You don't understand." The Crane sounded like a nebbish. "You don't have wings."

"Well if I did have wings, they would have been torn off by Doodad's robot once you left the fight," Pallas said as people in white Academy coats tended to her few wounds. "I thought you were getting treatment for that OCD."

"I don't have a disorder!" The Crane yelled, his hand pulling feathers in his panic to remove the blood from his wings.

Peter unraveled his shirt from his hand and grabbed the wing brushing his face. The hand was still bleeding heavily, and blood soaked the white feathers.

The Crane screeched and leapt back. His arm stretched out and he punched Peter. Darkness brought blessed release from the pain.

#

Peter woke up in the room alone. He tried to move and discovered he was tied to a chair. He could feel blood trickling from his wounds. His right eye was swollen shut and what he could see through the left was blurry.

The door opened with a click and Peter squinted.

"Man, you guys are a mess of trouble," said Clever Jack.

11

Keepsie was aware of chaos around her before she opened her eyes.

"Stop pulling him, you fool, it's not going to work," a woman's voice said.

Keepsie's eyelids felt welded shut. She took a deep breath and forced them open.

She screamed.

White Lightning hovered above her, his blue eyes wide in surprise. He didn't move. Tattoo Devil had grabbed him by his foot and was struggling to pull him away from her.

Oh. She looked beyond White Lightning and Tattoo Devil to see the hero Heretic, dressed in black flowing robes, looking positively murderous. Dr. Timson sat beside her near the door, tense and quiet.

"Keepsie, let him go," she said quietly.

Keepsie sat up, holding her head in her hands. She wanted to shake it to clear the ringing in her ears, but the headache wouldn't let her. She reached up and pushed the hero away from her—he moved as if he were merely a manikin, drifting until she stopped pushing.

"You tried to kill me," she said.

The heroes surrounding her didn't flinch. Their faces showed hostility and anger, but no understanding, no pity.

"Keepsie, you need to let him go," Timson said again.

"Or what? You'll try to kill me again?"

Timson took a deep breath. "We have other ways. We have your friends. Their powers will not serve them quite as well as yours. Give us the device and release White Lightning and your friends will come to no harm."

They had Peter, Michelle and the others. Keepsie reconsidered her defiant stance. She stood. White Lightning moved with her, gliding over the floor as if he were made of Styrofoam.

"You have my friends. But I have your hero. I guess that makes it a standoff?"

Tattoo Devil tugged again at White Lightning, who didn't move. "You know, you Third Wavers are pretty pathetic. We're sick of your bitter conviction that you're just as good as a hero." His voice was muffled slightly from behind his Japanese mask.

"And yet you still can't get what you want from me," Keepsie said.

Tattoo Devil dropped his hand from White Lightning's leg and glared at her. His eyes narrowed and he raised his right hand.

A katana-wielding samurai shimmered along Tattoo Devil's palm and wrist. The tattoo turned its head and looked straight at Keepsie. He streamed out of Tattoo Devil's hand to take shape next to him.

"Take care of her," Tattoo Devil said.

Keepsie didn't have time to duck as the samurai, clad in bulky Japanese armor, aimed his strike at her neck.

She fell back onto the cot with the force of the blow, White Lightning falling with her. She closed her eyes and coughed until she retched.

After what felt like several minutes, she staggered to her feet. She opened her eyes and failed to see blood streaming down her chest. The katana lay on the floor. Keepsie felt her neck, and although there would be a significant bruise, the sword hadn't pierced her skin.

Tattoo Devil—and his tattoo samurai—were frozen in place, glaring at her.

"Heretic?" said Timson in her calm voice.

Keepsie couldn't gather her thoughts well enough to defend herself, to think of something quick to do. Heretic was one of the Academy's strongest heroes.

Flames billowed up around her, and she thought she heard Timson scream to keep White Lightning, Tattoo Devil and his warrior safe. The fire was hot, unbearable, and she screamed as it seared her flesh. She collapsed, and the flames went out.

"What happened, Heretic?" Timson said. "Go on and finish it!"

Heretic didn't answer. She was frozen in place, hands raised, manic look plastered on her face.

Keepsie had covered her head in her hands, but realized that the burns on her skin were superficial. First-degree sunburn, if that. Her hair and clothing were untouched. In the back of her mind, away from the animalistic panic, a rational voice demanded her attention. They had tried three times to kill her, and they failed. Why?

Timson's feet scraped along the floor, and Keepsie looked up. The scientist stood over her, frowning at a cell phone. "This is getting ridiculous. Get in here."

A woman entered the room so quickly she must have been right outside. She had her brown hair tied into a severe bun, and wore tortoise-rimmed glasses attached to a chain around her neck. A nondescript blouse, a red silk scarf around her neck, a knee-length skirt and sensible flats completed the ensemble.

The woman glared at Timson. "You know I was almost here. You didn't need to yell."

"I needed you, Librarian," Timson said. "This woman is proving to be more trouble than she's worth, and we don't have all of her powers on file. What can you tell me about her?"

The woman walked over to Keepsie and appraised her with a cool stare. She looked at Timson and said, "Laura Branson, better known as Keepsie. Third Wave. Her power level was set at 2 when she applied to the Academy in 2025. She is able to keep anything she owns. She cannot be stolen from. Anyone who attempts to steal from her will be trapped in stasis until she releases them, which she can do with a thought. A very useful power when it comes to keeping her own belongings safe, but useless for crime fighting."

"And that's it?"

"That is all that is in the Academy's records about this woman's power. There is considerably more about her bar and her secret cabal of Third Wavers," the Librarian said. Keepsie guessed she didn't like being questioned.

"Nothing about invulnerability?" Timson asked.

The Librarian shook her head slowly, still staring her icy stare at Timson.

Timson slammed her fist onto the table and glared at Keepsie. "How could we have missed this? Our strongest heroes can't take her out."

She walked over to where Keepsie lay in a fetal position and kicked her. "Damn you, give us the device!"

Keepsie reacted without thinking and caught Timson's foot after it had connected with her forearms. She gave a jerk and Timson toppled with a cry, falling heavily on her hip. The Librarian just watched.

They can't kill me. The burns on her hands and her face stung, and her throat ached. *They can hurt me, but now I have hostages.* The samurai's katana lay beside her where it had bounced off her neck. She wrapped a hand around it and levered herself off the floor.

She glared at the Librarian and slid the tip of the katana under White Lightning's chin. Tattoo Devil, his samurai and Heretic moved slightly with her as she walked forward.

"Listen, you failed. I'm not dead, now I have three heroes," she said. "Now let me out of here."

Timson remained motionless, grimacing. The Librarian sighed and took a key ring from her pocket and unlocked the door. "The problem with the Academy is that no one knows when she's been beaten."

Keepsie moved forward, dragging her four hostages behind her. "I didn't actually think that would work."

Emergency lighting illuminated the hall every ten feet. Other doors, identical to the door she was exiting, lined the hallway.

She paused and turned to look at the Librarian. "Hey, can I have those keys, please?"

The Librarian smirked at her.

She pressed the katana into White Lightning's chin, wondering if he were invincible. "Look, I could be a bitch and demand them, reminding you of my hostages, but you were nice to me so I thought I'd be nice to you."

The Librarian shook her head and opened her mouth.

"Oh for the love of God!" Keepsie said. She stomped back and grabbed the keys from the Librarian, pushing the surprised woman back as she did so. "I'm tired of arguing with you people. You keep trying to hurt me afterward."

Keepsie got one last look of Timson writhing on the floor and closed the door and left them, running down the hallway. The heroes trailed behind her helplessly, like kites.

"Where the hell are the exits in this place?" she mumbled, seeing no end to the hall. There was a turn to the right up ahead, so she headed for that.

One of the doors opened and Tattoo Devil's sidekick, Cage, exited. Keepsie nearly ran into her and stopped short. She yelled in surprise and lurched forward, reaching for Keepsie's katana.

She stopped inches from the weapon and her body went rigid. Keepsie laughed.

"You seriously didn't think that would work, did you?" she asked. "But dammit, I wish one of you could tell me how to get out of here."

She took a step forward and Cage turned and fell into the odd gliding pace beside White Lightning, Heretic, Tattoo Devil and the samurai. They bumped together but otherwise moved without incident. Keepsie stopped when she heard a voice from inside a room.

"Keepsie? Is that you?"

The room Cage had exited was dark, but Keepsie recognized Michelle's voice. Keepsie turned on the light and her friend winced. Michelle was tied to a chair and had a swollen eye and bloodied lip. She stared at Keepsie as if she were a ghost.

"I thought you were dead. Jesus, what happened?" Michelle said.

Keepsie used the tip of the katana to cut through Michelle's ropes. "Not a good time for explanations. Do you know where the others are?"

"I think Peter is on the floor above this one," Michelle said, staring at Keepsie's burns.

Michelle led them down the hall. They spotted an EXIT sign, but Keepsie heard a shout behind them. A girl, about fifteen, appeared in front of them to block their way.

"You're not getting out of here," she said. Her eyes were wide and her hands shook.

"Aw, come on, kid, if you knew what had—"

"Stop, Blink," came a voice from behind them. The Librarian ran up behind them, glaring at the girl.

"Who's Blink?" Michelle whispered to Keepsie. "I didn't know there was a new one."

"And that's the weirdest thing to have happened today?"

"Let them go," the Librarian said to Blink.

"But—they have White Lightning!" the girl said.

"And they'll take you too, if you cross them. This is one woman you are powerless around."

The girl looked on the verge of tears. "How do you know?"

"Idiot," the Librarian said. "How do I know anything?"

Blink scowled at Keepsie. "You're going to have to let them go at some point. And when you do, they're going to be pissed."

Keepsie grimaced. "Yeah, I expect they'll be mad enough to kill me. Don't worry about me, Blink, I can take care of myself as soon as I get some aloe."

She dragged her prisoners to the elevator and pushed the up button. Blink disappeared again.

"The kid was right, though," Michelle said. "We can't take these guys with us forever."

The elevator arrived with a ding, and Michelle stepped aboard. Keepsie stayed outside, a smile spreading across her face.

"Are you coming?" Michelle asked.

"I want to try something." Keepsie stepped into the elevator and kept right inside the doors. Her hostages stayed behind her, but outside the elevator. "Push the button."

The doors closed, and Keepsie and Michelle left Cage, White Lightning, Heretic, Tattoo Devil and the samurai frozen and outside the elevator.

Michelle laughed. "That's awesome! What's going to happen now?"

"I have no idea," Keepsie said. "I've never done that before. Never had a chance to."

"But Keepsie, you don't have any hostages anymore," Michelle said.

Keepsie made a face. "Crap."

The elevator opened to an identical hallway to the one they had left. Michelle ran ahead of Keepsie, peeking through the windows on the doors.

"You sure they're here?" Keepsie asked.

"No, but Peter stopped here. It's a good place to start—oh here he is!" She stopped at a door near the corner and motioned for Keepsie to give her the keys.

The door was unlocked, though, and they opened it to find Peter being untied by Clever Jack.

"Oh, hi. I was just coming to get you guys," Clever Jack said. "I found Peter first."

Peter looked very much the worse for wear. He had lost his suit coat and his white shirt, and his undershirt was spotted with blood. A bruise on his face kept one eye shut. When Clever Jack untied his hands, Keepsie winced at the mess that was his left hand. He opened his good eye and it widened when he saw Keepsie.

"Man, Peter, you've been through hell, haven't you?" she said.

He coughed dryly. "You're alive."

"Yeah, funny story, I'll tell you when we're safe." Keepsie said. Peter nodded, his good eye still wide.

"Let's go," said Clever Jack.

12

Keepsie and Michelle hissed when they saw Peter's bloody hand. He grimaced as Clever Jack helped him to his feet.

Keepsie appraised him. "Well. You look like shit."

"Jesus, Keepsie, that's nice." Michelle said. She paused. "But really, Pete, you do look like shit."

Peter snorted and coughed out a laugh. He looked at Keepsie's bright red skin and said, "You look positively ready for the inaugural ball, yourself."

"Glad you're OK. Relatively, you know."

Peter opened his mouth, but Clever Jack interrupted him. "Let's leave the tearful reunions until later, kids. We have more daring rescues to do. There's your friends and of course, Doodad. But first—" He didn't finish, but instead strode off toward the elevators, leaving Peter with Keepsie and Michelle, all attempting to catch up.

"So how are we going to do this daring rescue?" Keepsie said.

Clever Jack closed his eyes and stabbed at the elevator buttons. The second floor button lit up and he grunted. "Huh. That's not what I expected."

"Why are we going up?" Michelle asked. "I thought all the cells were downstairs."

"So did I," Clever Jack said. "But this is where we need to go, apparently."

"Your power is impressive," Peter said. "That is, if this works."

Clever Jack looked at him with narrowed eyes. "I got you out, didn't I?"

Peter made a placating gesture, and Clever Jack smiled. "Although, you were pretty clever. The Crane went running past me in the hallway, blood all over his wings, not a care in the world except getting clean. How did you know about his little problem?"

"My power is weak, but useful at times," Peter said, focusing his gaze on the rising numbers above the elevator door.

They arrived at the second floor. Clever Jack stuck his head out of the elevator and motioned for them to follow him into the hall. The hallway was deserted, but well-lit and much more welcoming than the lower levels. Frames containing caricatures looking like a Hero Hall of Fame lined the walls and moonlight shone from the windows at the end of the hall.

Clever Jack turned left down the hall and walked with a purposeful gait. Keepsie, Peter, and Michelle followed, casting nervous looks around them.

"Nine is my lucky number," Clever Jack said, counting the doors as he walked. When he got to the ninth door, he paused and motioned the others out of the way. They flattened themselves against the wall, and Clever Jack opened the door.

He stared inside for a moment. "Hey Keepsie, do you know this guy?"

Keepsie peeked inside the room. It was an elaborate office containing an oak desk, bookshelves, and a visitor's chair, which was occupied by the only person in the room.

"Jason," she blurted. Her uncooperative customer stared at her. "What the hell are you doing here? You left."

Jason's brown eyes were very wide. "I don't know. Cops showed up at my place and brought me here to ask me questions about you and the bar. I met with Timson and then she said to wait here."

Clever Jack leaned into Keepsie and whispered, "What's his power?"

"Elevator control," Keepsie said out loud.

"Oh, excellent," Clever Jack said. "We can use you."

Jason looked terrified. "I don't know."

Keepsie stepped forward and leaned into Jason. "Check us out, Jason. Look at what the heroes did to me and Peter." Peter stepped into the doorway, his face stony, and Jason gasped.

"I have it on good authority that they have been torturing Ian as well," Peter said. "We need to free them, Jason. Clever Jack thinks you could help us. Will you?"

Jason nodded. "But, what can I do?"

Clever Jack grinned the smile that was starting to make Keepsie uneasy. "The most secure cells are only accessible by elevator key card."

"Oh. Well I can help with that," Jason said. "I thought you needed me to fight or something." He snickered nervously, raising his thin arms.

Clever Jack motioned for them to follow. "Not even a little bit." The four of them followed him back to the elevators.

"Any idea where the others are?" Clever Jack asked.

"I think Ian is in the eighth basement," Peter said. "Barry and Tomas, I have no idea."

"Eighth basement sounds about right. Take us there," Clever Jack told Jason. Jason pushed the button marked "B8."

"That's it?" Keepsie said.

"What did you expect?" Jason asked. "I can get us there without stopping anywhere else."

"I thought Clever Jack's power would keep us from running into heroes," Peter said.

"Only an idiot doesn't use the tools that fall into his hands," Clever Jack said. "If I were hunting, I could probably find a deer that had broken its neck in a fall, but it's much easier to just rely on a clear shot with a gun."

The elevator descended, with no interruptions, to the eighth basement floor. When the door opened, Clever Jack looked at them. "Keepsie, I need you to come with me. The rest of you wait here. Keep the elevator here. If someone comes down the hall who isn't us, take the elevator to the topmost floor and wait for me."

"Wait, how will you get there?" Jason called after him.

"Luck," Clever Jack said.

Clever Jack paid Keepsie no attention as she followed him. He looked at every door, placing his hand on each one, shaking his head, and moving on.

"Jack, why me? I'm not really useful in a fight."

Jack didn't look at her. "I need the device now, Keepsie. I need it to free the rest of our friends."

"So you can't just luck your way into their cells?"

"What did I just tell you about tools? I need that tool to open the cell quickly before anyone finds us."

Keepsie fingered the ball in her pocket and hesitated. Jack sighed. "Do you want Ian out or not?"

She handed it to him, a sense of powerlessness coming over her as she lost her final bargaining chip.

Jack took it, a look of reverence on his face. "Thank you."

He crouched down and put it on the concrete floor and spun it, just so. As it whirled around, it began to open, unhinging and revealing a small cavity inside where a handful of small, blue pills lay resting on some cotton.

"That's it?" Keepsie said.

"Don't discount it, you have no idea what these are. What they can do," Jack said. He reached into the cavity and pulled a pill out. He dry-swallowed it and waited.

Keepsie stepped back, not knowing what to expect. Clever Jack closed his eyes, took a deep breath, and then opened them, focusing intently on one of the doors. It was large and metal with a keypad containing several symbols on it. Keepsie had no idea what the symbols meant, but Clever Jack went to the pad and punched in a long code. A light came on over the keypad, bright red. Jack smiled and keyed in another code. The light began to blink.

"Finally."

Jack bent down and picked up the device. It shut at his touch, and he slipped it into his jeans pocket.

"This is all I needed. I'll get the rest. You go back to the elevator now."

Keepsie watched the red light blink. "Is Ian in there?"

"Not that one. It would be best to go back to the elevator now."

Keepsie backed away. Jack's eyes glowed in the dim light of the hallway. He giggled at her, a high, mad sound, and she ran.

#

Michelle was ripping Peter's shirt to use as bandages—with Peter protesting—when Keepsie got back to the elevator.

Michelle looked up from wrapping the cloth around Peter's hand. "What's up?"

Peter glared at Michelle. "That was Italian."

"Well, I found out what the device was," Keepsie said.

That got their attention.

"It's like a high-tech pharmacy bottle."

Peter frowned. "You mean it had drugs?"

"My mother's going to be pissed," said Keepsie. "She always said I'd get in trouble because of drugs."

"What were they?" Michelle asked.

"No idea. He took one and started putting in a code at one of the cells. Then he told me to come back here and wait with you guys."

They didn't say anything. Michelle turned her attention back toward Peter. Keepsie sank to the floor of the elevator, worry gnawing at her stomach that she had done the wrong thing.

Michelle sat next to her. "Hey, Keepsie, how did you survive that lightning?"

"Or Heretic's fire," Peter added.

Keepsie shook her head. "I don't know. I—"

She was interrupted by the elevator doors opening. There was a tense moment before Clever Jack lowered an unconscious Ian into the elevator.

"Present for you!" said Jack, giggling again.

Keepsie tried to let her concern and joy at seeing her friend keep her from retching at the smell. Ian had clearly fought back, and was covered in shit for his efforts.

Barry and Tomas entered the elevator behind Clever Jack, looking astonished and gratified to see them. They did not look as if they'd gone through the same hell as Keepsie and Peter.

"Gosh it's good to see you," Barry said. "We thought you were dead."

"I feel dead but I keep moving." Keepsie grimaced as she struggled to her feet. "Is Ian OK?"

"Oh he's fine," Clever Jack said. "Just the recipient of the powers of the up and coming hero, Inert. The Academy couldn't have him filling the place with shit."

"Inert?" Keepsie asked.

"One of their teenagers. Knocks people out with a touch. Right bastard in a fight, cause you don't expect it coming from him."

"Oh. Where are they all, Clever Jack?" Keepsie said suddenly. "Why haven't they launched the red alert or something? I mean, I took care of Tattoo Devil, Heretic, Cage and White Lightning, but I know there are more."

"No doubt they're on their way," Clever Jack said. "In a moment, they will see a group of rogue Third Wavers as the least of their problems."

"What did you do?" Keepsie asked.

Clever Jack ignored her. "One more to go, and we can blow this popsicle stand." He ran back down the hall.

"What is going on?" Tomas asked.

Keepsie stared after Jack. "A rescue. I think."

"Where are the heroes?" Barry said.

Michelle patted Keepsie on the shoulder. "Keepsie caught them in her power. How many did you get?"

"Four," she answered.

Barry and Tomas made impressed noises, but Keepsie focused down the hall. A door opened, sounding as if it was held closed by hydraulics. Then Clever Jack and Doodad came running back, shouting at them to close the door and hit the main lobby level.

Jason scrambled to comply, and Clever Jack and Doodad made it onto the elevator as the others got to their feet.

"Why the hurry?" Keepsie said.

"You'll see," Clever Jack said.

"Hello Doodad," Keepsie said.

The massive man bowed to her. "Please call me Eric."

"Eric?"

"Yes. Doodad was the name my mother gave me. I'm not fond of it."

"I see. OK, Eric—"

A loud rumbling interrupted her, shaking the building.

"Shit! What was that?" Michelle said.

A crack sounded above them. "Was that a cable snapping?" Keepsie asked, her voice cracking.

Jason put his hand against the wall of the elevator. "Yes. It's broken now."

"Why do we not fall?" Tomas said.

Jason grinned at them, and Keepsie tried to remember if she'd ever seen him smile. "It won't fall. I'm here."

"Wow," said Clever Jack. "Is that lucky or what?"

They arrived at the ground floor as the building rumbled again. Clever Jack smiled at Keepsie as they got off. "You wondered where the other heroes are? They will soon be there, trying to deal with what I set free. Thank you for the pills, Keepsie, I couldn't have done this without you."

Doodad bowed to them again and they ran down the hall and out the front doors.

Michelle and Tomas hefted Ian between them. "We have to get out of here!" Michelle said.

Jason stepped off the elevator last, releasing his hold on it to send it crashing down to the bottom level. Keepsie swallowed the panic in her throat.

"I think running is a good idea," she said. "Who's with me?"

They ran, dragging Ian, following the villains. Outside, night had fallen. Keepsie had completely lost track of time. In the light of the streetlamps, she saw that Doodad had created a climbing machine out of a fire escape and he and Clever Jack stood atop a Moroccan bakery. They watched the Academy with glee on their faces.

When Keepsie and her friends had crossed the streets, they ventured a look back.

The Academy was imploding, the walls caving in and dust flying everywhere. From the ruins rose a woman—no, a teenaged girl—bathed in a halo of light that was difficult to look directly at. She wore a white bodysuit that looked less like a hero costume and more like a futuristic suit out of a sci-fi movie, complete with dials and gauges.

Peter's voice sounded very far away. "Keepsie, I think it might be time to release the heroes."

She gasped—she still held the heroes paralyzed in the lower levels of the Academy, where they likely could be dead by now. She freed them with a thought and held her breath.

They came, then, from all directions. White Lightning burst from the Academy, at a speed that, despite her dislike of him, impressed Keepsie. The others teleported in, holding on to Blink. She must have rescued them before the Academy fell. The heroes went into immediate action, heading for the young woman.

"This is not our fight," Peter said.

"But it's my fault," Keepsie said.

"Let's go. The bar is closest."

"But it's my fault."

Peter's panicked eyes softened as he took her arm. "There's nothing we can do, we need to get somewhere safe. Please, Keepsie."

She nodded and let him lead her down the stairs to her bar. Michelle struggled to hold Ian up as Tomas grasped the lock on the door, concentrated briefly, and pulled it off. The doorknob came with it and he shoved the door open. They tumbled inside, shoving the door closed behind them.

Michelle and Tomas went to lay Ian down. Jason and Barry collapsed into a booth. Keepsie stayed by the door, watching the light show outside.

"Do you know who she is?" Peter asked.

"I have no idea, but I'm betting she's not a hero," Keepsie said.

Peter looked up the stairs. "Well, that's not something I expected to see."

Clever Jack was floating, drifting down the stairs. He touched down lightly outside the door and opened it.

"Did you know he could fly?" Peter whispered. Keepsie shook her head.

Clever Jack still had wild eyes and a half-smile. He looked around at the bloody, excrement-covered group. "You might want to get your friends cleaned up and get the hell out of town. This is going to get interesting."

"What happened out there?" Keepsie asked.

"We just released another unjustly imprisoned person, like Ian."

"Who is she?"

He just smiled at her. "Remember. Leaving town would benefit you. Thank you for your help, Keepsie, and please let me know the next time you screw with some heroes. I'd love to hear the story."

"I hope I never have to again," Keepsie said. Clever Jack, never losing that grin, took the drugs out of his pocket and winked at her, then left, jogging up the steps.

"I wonder why he didn't fly that time," Peter said. "What was in that drug?"

#

"Keepsie, we're in need of medical attention," Peter argued.

"They patrol ER's for criminals, Peter," Keepsie said, washing his still-weeping wounds. "They'll throw us back into jail immediately. And do you think they're going to listen to how we got this way?"

Peter pursed his lips as she bound his hand in gauze. Keepsie felt guilty, having the job of tending to Peter's blood while Michelle and Tomas did their best to wash Ian so he was less offensive. Both Peter and Ian had their tattered and filthy shirts replaced by Keepsie's Bar t-shirts, and seeing suit-wearing Peter in a t-shirt made the day all the more surreal.

Peter had wanted to go to an ER but Keepsie could think no farther than getting the hell out of town.

"Where are we going to go?" Peter asked.

"I don't know. My mom lives in Raleigh. I guess I could go to her place."

Peter shook his head. "They'll be looking at our relatives first."

Keepsie slammed the gauze back into the first aid kit. "Then you lead, Peter, because I'm sick of it! We're hurt and we need to get out of town. You figure it out! If you don't like my suggestions, why don't you come up with some?"

Peter opened his mouth to reply, but Keepsie stormed out of the kitchen.

Michelle sat on the floor watching Ian with a concerned look on her face. She raised her head when Keepsie stomped into the bar. "What was that all about?"

"I've just had a really bad day," Keepsie said. "How's he doing?"

"I think he's waking up, but it's coming slowly. The others are in the bathroom. Barry and Tomas are patching each other up."

"I'm glad they stayed. We need to stick together on this," Keepsie said.

Ian stirred as Peter came into the room. He avoided Keepsie's eyes and went to Ian's side.

Ian opened his eyes. "Dude. You got me out. And what the fuck happened to you?"

Peter eased himself onto the floor and started talking. He told Ian an abbreviated version of the night's adventures, glossing over the torture. Keepsie stood with her back to them, staring through the front window up at the battle that still raged. She wondered if Ian was getting shit on her floor, and then felt guilty.

She eased the door open and ventured up a couple of steps. She'd caught the sound of clockwork, the sound that usually came with Doodad's attacks. The heroes still battled the girl, or tried to, anyway. She still hung motionless in the air, but a globe of impenetrable light had surrounded her despite the heroes' attacks.

The clockwork sound came from the ground level, however. Up the street came a walker, another one of Doodad's vehicles, surrounded by scores of smaller machinery, each with several appendages.

Some sported items that looked like artillery. Others buzzed about his head like drones.

He and Clever Jack had an army.

13

Peter ignored Keepsie's cold manner and focused on Ian.

His friend grimaced at him. "I'd ask who had the worst night, but I think we're going to need a lot of beer for that story."

Michelle choked out a laugh and Peter smiled.

"The bad news is that it may be a while before we get that beer," Peter said. "We have to leave—"

Keepsie stormed back into the bar. Peter hadn't even noticed she'd left.

"We have to stop them," Keepsie said. "Get up."

"What? What are you talking about?" Michelle said.

Keepsie's eyes were wide and unfocused. "Doodad and Clever Jack. We have to stop them."

"Keepsie, we've been through enough tonight," Peter said. "We need to rest up and get out of the city. You can't expect us to go back out there and go through more, can you?"

Keepsie focused on him, and he saw a desperation in her eyes that he'd never seen. It was a naked look, all confidence and bitterness gone.

"Fine." She opened the door and was gone.

"Shit," Ian said, and struggled off the floor. Peter and Michelle didn't stop him. They just stared as Ian limped to the open door. He turned around and gave them a withering look. Then he left.

Peter's wounds throbbed and his hand felt as if someone had shoved an ice pick through it an hour earlier. The thought of getting off the floor nearly brought tears to his eyes. Michelle looked at Peter once, then followed Ian.

Keepsie hadn't steered him wrong before. Well, there had been all that with standing up to the heroes, dealing with super villains, forming an illegal group and getting them all captured. But they always followed her. Because she was, well, Keepsie.

He struggled to his feet, hissing with pain, and looked out the window. He couldn't see Keepsie, but Michelle was sprinting up the stairs. Peter dragged himself up the stairs and followed Michelle, taking a moment to check the road for cars.

The road had no cars, probably because of all the robotic soldiers Doodad controlled. *Oh hell.*

Peter joined his three friends on the sidewalk. Clever Jack and Doodad sat in Doodad's walker, triumph on their faces. They pointed to the Third Wavers.

Keepsie stared blankly at the hero battle overhead.

Doodad's walker stopped in front of them. Clever Jack grinned and waved. "Glad you could make it. What do you think? We're going to drive the heroes out with this army. No more holier than thou heroes. No more spandex. Join us." It was not a question.

Keepsie opened her mouth, but Peter put his good hand on her shoulder. "This is amazing, Clever Jack. I had no idea you two were that powerful."

Michelle looked at him sharply and Ian simply watched the drones fly around the villains. Clever Jack pulled the ball bearing from his pocket. "This drug is something similar to what your grandmothers took—it's like super-Zupra. It boosts power. Dr. Timson created it, but Doodad stole it."

"That is brilliant," Peter said, nodding. Keepsie turned her head to look at him and he squeezed her shoulder harder.

Realization dawned on Keepsie's face. She shielded her eyes from the glare and looked at the girl floating above them. "So you were lucky enough to release your friend up there, and Doodad is now strong enough to control all of these soldiers. Is she OK up there?"

"We don't know. We're going to rescue her now." At Jack's word, several of the robots ignited jets and rose into the air.

"Right," Peter said. "Well, good luck with that. I guess we'll get out of your way; we're a little minor league for this kind of fighting."

Clever Jack gave them a paternal smile. "You guys get some rest. You've helped out a lot tonight."

"Thanks, and good luck," Peter said, carefully steering his friend back down the stairs.

"Count on it," Clever Jack said as they left, and Peter felt stung by his words.

"Peter, what—" Michelle started before Keepsie shushed her.

"Wait till we get back inside," she hissed. Peter was relieved to hear the sense come back into her voice.

"Oh dear God," Peter whispered as the door shut behind him. He leaned on it and panted; fear and adrenaline taxing his already exhausted body.

"What are we going to do?" Keepsie asked.

"What do you mean?" Ian asked. He went over to the window and peered out.

"What do you mean what does she mean?" Michelle asked, her voice high and strained. "We helped them get that drug, we helped them release that woman, we helped them build that army! God knows what they're going to do with them!"

Tomas, Barry and Jason emerged from three booths. They looked as if they'd been sleeping. "What's going on?" Jason said.

Peter started to explain but Ian interrupted him. "Clever Jack and Doodad have a way to get those torturing bastards out of the city for good, they've got an army and a new ally, she looks pretty powerful," he said, glaring at Peter. "As for these guys, I not too clear on what's going on. We hate the heroes. Those bastards *tortured* us. Clever Jack and Doodad have been sticking up for us, freeing us from their little torture chambers, getting us here safely, and we're wondering how to stop them?

"Guys, they have the recipe out there to get rid of the heroes once and for all. Why not help them?"

"You can't be serious," Peter said.

Ian gestured to Peter's bandaged hand. "Dude, those heroes fucked us up. Have you looked at yourself? How can you be on their side?"

Keepsie leaned on a stool by the bar. "We're not on their side, Ian. But we're not on the side of flooding the city with robots, either. We have enough problems with the rats."

"You let them get to you, didn't you?" Ian asked, disbelief on his face. "I can't believe you let them get to you. Their whole spiel about goodness and heroic action and leaving the city to those with the special powers."

"Ian," Michelle said, extending her hand to him. "Let's just talk about this, OK?"

"No. Fuck that," Ian said. He walked over to the door. "I'm done talking. I'm done with the hiding out in a fucking basement bar and drinking beer and whining about how I can never use my power for anything and how the heroes step all over us. You didn't spring me from that place, and I was put there defending you. Clever Jack freed me. Maybe he's the person I should be sticking with."

"Ian, this is a really bad idea. This isn't like you," Peter said.

Ian paused with his hand on the door and said, "Christ, Peter. Grow a pair, why don't you?" He slammed the door on his way out.

"Ian, don't, wait!" Michelle said, and Peter caught her arm as she tried to run after him.

"He's gone, Michelle, I'm sorry," Peter said.

"Let me go!" Michelle didn't fight him; her anguish diminished her. "He left me."

Peter nearly fell back in surprise when she buried her face in his chest and sobbed. He winced at the pain in his shoulder, but held her awkwardly. Her head was right below his nose and avoided breathing as long as he could, but she wouldn't let him go and he had to inhale. He sucked in as little air as possible, but the images still flooded his mind. Michelle, Ian, candlelight and—*oh*.

He wondered why he hadn't realized Michelle and Ian had been lovers. Then again, he didn't really notice that kind of thing.

"So what now?" Peter asked Keepsie. "Ian is going to tell them we're not on board."

"It doesn't matter anymore, Peter. I've fucked it all up. All of it." Keepsie climbed atop her stool, burying her head in her hands. She did not cry; she merely looked too tired to do much of anything.

Peter felt something heavy in his chest. He was comforting the wrong woman. His natural instinct had not been to take care of Michelle, but to help and support Keepsie. He wanted to hold her and tell her everything would be all right.

Not knowing at all how to deal with the etiquette of removing a sobbing woman from your arms in order to hold a non-sobbing one, he stayed where he was, staring at Keepsie and overwhelmed by feelings he hadn't allowed himself to feel since high school.

And if he could have been able to go to her, which he couldn't, if he would have had the courage to hold her and comfort her, which he didn't, he would have been lying to her anyway. They were badly wounded fugitives. The heroes were after them. The villains had flooded the city with a nightmare—with their help. And their strongest ally and best friend had just deserted them.

He had no idea how everything was going to be all right.

#

Keepsie wouldn't respond. She lay in a booth curled into a fetal position. Michelle tried to talk to her, but soon gave up.

"She's completely overloaded," she said flatly. "She probably just needs time. I think I know how she feels."

Peter sighed. "Just give her some time to process all of this. We have to plan out our next step."

"We need help," she said. She hadn't mentioned Ian again, and Peter didn't bring up what he had learned while holding her.

"I'm thinking we need to call some more Third Wavers," said Peter. "We also have to think about the city. Are they still fighting out there?"

Barry had the post by the window. "I don't see Doodad or Clever Jack, but there are those flying drone things doing a kind of patrol, I guess. And actually…"

Barry backed away from the window as one of the drones descended into the stairwell, a bright red light shining through the window.

Peter fought the urge to hide his face from the eye. "Well, I guess Doodad and Clever Jack know we're not on board now. We need to get out of here."

"Where are we going to go?" Michelle asked. "If you think that we'll be safer carrying Keepsie out in the open than staying here, I'd like to see what superpower you're hiding under that stuffy exterior."

Peter pointed at the drone. "Look, everyone knows we're here, heroes and villains. It's a matter of time before they come for us. The heroes discounted Keepsie's powers, but the villains never did. They never underestimated any of us, actually."

Michelle got a Rolodex from under the bar. "I'll call some people, then. I have to admit that after the incident with Samantha, I don't know who to trust. It would be good to get Colette here, and Vincent, to clean up the stench."

"The busboy?"

"Busboy, dishwasher, cleaning crew. If it had dirt involved, he was in charge. As for the customers, we don't know everyone's full names or their powers. A lot of people come to the bar for the sense of belonging, not to dump their names and histories on us. I serve beer, I don't take a census."

Peter lifted his bandaged hand. "We have to get medical help before we do anything. I'm useless now, and I think Keepsie would be better without those burns and bruises."

Michelle frowned. "I remember a guy, he didn't come in often, but he had healing powers. Alex or Alan or something. His power's pretty weak, though."

"Well, that goes without saying," Peter said. "But it's the closest thing we have to a hospital now. How can we contact him?"

Michelle thought for a moment. Her eyes got momentarily bright, then she deflated. "I know who would know his number."

"Who?"

"Ian. They used to surf together."

"Done," said Peter, and stood up. "Take care of her. Do what you can to get some fluid into her, preferably something with sugar. Also, some painkillers should help her out, if you can coax her to swallow something. Try to get her alert and moving. She'll be due for more painkillers in about two hours. And tell her I'll be back shortly."

"How are you going to find him?" Michelle asked.

"I have an idea."

"An idea, great."

Keepsie slept with her head on the bar, breathing shallowly and with a small groan after every breath. Beside her on the floor was Ian's jacket; he'd forgotten it in his rage.

Peter bent beside Keepsie and picked up the jacket. He leaned close to her. "Don't worry, Keepsie, everything's going to be all right."

She didn't respond. With a quick look behind him to make sure Michelle wasn't watching—she was discussing the phone list with Tomas and her back was to him—he leaned over and kissed Keepsie on her warm forehead.

The effect was unexpected—he'd been holding his breath—but explosive. Keepsie filled his mind, everything about her odd passive talent, all of the details, details he was sure even she didn't know.

He fell back in surprise, hitting the floor with a pained grunt.

"What the hell happened to you?" Jason asked, picking him up.

"I—uh—fell..." Peter said, staring at the sleeping powerhouse that was Keepsie. He was frankly astonished that he'd been able to steal a kiss, considering the span of her abilities.

"What happened?"

"Exhaustion, I think. Excuse me, I need to talk to Michelle."

His lifelong pragmatism warred briefly with the new emotions that were roiling, but he realized that being shy was not the safest way to go at this juncture.

He took Michelle's hand and took her into to the kitchen.

"This is hard for me to say. I will preface it by asking you to keep a secret for me," Peter began.

"Huh?"

He sighed. He was usually more concise than this. "You know my power—I can find out things about people by smelling them. I just, well, found out some rather amazing things about Keepsie."

Michelle looked repulsed. "You smelled her?"

"No, I, ah, kissed her. I have never gotten this much information about someone. Never."

"Wait, so, let me get this straight. You haven't ever kissed anyone before?"

Peter's face burned. "Of course I have. But I have never kissed a Third Wave woman before. All my life I've tried to respect others' privacy and avoid using my powers on them. I find out all sorts of things I don't want to know." He looked pointedly at Michelle.

"What do you—oh. You mean me and Ian," she said, looking down.

"I didn't mean to find out, but after he left you were holding me so close, and..." He trailed off.

Peter's excitement finally overshadowed his embarrassment. "But that's not what I wanted to talk about. My point is that Keepsie is much more powerful than she knows. I think I know how she survived the heroes' attacks."

"I'm not following," Michelle said.

"Killing someone is nothing more than stealing their life. Keepsie can't be stolen from. Therefore—"

Michelle interrupted him, her brown eyes very wide. "Keepsie's immortal."

14

Peter and Tomas stood in Keepsie's stairwell, staring out into the street. Doodad's drones were everywhere: perched in trees, exploring the Academy ruins, following early-morning joggers. A news van had attempted to set up, but a drone severed its antenna. Where there weren't people to harass, drones did little more than common vandalism. They broke windows, destroyed storefronts, and set cars on fire.

The battle with the girl had moved on; a light on the horizon in the west showed that she was still airborne, and thunder still rumbled in the air. White Lightning was still active, then.

Was this Clever Jack's master plan? To annoy the city and cause damages? What were they really planning? All he needed was a name and a phone number. But if he could find out more, then he would. If he could accomplish this alive, that is.

Michelle and Peter had agreed to keep silent on the secrets they had found out about each other. Before Peter left, with Ian's coat slung over his damaged hand, Michelle asked him to kiss her.

"What?" he asked, entirely flummoxed.

She laughed and held out her hand. "I want to know if there's something about my powers that I don't know either. Keepsie has a hidden talent, and apparently so do you. So what can you tell me about myself?"

Peter took her hand and kissed it.

The effect was not the surround-sound iMax experience that Keepsie's had been, but Keepsie was clearly the most powerful among them. Michelle was more like reading a magazine. She could hold any flat, tray-like surface with little difficulty, even throw it. The items on the tray would obey her will, staying upright until she let go.

She frowned when he told her the report.

"Well, look at it this way," he said. "Have you ever tried throwing a full bar tray? As a weapon, I mean."

"No, actually. Thanks, Bloodhound. You be careful out there, OK?"

"'Bloodhound?'"

She grinned at him and waved him out the door. Tomas had insisted on coming with him as a guard.

Ian's scent was all over the jacket; one didn't need superpowers to be able to tell that. It reeked from the shit splattered on it during Ian's fights with the heroes. Peter didn't relish inhaling the scent, but figured it was his best bet to track Ian. It had worked in the Academy, it might work here.

He made a face and steeled himself. He hadn't eaten anything since Keepsie had offered him a snack last night around dinnertime, so luckily there was nothing in his stomach to come up. However, it did register a complaint as he inhaled Ian's scent deeply. The stench of feces was overpowering, and Peter staggered.

The image was clear in his mind, though, and he laughed ruefully when he realized Ian was very close to Keepsie's apartment. His friend was standing near the woods in the park, with Clever Jack.

How the hell am I going to do this? He didn't ponder the answer to the question.

"He's in the park, about eight blocks away," he said to Tomas. The large man nodded. They went up the street at a jog.

Peter's pain was back, throbbing and aching. Were the wounds seeping again? He had warred with the idea of sending someone else to find Ian, but he was closest to him, not to mention if Ian moved, only Peter could find him.

The drones turned their red eyes toward the two men, but they didn't harass them. Many of the larger automatons paused in their mayhem to watch them and Peter wondered if they were reporting to their master.

By the time they reached the park, the robots had changed their tune. Drones buzzed around their heads, and larger ones began following them. One finally leaped onto Peter, its sharp feet digging into his back for purchase. It grabbed onto his bandages and Peter cried out in pain.

Tomas plucked the robot off his back and threw it, smashing it against the stone wall that surrounded the park. Peter ran for the trees. An aerial robot attached itself to his shoulders like a bronco rider and beeped loudly as Peter ran. Tomas didn't help this time: he'd been attacked by his own menace.

Peter backed up to a tree and swung his head back, intending to slam the robot against the tree and get it off him.

It was apparently smarter than it appeared. It was certainly quicker than it appeared. Peter's thought as his head connected with the tree was embarrassed realization of his idiocy; he'd thought only fools fell for that trick. He slumped onto the ground and passed out.

#

A foot nudged his ribs. It wasn't a cruel kick, nor was it a concerned gesture. Peter opened his eyes.

Clever Jack smiled down on him, his wide friendly smile that now set Peter's hair on end.

"Pete! Tomas! How's it going? Come to hang with us, have you? Wanna see what we're doing with our new pets?" he asked.

Ian stood back from Clever Jack, hesitation and anger on his face. Peter tried to focus on his friend, but found his vision blurry. "I need help."

"No kidding," Clever Jack said amicably. "Looks like you've got a concussion there. And not to mention your little perforations that Frankie the Crane gave you."

Peter tried to sit up, saying, "No, that's not—" but Clever Jack pushed him back down.

"Before you get up, Petey, I need to know some things from you."

Peter groaned. "It's unlikely I have more information than you do on anything."

Clever Jack pressed on Peter's chest harder, and he grinned. "I think you're wrong. For example, I think you know what you're doing here, and I don't. I also think you know why you lied to me a little while ago, and I don't know that either. I thought we were friends, Peter Peter."

"I need to talk to Ian," Peter said. "I lied to you because I wanted to keep Keepsie from saying something she shouldn't. And although I am quite grateful for the help you gave us in escaping the Academy, I really don't think we're friends."

"Told you he wouldn't hold up under pressure," Ian said, not looking at Peter.

Clever Jack sat back on his heels. "That's not entirely true, Ian. He held up very well at the Academy. Well, he's no threat, that's for sure. How you both ended up Third Wave is beyond me."

Clever Jack waved his hand. "Talk to Ian. I'm interested in hearing this."

"Didn't Tomas tell you?"

Tomas looked abashed. "I wasn't sure what to say."

Peter sat up, unhindered this time, and gingerly touched the back of his head. It was wet. No surprise there. He looked at Ian, who looked defiant.

"I need Alex's phone number."

Ian's eyebrows shot up. Clearly he'd been expecting something else. "Huh?"

"Your surfing buddy? Alex? Minor healing powers? We need to contact him. Keepsie's not dealing with her injuries well and the heroes will likely be having the ERs watch for us." Peter held the bloody hand up to Ian. "I could use him too."

Ian shook his head. "She wasn't that hurt when I left."

"Adrenaline can make you forget a lot of things," Peter said. He hadn't meant to make a subtle point with that, but Ian colored anyway.

Peter pressed on. "Still, Ian, she's hurt. She could really use his help. I'm not here to infiltrate you, not here to convince you to come back. For one, you're a grown man and I'm not your father. Secondly, if I were here to try to reduce Clever Jack's army's numbers, I don't think I'd make it out alive."

Clever Jack looked at him, head cocked to the side. "The dog look," Ian had called it once. "Now, there's an interesting choice of words. Clever Jack's army. I like the sound of that."

Peter ignored him. "All I need is a phone number and an address. We won't bother you. All we want is to get some medical help. Please, Ian, if any semblance of friendship remains between us, or between you and Keepsie..."

Ian looked at Clever Jack, who shrugged. "Don't look at me. Like Petey said, you're a big boy now, Ian."

Ian nodded. "His phone number's 555-7140. He lives in Mountain Island apartments in 34C. It's a couple of blocks away."

Peter got to his feet with Tomas's help. "For what it's worth, thank you."

A weight settled on his throbbing head as he left them. Ian had been hurt that he hadn't been there to talk him back to their side. That was clear enough. But if Peter couldn't talk him out of it back at Keepsie's Bar, then how was he going to talk him out of it in front of a super villain whose power was insane luck? Improved, insane luck.

He turned around. "Ian, if you change your mind..." But they were gone, having disappeared into the trees.

Robots did not attack them on the street. It seemed odd that the villains had a stronger sense of rules and decency than the heroes, that even though they were attacking the city, they were allowing Peter passage to do something he was fairly certain the heroes wouldn't allow.

#

Peter found the walk to Alex's apartment to be quick. There was no traffic on the streets and what few pedestrians were out were driven back inside as soon as a drone spotted them. No one seemed to notice that Peter walked unmolested, and for that he was grateful. All he needed now was people to think he was on the villains' side.

The heroes—the ones who were free, anyway—were already sure of it.

And whom were they fighting, anyway?

15

The pain—the physical pain—was not overwhelming, but it did stop her from focusing on Ian's betrayal. People had wanted her dead, and had tried very hard to make it happen. It felt so good to just shut down.

Relief.

"There, that's the worst of it." A familiar voice.

"Can't you do more? She's still got some burns." More familiar. Peter. Loyal Peter.

"Look, I can heal one inch at a time. And it takes a lot out of me. If you want me to work on those holes of yours, I'm going to need a break. She'll be fine. Let her sleep."

"All right. We could all use some sleep, I guess."

"Go ahead and sleep, man. I'll start working on you when I can. You won't even know it." Healing guy. Didn't visit the bar often.

"You should stay here till we wake up. I don't know what will happen if we let you head home alone."

"I'll be here."

"Good. Thanks, Alex." Peter sounded so tired.

Silence. Relaxation.

Memories.

Keepsie's eyes flew open. The burns no longer chewed at her scalp and hands. The ache in her neck where the katana had hit her was gone. The jittery buzz she'd felt since the lightning incident was gone.

She sat up. Peter lay close by on the floor cushioned on a rolled-up kitchen towel. Blood seeped onto the towel. What had he gotten himself into? He was asleep already, exhaustion bringing out lines in his face. Blood had seeped through his bandages to dot the shirt she'd loaned him. Her other friends were in various states of repose around the bar, most resting in the secluded booths.

The Elvis clock on the bar wall said ten forty-five.

Keepsie took a few deep breaths and swung her legs to the floor. Tiptoeing, she stepped over Peter and through the bar where her friends all dozed. Alex didn't open his eyes as she quietly opened the door and slipped out into the morning sunlight.

16

Peter cracked open his eyes. From very far away, he was aware of someone shaking him. He briefly considered the idea of trying to sleep through the intrusion, but it was insistent, and getting increasingly violent. He opened his eyes fully and saw Michelle kneeling over him.

"Where the hell did she go?" she said.

Peter looked around the room. Alex stared at him, stricken. Keepsie's bar stool was empty.

"I don't—you mean she's gone? Are you sure?"

Michelle gave him a scathing look and let him go. "You were sleeping four feet away from her and you didn't hear her leave?"

"No, I didn't hear anything," he said. "I must have been tired after staying awake for thirty hours, getting tortured and then betrayed by my friend. Not to mention a concussion. Terribly sorry."

"Don't try to sound like Ian," Michelle said. "You can't pull it off."

"What time is it?" he asked, ignoring her barb.

"Noon. You've been asleep for about an hour," Alex said. Dark circles were under his eyes.

"You didn't hear anything?" Peter asked him.

Alex looked down at the floor. "After healing someone I sort of black out for a while. I told you it took a lot out of me. Healing you and Keepsie was more than I've ever done before."

Peter realized that his wounds were no longer throbbing. He took an exploratory poke at his chest and shoulder and found them scabbed but much better. He flexed his hand; it was stiff and he wouldn't feel comfortable using it for some time, but the hole was gone.

"What are we going to do now?" Michelle asked.

Peter's mind was still fuzzy from sleep. "I don't know."

"Can't you do that bloodhound thing and track her?" she asked.

Bloodhound thing. Right. He'd forgotten that he had an extremely useless superpower. Only it helped him find Ian—twice, in fact.

"Ian had left a rather... strong smell behind. I don't know if I can smell Keepsie."

"So what are you waiting for, dumbass, at least try!"

Try. OK. He would try. If only he could make his brain work a little faster. He shook his head in a futile attempt to clear it.

His body felt as if it were made of lead. He struggled to his feet and went to the bar where Keepsie had slept. He put his head close to the bar and inhaled.

After a moment, he stood. "She's feeling guilty, consumed by it. She feels alone, like this is her problem to fix. She left and just went to wander the city. I don't think she knew where she was going. But I think she's at the Academy."

The others were aghast. "The Academy? Why?" Michelle asked.

"I don't know. Maybe that's where the answers are."

"What answers?" Jason asked.

"Whatever she's looking for."

Alex went to the window and peeked up to the street. "Nothing out there. It's dead."

"We have to go find her!" Michelle said. "The Academy's a wreck! It's not safe!"

The words took a long time to reach Peter's brain. "You're right. Let's go."

Michelle insisted they raid the kitchen before going, as they hadn't eaten in almost a day. Armed with little more than sandwiches, they left Keepsie's Bar.

"Peter, why were we able to take Keepsie's food?" Alex asked.

Peter swallowed a bite of ham sandwich. "She wants us to take it. If we didn't have her permission, we'd be stuck in her kitchen. It's a subtle distinction with fascinating—" he stopped when he heard a familiar clockwork clanging nearby.

"Doodad," Michelle said. They ran back into the stairwell and hid until the walker clanked by.

Something drifted down to the street. Michelle darted out and grabbed it: a bright red silk scarf.

"Hey, wait a minute. I've seen that before," Michelle said. "It was on that hero in the Academy—the Librarian. She was with Doodad?"

She handed the scarf to Peter. He took it and belatedly realized what he was supposed to do with it.

"Well?" Michelle asked.

"Look, I've spent my life trying not to use this power. It takes some getting used to," Peter said. He smelled the scarf.

Peter closed his eyes against the fear radiating off of it. "It is the Librarian. Doodad and Clever Jack have her."

"Why would they want to kidnap her?" Alex asked.

"She keeps the Academy's secrets." Peter said.

"That's bad," Alex said.

"But Keepsie..." Michelle said.

Peter sighed heavily. Every fiber of his body was screaming at him to go after Keepsie. But she was immortal, or at least she couldn't be killed. The Librarian was not, that he knew of.

"If we let them keep The Librarian, we'll be giving them another weapon. We've already given them too much," he said finally. "We have to split up."

Michelle nodded. "Peter, you and I and Alex can go after the Librarian. Alex has a cell phone. Tomas, Jason, and Barry can go after Keepsie."

"How do we find her?" Jason asked.

"Oh! Wait! I just got an idea!" Michelle said, and ran back inside Keepsie's bar. She came out a moment later with a pair of panties.

Peter blushed furiously. "What are you planning on doing with those?"

"I figured you should have some dirty laundry so you can track her better."

"Good Lord, Michelle!" he said. "Can't you get a dirty sweat-shirt or something?"

Michelle made a face at him and went back inside the bar.

Jason grinned while Alex and Barry howled with laughter while Tomas looked puzzled. "Why does she have dirty panties in her bar?"

Peter willed the blood to leave his hot face, and felt close to normal when Michelle emerged carrying a rumpled tank top.

"That's fine," Peter grabbed the shirt and held it to his face, as much to get away from the laughter as to smell Keepsie. He nodded. "She is on her way back to the bar. I think all you guys need to do is wait here." He stuffed the shirt into his back pocket, where it dangled like a white flag.

He fixed his gaze on Tomas, the tall Norseman staring at him impassively. "Please protect her." Holding the gaudy scarf to his nose, he jogged down the street, away from Keepsie.

#

The Seventh City park was a masterwork of public planning. It was fifty acres alongside the Weaver River and had incorporated a naturally occurring large ridge that some city officials had wanted removed, but the planners said it could be part of the park, adding hiking to the draw of Seventh City.

It took on an L shape, with the large hill at the right angle. Underneath the hill were some fox holes that no one had ever worried about filling, as they'd wanted to keep the park's wildlife balanced. A couple of animal rights groups made some arguments on the rabbits' behalf, but not very convincing ones.

It was to the base of the hill and these foxholes that Peter tracked the Librarian and Doodad.

"In there," Alex said, his voice tinged with disbelief.

"Yes. They came here. The hill opens up somehow," Peter said, looking around for some sort of switch. Sparse bushes around the nearly hidden foxhole proved to hold no hidden switch, and there was no nearby tree with a convenient branch to pull on.

He threw up his hands in exasperation. "I don't know. But that's where she is."

"But we can't go down there, Peter," Michelle said.

"Yes, thanks, Michelle," Peter said bitterly.

"So now what?" Alex said, and as if in answer, the hill began to rumble. They stumbled back as a round portal appeared in the side of the hill, rolling in and aside to reveal a dimly lit hallway.

Clever Jack peeked out. "Oh, what luck!" He exited the hill and stepped aside. An older man peeked out after him, and Michelle gasped.

"You told us Seismic Stan was dead," Peter said.

"Yeah, I lied about that," Clever Jack said, giving the man a hand out of the hill.

Stan was about fifty, the same age as Pallas, but he looked much older. His hair was steel gray and his face was heavily lined. He wore a hard hat and a pair of goggles. He looked ridiculous, but his absurdity was more frightening than silly.

"Run," Peter said.

He'd barely made it ten steps when the ground turned to liquid and covered him in a wave. Dirt knocked him over as his legs gave way into the grassy, bubbling earth. He sank, flailing, and came to a stop when he was buried to his neck. His heart hammered in his ears as he tried to crane his neck around and see where the others were and if they had made it.

Michelle lay on the grass, unconscious. She bled from a head wound and Peter saw a rock nearby, also bloody.

Alex was buried similarly to Peter, glaring at their captors. Peter faced away from them and could only hear the footsteps by his ears.

Clever Jack squatted down. "Heya Petey. S'up?"

Peter was done being diplomatic with Clever Jack. He was a villain, and there was nothing Peter could say that would make things better for him.

"Where's the Librarian?" he asked. He sounded very impotent.

"Wow, you tracked her here? You're impressive," Clever Jack said, losing the tone of superior amusement. "Come on, we'll take you to her."

Where the Academy's cellblock was the epitome of technological superiority, the villains' caves stank of medieval torture. To be fair, it was the heroes that had tortured Peter and Keepsie, and not the villains, but their hobbit-hole of a hideout was complete with iron-gated cells. Clever Jack led them down the narrow tunnel, the silent and glowering Stan following them.

"That one's White Lightning's," Clever Jack said, leading them down underneath the hill, pointing at a cage. "That reinforced one is Pallas's. See that hole over there? That's where The Crane is going to go. Stan dug us a really deep pit for that stretchy bastard. There's a puddle of mud at the bottom." He chuckled. "You guys, you're going in with the Librarian. You wanted to see her, and I'm nothing if not accommodating."

"Then he must be nothing," Alex whispered to Peter, who was still trying to remove the dirt from his ears.

Doodad stood outside a cell with apparently no door, only iron bars. The Librarian sat in the corner, her pristine hair still knotted into its bun and her clothes immaculate. Peter wondered if part of her power was to look the part of the librarian as well as have super informative powers. He wondered if now was perhaps not the right time to ask her.

Doodad placed his hand on the bars and there was a low rumbling and a soft clink, and the bars parted. The Librarian looked at each of them in turn and did not move.

Clever Jack ushered them inside. "Your new home! Dinner is at six. I hope you like pizza." The villains walked back up the hall.

The Librarian addressed each of them in a wooden and disinterested voice. "Peter Ross. Olfactory knowledge of people. Michelle Cooper. Unable to lose balance of a loaded bar tray. A very detailed power. Alex Cardon. Healing power in the area of one square inch at a time, which drains you terribly."

Michelle snorted. "And you are?"

Her glasses glinted in the firelight. "I am the Librarian. I store and retain all knowledge given to me."

"You've got all of the Academy's secrets?" Alex asked.

"Yes." She sat down and leaned her head against the dirt wall.

"So, no magical digging powers?" Michelle ventured.

"None. Seismic Stan, previously thought to be dead, is to date the only known human who can manipulate the land," The Librarian said.

"And he is unlikely to help us," said Peter, sitting down beside her.

"How did he catch you?" Alex asked.

"I was hiding at Heretic's apartment. I thought she could keep me safe, but Doodad found me after Dr. Timson called Heretic away to fight... the newest threat."

"And the new threat would be?" Peter asked.

The Librarian shook her head. "That is classified."

Michelle ran her hands along the bars, pulling at them. "Well guys, it seems our rescue effort failed."

"Well, it's nice that our days are having consistency," Peter said. "We might as well wait for pizza."

"I hope it's vegetarian," Alex said. Peter looked at him for a surprised moment and then started to laugh. Michelle joined them, and for a moment, it really did seem funny.

17

Keepsie regarded the chaos around her with a sick disinterest. She knew it was her fault. There was no "almost" here. Entirely her fault. Although they may be pigheaded torturing bastards, heroes did keep the city free from harm. And the villains clearly did not.

She had headed away from the Academy and the bar, first, wanting to clear her head without being met with her responsibilities.

Where was Pallas? The strongest of the heroes should be here to deal with everything, but she was gone. Keepsie hadn't seen her in weeks. She was probably the one hero Keepsie could stomach.

Of course, Pallas hadn't caused all this damage.

The heroes still battled the glowing girl, and it didn't seem as if she was fighting back. They were high in the air, on the outskirts of town, away from the wreckage of the Academy. The Academy Keepsie had helped wreck.

She shook her head slowly, and started walking toward it.

The chaos got worse closer to the Academy. What had looked like simple mayhem on par with something Bugs Bunny would do was now turning into serious violence. A storefront burned brightly with no promising sirens in the distance. A woman lay on the hood of a car, blood caked and tacky around her, shattered glass indicating she'd been dropped. Her legs and neck bent at odd angles that made Keepsie light-headed to look at, but she didn't turn away.

The drones still hovered in the sky above the Academy, diving in and out of the thick smoke that billowed from the formerly white building. More proof of their carnage littered the streets in the form of dead dogs, cars lying on their sides, and more burning buildings. The walk to the center of the city seemed shorter than usual, as walks usually did when one was about to face something unpleasant at the end.

She stood in the middle of the street with her bar on her left and the Academy on the right. The eerie silence that had engulfed the previous blocks was now gone, replaced with the buzz of the drones.

They surrounded the Academy, smaller ones rooting around inside, larger ones clearly guarding it. As she approached, they clacked toward her, raising their weapons. She backed off and they returned to their posts.

She wondered if anyone had been trapped inside. She considered her options.

She could run in there and die. She could go home and go to bed and let more innocent people die. Or she could go back down to her bar and talk to her friends. Peter would have an idea what to do, and Michelle would back him up, if she didn't think the idea was stupid.

#

"They went where?"

Tomas patiently repeated himself. "To rescue The Librarian, a hero you apparently encountered at the Academy."

"But why rescue a hero? Why not let the other heroes do it?"

"The heroes are otherwise occupied. The villains seem to be gathering resources, and The Librarian holds the secrets of the heroes."

"Oh crap."

Tomas nodded.

Barry brought Keepsie a soda. "You back with us, Keepsie?"

Keepsie grinned at him, enjoying the paternal-like attention.

"I'm OK. I could be better. We need some more reinforcements. Did Michelle manage to call anyone?"

"I think she got through to Colette, who was going to try to find some other people. She said she'd be here soon. She's bringing her car."

Keepsie took a deep breath. She had several doubts about her plan, especially considering her previous attempts at getting involved. She was an ant trying to meddle in the affairs of giants.

She went to the kitchen and grabbed a bag of chips, and became aware of an increasing need for more food. She turned the knob on the grill and went back out to the bar.

Underneath the counter was a Rolodex of emergency numbers; people Keepsie felt she could count on. She hadn't been able to get to them yesterday, but now she felt more grounded with the numbers available.

The first one she called was Wanda, the waitress with the perfect memory.

"Wanda, it's Keepsie Branson."

"Holy shit, Keepsie, bad time to talk to me about that job. Have you looked outside? The shit's coming down," came the deep, feminine voice on the other end.

"Well, I'm not exactly calling about that job, Wanda," Keepsie said patiently. "But I do need your help."

"Sure thing, kiddo, as long as it doesn't require me to leave home. And where the hell are the heroes, I ask you?"

Damn. "They're fighting a big bad, Wanda. There's shit going down everywhere. You can stay home. I just need to ask you some questions about some phone numbers and some powers."

Silence at the other end. Then Wanda said, "You know, kid, when you asked me to catalogue all of that stuff years ago, I thought you were just getting your kicks spying on your customers. I didn't actually think you'd ever use it."

"I didn't think I'd ever need it, sorry to say," Keepsie said, blushing a little. It had made her feel sneaky to keep track of everything she knew about her customers, but Wanda's memory banks were infinite, as far as they could tell, and she didn't mind loaning a bit of her space to Keepsie.

"So what exactly do you need?" Wanda asked, her voice getting the waitress matter-of-factness she used at work.

"Names. Phone numbers. Powers. And anything you know about any Third Waves that I didn't tell you."

"Right. OK. There's you, Laura Keepsie Branson, who can't have anything taken away from you. You place anyone who attacks your personal belongings in a full stasis mode, whatever that is, and anyone robbing something of yours that is not on your person is trapped with the offending extremity, usually an arm, held until you free them. Ian Smith, also known as Feculent Boy, who can shoot feces from his fists. Totally gross," she added.

Keepsie clamped her teeth together to avoid interrupting her. Wanda had her way of regurgitating information, and didn't appreciate being interrupted even if her information was useless. Once she had gone through Keepsie's closest friends, she started giving useful information, and Keepsie started to write.

#

Few people were game for venturing out, Keepsie discovered. Those she had talked with last night who decided not to help her were openly hostile. Coming across Alex's name on the sheet, she tried his cell.

The voice that answered was quick and whispered. "Hello? Who's this?"

"Hey Alex, it's Keepsie," she said. "I just wanted—"

"Keepsie, where the hell are you?" he asked. He sounded terrified, his voice a hoarse whisper.

"I'm at the bar. Listen—"

"Keepsie?" It was Peter this time. His voice was much more calm than Alex's, but still hushed. "Are you all right?"

"Yeah, I'm at the bar. Did you find the Librarian yet?"

"We've been captured by Clever Jack and Doodad. You have to tell the heroes that Seismic Stan is alive and with Clever Jack and Doodad."

"Oh my God, are you guys OK?" Keepsie asked, her heart pounding.

"We are fine. They also have the Librarian. I believe they are torturing her into learning the heroes' weaknesses so they will know how to best defeat them. You have to tell them, Keepsie, tell the heroes, tell them before—oh no," his voice dropped in despair.

"Wait, where are you guys? Where are they keeping you?"

The phone went dead. "Peter! Peter! Dammit, Peter!"

Tomas and Barry looked at her with concern.

"Clever Jack and Doodad have Peter, Michelle and Alex," she said in a wooden voice.

There was something else Peter had said, but Keepsie couldn't remember it.

"Where are they?"

"I don't know. He didn't get a chance to tell me, I guess Clever Jack found out they had a cell phone. What are we going to do?" she asked him, her voice shaking.

"There's not much we can do, not with Doodad's drones watching us. If he and Clever Jack see us coming—"

Shit. "Tomas, it's not just the two of them. It's Seismic Stan too. Peter said we have to tell the Academy."

Tomas stared at her, his face growing white.

"We need to get out of here," she said.

He shook his head. "But Colette is on her way here."

Keepsie swore and ran past him and up the stairs to the street. A car drove down the cluttered street, and Keepsie saw Colette behind the wheel. She waved at her and turned to look east.

A rumbling sound echoed over the buildings, and Keepsie stumbled. The glass in several storefronts cracked.

"Inside, now!" Keepsie yelled to Colette, who climbed out of her brown sedan.

Keepsie stood still for a moment, bracing herself on the railing, as her cook ran past her down the stairs. She then followed her.

When she got into the bar, Barry and Tomas were white-faced and talking in low voices. They looked up when she walked in.

"This is it," she said, running behind the bar and rummaging in a toolbox. "Ian is a turncoat; Peter, Michelle and Alex are captured, the villain who makes Jack and Doodad look like Boy Scouts is alive, and no one else will help us."

She stood up, a short bat in her hand. She flipped through the Rolodex, grabbed a card that was outlined in black and handed it to Barry. "Call the Academy, let them know what's coming and the information they're likely to need. Barry, Jason, Colette, let's, uh, arm ourselves, I guess."

"But the Academy is gone. That glowing girl blew it up," Tomas said.

"They have an answering service in case the phones go out," Keepsie said. "They're really efficient, if we take a moment to stop hating them."

Tomas returned to the phone with the card in hand and started dialing. Keepsie put the toolbox on the bar. Inside was an assortment of bludgeoning weapons from wrenches to short bats. Barry stared at her.

"Would you prefer a knife? I think Colette can lower the 'no one touches my knives' rule for today," Keepsie said. Colette nodded grimly, her blonde braid bobbing off her neck. "But this is what I have to keep the bar fights to a minimum."

"Keepsie, I'm fifty-five years old," Barry said. "My dreams of fighting super villains died about twenty-five years ago."

"Then why are you here?" she asked. "You, Tomas, and Colette are the only ones who showed up. Jason's here by chance. I need someone to help. I need someone to have my back because I'm not sure I know what the hell I'm doing. I need someone who has planned his whole life to be a hero but the Academy decided otherwise. But if you are too old, then by all means, stay here. Of course, if Stan decides to get his revenge on the city, you'll be in a basement in an earthquake with two stories of steel and stone above you."

Barry stared at her for a moment. Without moving his eyes from her face, he reached into the toolbox and pulled out a wrench. "I'm set."

"Good," she said with a nod. "Tomas, there's a bat in the back if you want. Colette, get yourself a knife."

Colette walked into the kitchen, her jaw set.

Tomas slammed the phone down, causing Keepsie and Barry to jump. "The answering service will not believe me. They said the heroes are too busy keeping the city safe to start chasing ghosts. They will not listen!" He broke off into a string of Norwegian.

Keepsie sighed. "Then it's just us, then. Great."

Colette returned from the kitchen, her apron on and her chef's knife tucked into the strings. "I'm not going. Someone has to hold down the fort."

Keepsie stared at her. "Did you hear us? Seismic Stan. Here. Earthquakes. Basement bar. Besides, you know best how to filet someone, we need you and your knife."

Keepsie expected Colette to go red with rage, but the color drained from her face. "So I'm dead if I stay, and I'm likely dead if I go."

Keepsie put her hand on her arm. "If you stay and die, you'll be alone, and won't help anyone. If you go and die, you'll be with us, and you'll have tried to help Peter."

Colette grunted. "Fine. We'll take my car."

Her motley crew assembled, Keepsie took a moment at the door to compose herself, then opened it.

The street was deathly quiet. Keepsie wondered for a moment where the townspeople were; had they had evacuated or were they hiding in their homes? Another rumble sounded from far away and Keepsie staggered.

They piled into the car and sat panting for a moment, Colette at the wheel.

"So leader," Colette asked, "where are we going?"

Keepsie swallowed and pointed east. "Go that way. I hate to say it, but that's where the rumbles were coming from, and wherever Stan is, is where Clever Jack and Doodad are. And wherever Clever Jack and Doodad are, that's where the others are."

Colette nodded, and floored it.

Keepsie turned around in her seat. The Academy still belched smoke from its innards, and Keepsie felt a shameful but true sense of satisfaction.

Colette drove them away from the carnage, swerving in the road to avoid more of Doodad's robots that tried to jump onto the car. The rumbling continued and Colette swerved again to avoid trashcans and displaced parked cars. The road started to split ahead of them, a black crack in the asphalt.

"Oh, shit, Colette," Barry said, bracing himself on the dash.

"Hold on," Colette said, her voice low and concentrated. "My suspension's going to be shit after this."

She floored it and they bounced high as the car barreled over the broken road. The car gave a great groan and limped to a stop at the park. The rumbling stopped for the moment, and Colette turned in her seat, wincing as her she did so.

"I'll probably need a raise to pay for a new car," she said.

Keepsie took a deep breath, realizing she'd been holding it. "You've got it."

18

Peter stared at the dropped cell phone, which had begun to short circuit against his face. He looked up and Doodad was glaring at him.

"Where did you get that?" he asked.

"We had it, you dumbass," Michelle said. "Should have frisked us, shouldn't you?"

Doodad colored. Peter remembered the reports on the news warning the populace of this man's intellect as well as his physical strength, and he groaned. The stereotype of being big and dumb was not one Doodad appreciated.

The cell phone animated at his feet at sprouted spindly metallic legs. It skittered across the floor towards Michelle. She gave a disgusted cry and shrank against the wall.

The cell phone leapt onto her thigh and dug its sharp legs through her jeans and into her flesh. Michelle screamed. "Get it off me!"

Doodad smiled coldly, watching her writhe as his construct dug itself into her leg. Michelle plucked it from her leg with a cry and with shaking hands threw it at the bars where it ricocheted and bounced onto the hall's dirt floor.

Doodad took a step towards the bars that separated him and Peter.

"Any more electronics in there?" he asked.

Peter opened his mouth, and Doodad held up his hand. "Never mind. I'll find out on my own." He concentrated and Peter felt his pocket writhe as his pocket change came to life and melted together, forming a small metal humanoid that crawled out of his pocket. Alex had a similar item crawl out of his, and Michelle swore as her rings and earrings slithered off of her like snakes.

The metal followed Doodad, who smirked and left.

Michelle to sat and rubbed her leg while Peter stared after Doodad thoughtfully.

"I didn't know he could do that with metal," he said. "I thought he was only good with machines."

It had been an hour since the Librarian had been taken from them. Peter wondered if the villain's method of torture was worse than the heroes'. He hoped he wouldn't have to find out.

A metallic cot clinked down the hall, walking on stiff legs, followed by the stony-faced Doodad. The Librarian lay on top of it, dirt and twigs caught in her face and hair. She looked as if she'd been buried alive.

Peter rushed to the bars, Alex beside him. "Is she alive?" Alex asked.

"She's unconscious," Doodad said. "Lucky we caught you guys, now she won't die after all, will she, little healer?"

The cot walked into the cell as the bars bent themselves back. "She held out for a lot longer than Stan figured she would. Good luck with her," Doodad said, and left them alone.

The Librarian breathed shallowly, coughing weakly every few breaths.

"Can you help her?" Peter asked.

Alex placed his hands on the Librarian's ribs. He closed his eyes and nodded. "I think Patricia would be more useful here, but I think I can help."

"Patricia can only remove alcohol, not dirt," Michelle spoke up, and closed her mouth when Peter glared at her.

Alex's face relaxed. "Ohh... it's like an infection. I can do this. It will just take time."

Peter ground his teeth and forced himself to step back, knowing he could do nothing to help Alex.

"Do you think she gave them information?" Michelle whispered to him.

"Doodad says she did. I can't figure out why he would lie to us. It's not like he can trick us into giving him information—we don't have any," Peter said, watching Alex concentrate.

His healing powers were so slow. Peter couldn't see any change in the shallow, labored breathing of the Librarian. He paced the length of the cell, trying to think of a way out.

He hadn't had a chance to tell Keepsie where they were being kept. And if Doodad's constructs and that glowing girl were attacking the heroes, they would be occupied with protecting the city, not tracking down the villains behind it all.

He sat against the wall and cradled his head in his hands. Michelle sat beside him.

"I was thinking about what you were saying," she said.

Peter raised his head wearily. "What are you referring to?"

"About my powers. That I might try using them offensively."

"Well, you can lift a lot of weight on a bar tray, right?" Peter asked, watching Alex.

"Yeah. That means I can probably throw something heavy, as long as it's on a bar tray, I mean. Or I could just throw a bar tray that had been shaved off at the edge."

Peter frowned. "You mean like a discus?"

"I was thinking something closer to Xena and her throwing circle thing, but yeah."

Peter looked around the sparse cell. "But we don't have a bar tray in here." There were torch sconces in the wall, but no torches. The only thing in the room besides the four of them was the mechanical cot that held the Librarian.

"No. I guess not." Michelle lapsed into silence and stared at Alex, whose eyes were still closed.

Alex relaxed and sagged, staggering backwards. Peter jumped up and steadied him.

"She's OK, now. All the dirt's gone, airway's clear," he mumbled, and slumped against Peter, who carefully lowered him to the floor.

Michelle bent over the Librarian, who was struggling to sit up. "How are you feeling?"

"Alex Cardon," she said, focusing on the unconscious man. "Very limited healing powers."

"Oh, that's nice. He saved your life, bitch," Michelle said.

"Yes, I suppose he did," the Librarian said. She looked at both of them. "So my rescuers are a woman who can control a bar tray and a man who can find limited information about someone by smelling them."

Peter ground his teeth. "So, what are your powers, anyway? We've got someone like you on our side, Wanda Greene, how are you a hero with a special name and a position in the Academy when she's a waitress?"

"Wanda Greene. Perfect memory, limited intelligence," she said. She was starting to sound like a computer. "My powers are perfect memory, enhanced intelligence, superior organization, cross-referencing, not to mention I am entrusted with the Academy's secrets. I am a hero, unlike a First or Third Wave human." She gave Michelle a pointed look.

Peter swallowed his annoyance. "But, then why did you help Keepsie escape last night?"

"Simple logic. Keepsie clearly had the upper hand. None of our heroes could kill her, and she had several hostages."

Michelle snorted. "I thought heroes like you didn't negotiate with terrorists."

The Librarian rubbed at her eyes and wiped dust from her face. "The Third Wavers are neither terrorists nor villains. You were in our way and we underestimated you. That is all."

Michelle opened her mouth to retort but Peter shushed her. "What about the villains. What did you tell them?"

The Librarian lowered her eyes. "Everything they asked. I am not a combat hero. I am not trained in withstanding interrogation and torture."

Peter knelt beside her. "Listen, we need to get out of here, we need to get you, and probably most of us, to a doctor. What can you tell us about Clever Jack and Doodad? Jack told us that the heroes and villains were engineered in the halls of the Academy."

The Librarian opened her mouth and then closed it. "No, there's no use in denying it at this point. Yes, they were raised within the Academy. Clever Jack Townsend: impossible luck. No weaknesses known. Eric Timson, Doodad, mastery of machines, bears an insane grudge against his mother. The villains weren't engineered, exactly. They were meant to be heroes. They were just bad seeds."

"What about Clever Jack's mom?" Michelle asked. "He seems to be a lot less bitter than Doodad."

"Clever Jack's mother came from the Appalachian Mountains. She had gotten herself in trouble but had read about the Academy's offer for free prenatal care and discreet adoption, so she came to Seventh City for the drug treatment. When Clever Jack was born, the doctor dropped him. At the same time, a nurse slipped and fell right under Clever Jack, giving him a soft landing."

The Librarian smiled. "Everyone pretty much figured out his power right then. His mother said he was like the Clever Jack of Appalachian folklore. The lucky bastard, she called him. So she named him Jack. When it came time to choose our hero names in our teens, Jack became Clever Jack."

"Sounds like he liked his mom," Michelle said.

"His mother left soon after weaning Clever Jack. She went back home with her future secured by the Academy. We do suspect that when Clever Jack escaped the Academy years ago that he sought her out. We don't know if he succeeded." She took a deep breath. "Either way, he has been working to free his delinquent friends. He already has Doodad, and he apparently found Seismic Stan, which was impressive considering the Academy thought him dead years ago."

Peter made an exasperated sound. "And?"

She was a crappy actress and tried to feign innocence. "And what?"

"The girl who blew up the Academy. Jack freed her. Who was she?"

She glared at him and swung her legs over the side of the cot. "You already know far too much and you don't need to know anything else. Look what you managed: you were manipulated into helping the villains, you broke the law to become a vigilante group, and then got locked up. Any more information would not help you break those bars."

Peter stared at her. "You know, you've never denied any of the things we found out. You really haven't taken the stance that the Academy usually takes when these questions are brought up."

She stood, wavering slightly. Peter didn't move to support her. "My name is The Librarian, not Public Relations Woman. I say what I think is in the best interest of myself and the Academy in my opinion. That's why I only serve the Academy internally. They don't really agree with me. I suppose I have the opposite of Ghostheart's lying power."

Michelle's head snapped up. "Lying power..."

Peter felt his mind clear as if by magic. Or a superpower. "Her power is lying. It makes perfect sense. Oh thank God."

The Librarian's face crumpled and she sat back down on the cot. "Oh my. You didn't know, do you? This was the one thing you didn't know. And I told you."

Peter smiled, feeling as if something had finally gone right. "We were entirely duped by her. I've been kicking myself for the last day, trying to figure out how none of us figured her out."

Michelle nodded. "Super lies. I guess this is why we never knew about her as a hero. But why do we see through them all?"

The Librarian sustained her stony silence.

Peter laughed. "Because that's her weakness. Her power doesn't work if you know what it is."

Michelle got up and went to sit beside the Librarian on the cot. "While this is great for our egos, it's not going to help us out of this cell."

"Wait," Peter said. "Get up, both of you." He offered his hand to help Michelle up, but simply waited for The Librarian to make her morose way off the cot.

The cot was made of flat metal plates jointed together in an odd, somewhat organic way. The metal forming it was dense and heavy; Peter guessed it was iron. He pulled at one of the legs experimentally, and it didn't budge.

"Michelle, come here," he said. "See if you can lift this."

Michelle gave the cot a dubious look. "What are you talking about? If you can't move it, there's no way I can."

"Sure you can. See here?" He pointed to the underside of the cot where one of the metal plates was. "This is just a bar tray with some extraneous things hanging off the edge."

"You're kidding, right?"

"Look, just try to lift it. You said yourself that you wanted to see if your powers could span farther than you'd thought."

Michelle stared at the cot for a moment. She knelt and put her hand on the bottom of one of the plates.

"One order of cheese fries, with a fucked up living metal walking cot on the side," she muttered, and stood, hefting the cot easily onto her shoulder.

Her face lit up. Even though she clearly carried it lopsided, with her hand at one side and not supporting the other at all, it sat easily and flat on her hand.

Peter grinned. "Excellent."

The Librarian stared at Michelle with a glazed look in her eye. "Michelle Cooper. Powers upgraded to include lifting possibly anything with a flat underside. Power level upgrade to 4, possibly higher."

"Give it a rest," Peter said.

Michelle put the cot down with ease, and Peter embraced her. "We have a weapon now."

19

Keepsie climbed out of Colette's car. "So do you guys know about a hero—or villain—who is all glowy like that girl?"

"You mean that light show?" Barry asked, slamming the car door. "Never. And I remember when Pallas and Seismic Stan had their first battle."

Tomas nodded. "My ex-wife was a hero groupie, and she tracked all of them. I do not remember someone who could do, well, whatever it was that person did."

"How are we going to do this?" Colette said.

Keepsie chewed her lip. The details were always the hard part. "Let's get out and get into the trees and see what we can find out. It's dark enough that we won't be seen."

"Yes, and we will not be able to see either," Tomas grumbled, but followed them.

"Sure we will," Keepsie said. "Can't one of you glow like that woman back there?"

The glow was still bright twenty blocks away. They couldn't hear anything going on, but it was clear the girl was still there.

Barry chuckled, coming up behind Keepsie. "Sure thing. You bet. My ass'll start glowing right pretty like a firefly, just a second."

They all laughed and the tension lifted. With the headlights off, the only light was an occasional building that hadn't lost power and that odd villain who still shone her light against the horizon. They headed for the trees and made their way towards the hill, where demons still flew out.

"Can you see anything?" Keepsie whispered.

"There is a hole in the side of the hill," Tomas replied. "And Doodad is there."

"That's where Peter is," Keepsie said, and inched closer. The hole was clear now. "So. Who has super-hearing?" Keepsie asked.

"Why are you asking us this? You know what we can do," Tomas asked, sounding annoyed.

"Sorry. I'm just feeling like we're the only ones that can stop them, but I have no idea what to do," Keepsie said, abashed.

Barry silenced them and looked at the hill. Clever Jack climbed out of the hole and looked at the horizon. He laughed, and Keepsie cringed at the sound.

"Doodad! She's on her way back!" he said. "She's waking up!"

Keepsie felt her throat close with adrenaline. Now was the time, before that door closed. Her legs locked up and her vision swam. What was she going to do? Yell at them?

"Keepsie? We need to do something now," Barry said mildly.

She took a deep breath to steady herself. "Right. You guys distract him. I've got to get in that hill."

"But how—" Barry asked, but Tomas interrupted him.

"Barry, your leg please."

"What? Oh," Barry said, and twisted his left leg off at the thigh. He held onto Colette's shoulder for balance and handed the leg to Tomas.

Tomas hefted the leg to his shoulder, javelin-style. The leg remained stiff, and Tomas grunted as he heaved it. His brief burst of strength gave it enough velocity that Keepsie actually heard the wind whistling through the leg hair.

While the leg was airborne, Keepsie shot forward and dashed towards Doodad. Tomas was right behind her; Barry had to wait for the new leg to grow in before he could run.

The leg hit Doodad squarely in the face, foot-first, and he fell backwards in a howl of pain. As he staggered and fell, Keepsie saw something shine against the unholy glow of—yes, the girl was approaching them fast. Keepsie dropped to her knees and felt around for it.

Doodad's voice was thick and garbled with pain as he swore. Keepsie remembered Clever Jack and shouted a warning to Tomas.

It was too late. Clever Jack's power kicked in as Tomas got to him, making Tomas slip in the grass and fall hard on his belly, knocking the wind out of him.

Clever Jack stood beside them, watching the three of them in their various positions in the grass.

Clever Jack bent down to where Tomas lay, struggling to get his breath. "You guys are certainly more entertaining than the heroes. Did you really think you could—" he was cut off when Barry slipped behind him and swung at the back of the head with his leg, baseball-style. Barry whiffed and toppled over on his one leg as Clever Jack ducked.

So heroic, Keepsie thought. Doodad was starting to rise and she scrambled around the grass faster.

Her eyes must have been adjusting to the dark because she finally spied the ball near Doodad's shoulder. He clutched his face with his hands and smeared blood all over his cheeks.

Her hand closed around the small, warm sphere right as Doodad's hand fell on hers. She nearly sobbed with relief as the villain froze beside her.

"No!" screamed Clever Jack lunging at her. He landed on her full force and she fell backwards with his weight on her.

What's wrong, why didn't I get him? She realized he was too smart to try to steal from her. He grabbed her lapels and shook her.

"You are your pathetic little friends are not going to ruin this for us!" he said. His breath was hot and foul. "Let him go or I'll make you wish the heroes had killed you."

Her left hand was closed tightly on the ball but her right was free. Tomas, Barry and Colette looked at each other and nodded. Could Clever Jack's luck protect him from all four of them?

Her right hand was close to Doodad's immobile fingers. She grabbed the frozen villain's hand and swung Doodad like a weapon just as the three standing attacked.

Barry was unlucky again, his right leg coming free from his body even as he swung his left. He fell on his left side and grunted. Colette swung with her knife, slicing into Barry's leg. Tomas also missed, growling low in his throat and swinging a punch at Clever Jack that Keepsie knew had his brief super-strength behind it. Right as he swung, Clever Jack leaned in again and opened his mouth to say something else, but Doodad's immobile body connected with his head and he fell off Keepsie and stirred briefly in the grass.

They sat panting. Barry groaned. "Did we win?"

"I think so…" Keepsie said.

Colette stashed her knife. "How were you able to hit him?"

Keepsie got to her feet, stashing the ball in her pocket. "No idea. Maybe we just overwhelmed him."

Tomas looked at the brightening cityscape as the girl flew toward them. "I think we should get out of here as soon as possible. You go inside, I will watch Clever Jack in case he wakes."

"Right," Keepsie said. She approached the hole in the side of the hill, Doodad floating behind her.

Barry came up behind her. "An honest to God villain lair. I can't believe this is so close to the Academy."

Keepsie nodded, climbing inside the hill. "You'd think they'd want to be as far away as possible."

Colette grunted as she followed them. "Not necessarily. The Academy has secrets they want. Like that drug. Which I'd like to take a look at when we get a chance."

"Sure," Keepsie said, brushing the floating Doodad out of her friends' way.

Colette stopped at the doorway to a room littered with metallic parts. "Go ahead, Keepsie. I'll catch up."

"Sure thing."

Their friends called from within. Keepsie ran down the dirt hall, deeper into the hill, until they found Peter's cell.

Peter, Michelle, Alex and the Librarian waved at them from a cell.

Keepsie hugged Michelle uncomfortably through the bars. "Are you guys OK?"

"Yeah. Alex healed what he could," Peter said. "What's going on up there?"

"Stan's hitting the city with earthquakes," Keepsie said. "The heroes haven't taken down that glowing girl yet and she's on her way here, the heroes behind her."

The Librarian clapped her hand to her mouth. "Light of Mornings. They haven't been able to cage Light of Mornings yet, and now it sounds like she's awake."

Peter glared at the woman. "So now will you tell us who she is?"

The Librarian didn't look at him. "She emanates nuclear radiation. She has been artificially asleep in a special cell of the Academy since her teenage years when she became too difficult to control."

"And let me guess," Keepsie said, her shoulders slumping. "She and Clever Jack were best friends."

20

Keepsie looked different. Peter couldn't put his finger on it, but it was beyond the physical injuries she'd gotten in the past twenty-four or so hours. She listened to the Librarian with a clear, concerned look on her face.

Light of Mornings had been born two years after Clever Jack and Doodad, in the Academy's third round of successful hero creation. She had glowed from birth, and the scientists who engineered her thought her power was merely one of light. Useful, but no more exciting than Third or First Wave.

Her mother died soon after childbirth. The autopsy revealed radiation sickness. Light of Mornings, her given name Olivia, was quarantined until she could be taught to control her powers.

She learned to control the radiation when she was around four, but it still burst forth in times of high emotion. She was trusted to be around her peers when she was 12, interacting with the other children of the Academy for the first time.

"Whoa, that must have been really tough for her, since she'd been isolated and all," said Michelle.

The Librarian nodded and continued with her story.

Clever Jack, Doodad, Tattoo Devil and Heretic made fast friends with Light of Mornings. She was uncomfortable around the other kids, who were learning their strength, speed or flight powers. Clever Jack and Doodad hadn't begun to exhibit any signs of delinquency at this point.

Keepsie exchanged a look with Peter and he flushed. *Stop it. You're thirty-four years old.*

It was Light of Mornings who caused Clever Jack and Doodad to turn "the way of Seismic Stan." Delighted with her new friends, Light of Mornings would try to focus her power to melt metal, and with Doodad's help, they sent molten, dripping mechs to follow instructors down the hall. One was burned badly from the hot metal and they got their first detention.

Tattoo Devil had even experimented with her, having her burn a design on his skin to see if his power would work on the burn as it did on the ink, but it merely scarred his shoulder.

Each time she was put in detention with a co-conspirator, she was warned that she would be isolated again if she misused her powers. Her friendship with Clever Jack made it more and more difficult for the scientists to catch her, and only the tell-tale radiation burns indicated that she'd been causing damage again.

Then the incident happened. The Librarian refused to say what had happened, only that it caused the scientists to research and develop a sleep chamber to contain Light of Mornings. Clever Jack and Doodad had escaped after the incident, and Tattoo Devil and Heretic had been left behind, shocked and submissive to their instructors.

"The fact that she is now flying means her powers have evolved while she slept, and there's no telling how strong she is now," The Librarian said.

"Does anyone else feel like they just want to stay down here until this all plays out?" asked Barry hopefully.

Keepsie shook her head. "We have to stop them. First Stan, then the most powerful super villain released, man, I'm having a productive day."

Colette came down the hall, looking preoccupied. "Everyone OK here?"

"I think the first order of business is getting us out of this cell," Peter said. He ran his hands up and down the bars. They showed none of the fluidity that they exhibited when Doodad commanded them.

The Librarian piped up. "Doodad's power allows him to manipulate machinery. It's likely only opened by his power alone."

Tomas got behind the immobile Doodad and placed his hands around his neck. "Keepsie, you can release him, and if he doesn't let our friends out, I can crush his throat."

Peter held his breath as Keepsie stared at Doodad. "We're letting you go, then you will let them out. Tomas is serious. He's from Norway. They don't fuck around."

"What does that have to do—" Michelle whispered to Peter, but he shushed her.

In a moment Doodad was freed. He snarled at Keepsie, but Tomas tightened his grip. Tomas was one of the few men who could match Doodad's size and girth, and he looked quite comfortable with the villain's neck in his hand.

Doodad didn't move, but the machinery inside the bars whirred again and they parted wide enough for the captives to get out.

"I knew we could make friends," Keepsie said. To the others, she said, "Let's go."

As they walked up the corridor, Tomas behind Doodad, Peter asked Keepsie, "Are you OK?"

"No. But I'm better," she said, grinning. "I got you guys out, didn't I?"

He stiffened as she wrapped her arm around his waist briefly and gave him a half-hug. "I'm sorry about all the shit earlier. I was kind of overwhelmed."

"Right," he managed to say.

She peered up at him. "You still mad?"

"Uh, no, it's just been a stressful sort of day, that's all. Thanks for the cavalry."

She dropped her eyes. "All of this—all of it—is my fault. I'm trying to fix what I can. But the thing that's bugging me is, where is Ian? He wasn't with Clever Jack and Doodad."

Peter blinked. "I have no idea. We haven't seen him."

He put his hand on her shoulder. "Keepsie." They stopped and the others moved on ahead.

She looked up at him, unhappiness scrawled across her face. With every fiber in his being telling him to kiss her, he squeezed her shoulder briefly and said, "We, ah, need to talk about your power. In the middle of all this excitement, I have discovered some new, well, aspects of my talents that I was previously unaware of. And through those talents I found out some things you need to know."

She stared at him blankly and stopped walking. "What are you talking about?"

"We can't talk in front of The Librarian, but we need to discuss this soon."

She nodded and ran her hand through her hair. "Let's go, we need to figure out what to do about that nuclear chick."

Peter followed her up the corridor toward the glowing light.

#

"So what's going on?" Keepsie asked as she reached the group clustered around the opening of the hill.

As her friends shielded their eyes, The Librarian spoke in her monotone, cataloguing every person battling outside.

"—of Mornings, who has apparently gained the power of flight along with her other nuclear capabilities. White Lightning, with super strength, flight, and command of lightning. The Crane, with flight and the ability to stretch his limbs."

She continued her monologue as the group stared in horror. Light of Mornings still looked groggy, but hovered with a golden force field surrounding her. The air was filled with the cracklings and booms of White Lightning's attacks, but the heroes looked much the worse for wear, with burns showing up bright on their skin, and Light of Mornings looking groggy but unharmed.

"Oh lord," Peter said. "They're using children."

Terrified-looking teenagers, heroes that Peter had never seen before, children he now knew were born and raised within the Academy, had joined the fight. Children with powers that seemed more likely to fizzle out than actually do damage to a villain. One teen had encased his entire body in ice and had approached the force field, fashioning a drill from ice sticking off the end of his hand. He tried to drill into her force field, but the ice melted before it could even touch it. Another had turned herself into a massive crane with a wrecking ball and was clanging the ball off the force field.

"This is too big for us," Peter said. "I think we should probably get to safety and let them duke it out."

"No, I'm responsible and I'm going to——" Keepsie said, but Peter interrupted her.

"Keepsie. Can you figure out how to fight a bomb? Because that's what she is. A confused nuclear bomb who is on Clever Jack's side. We're probably already getting heavy doses of radiation at this proximity!"

Keepsie opened her mouth, then closed it and nodded. "Let's head to my apartment, it's closest."

"I am not sure if close to the battle is the safest place to be," Peter said.

"Then what? The bar? We don't know where Ian and Seismic Stan are. Should we just hit the road and out of town?" Keepsie asked.

"No, no, don't do that—oh no," Barry moaned. He watched White Lightning leap to the street where Colette's car was parked. He hefted it over his head and threw it toward Light of Mornings.

"Our ride?" Alex asked, and Barry nodded as the car bounced off the force field and flew back towards White Lightning. He flew up out of the way and it hit the street with a crunch.

Colette's eyes bulged. "You could throw it but not catch it, you overpowered cocksucker?"

The car slid across the street, kicking up sparks, and crashed into the side of Keepsie's building.

"Shit. Colette's car and my apartment," Keepsie said.

Gas dribbled from a punctured tank. Peter wondered when it would explode. They always exploded on television.

Peter ticked off the options on his fingers. "We definitely can't go to your apartment, now we definitely can't get out of town, so I guess all that's left is the bar."

"But what about Seismic Stan?" Keepsie asked.

A rumble, very close by, answered her, and a tidal wave of dirt rose up from the park and flowed toward the heroes.

Keepsie shoved them out of the hill. "All right, it's settled, back to the bar."

Michelle pointed to The Librarian. "What about her?"

"She's worse in a fight than we are," Peter said. "We should take her with us."

Keepsie grimaced. "That's like inviting the perfect spy into our group."

Peter shook his head. "No, Ghostheart was the perfect spy." Keepsie cocked her head to the side. "Her power was lying. Anyone believes any lie she tells."

"Ohhhh..." Keepsie said.

"Exactly," Peter said. "But we should tell the others."

"All right, people, we're going to have to run. Is everyone up for it?" Keepsie asked.

They climbed out of the hill, keeping an eye on the battle.

Tomas cleared his throat. "What about him?" Doodad glared silently at them all.

Keepsie grinned in a way that made Peter's neck hairs rise. "Let him go," she said.

"Keepsie, is that the best—" Peter began, but Tomas had already released his hostage.

Keepsie's grin widened further when Doodad made a lunge for the ball she held out in her hand.

"You're not as smart as you'd like us to believe," Keepsie said to the again-frozen Doodad.

"How did you know what he would do?" Peter asked breathlessly.

"I know how people are about their things. He just forgot that it's mine again."

"So, ah, shall we go?" Peter asked.

They nodded. Everyone but Barry. In the glaring light he looked far older than middle age, and Peter was very aware of a large gut hanging over his detachable legs.

He chuckled. "Run? To the bar? I've run to bars before, but not in the past fifteen years."

Another car ricocheted off the force field and hit the hill above them. They cringed back from the wreckage that fell in front of them. Wheels and other debris popped off, littering the park.

Michelle set her jaw. "Barry. How much do you weigh?"

"Ah, that's a personal question," he said uncomfortably.

"If you don't want to run, you'll have to be carried. I've never carried more than three hundred pounds. Are you over three hundred?"

Barry stared at her.

131

"You're brilliant, Michelle!" Peter said. He scouted around and spied a car door lying not too far from them. "There, will that door work?"

She nodded and made sure the coast was clear. The door settled easily into her shoulder and she trotted back over to the hill.

"All right, Barry, hop on."

"You're kidding. You've got to be kidding me."

"Dammit, Barry, either stay and die of radiation or worse, or run and die of a heart attack, or let her carry you!" Keepsie said.

"Fine, all right, but you owe me a beer."

"If we get to the bar safely, I'll owe you a keg. Let's go."

Berry reached down and removed his right leg. Michelle crouched down so he could climb onto the car door, and then he removed his other leg.

"Are you all right, Michelle?" Peter asked.

She nodded. Barry might as well have been made of Styrofoam for all the effort she was putting into holding him.

Keepsie turned to The Librarian, who had stopped her constant monologue to stare at Michelle.

"Are you coming with us?" Keepsie asked.

The Librarian looked out to the heroes still trying to penetrate Light of Morning's shield, then nodded. "I am of no use here."

"All right. Keep track of the person in front of you. If someone falls behind, help them." Keepsie said.

"And the person at the end of the line?" Peter asked.

"That'll be us, I'll watch you if you watch me," she said.

"Deal," he said, and they ran.

Michelle carried Barry in the lead, her long legs easily outdistancing Alex. The Librarian and Tomas were next, he lumbering along and she tottering on her heels. Colette kept pace with them, running faster than her bulk suggested she could. Keepsie and Peter slowed their pace to keep the three in front of them.

The heroes continued their battle not one hundred yards away, trying to break Light of Morning's force field, and seemed not to notice them. Tattoo Devil screamed as a pterodactyl was birthed from his shoulder blades. It flew over Inert, the kid who could knock people out with a touch, and picked him up by the shoulders. The sidekick winced as the beast's talons cut into his shoulders. The pterodactyl flew over the massive golden sphere and dropped him. He readied himself to land on the top of the field, but Light of Mornings looked up, her eyes flashing golden, and she focused for the first time since Peter had seen her. As Inert fell towards her, she allowed a small hole in her force field to open.

It was over too quickly for Peter to register quickly what had happened. The hero fell through her force field, and as he entered it, he reached out to touch her, but there was a blinding flash as if the force field had become something made entirely of light. The small sun flared and everyone hid their eyes. Peter stopped when the flash subsided.

Inert had fallen straight through the force field and through the bottom. He lay in the grass, a charred husk. The corpse was badly burned, hair, clothing and eyelids missing.

"Oh God," Peter said. Keepsie had stopped running and was dashing back to him, Doodad trailing silently behind her.

The ground rumbled again and Keepsie clutched at Peter to keep from falling. Lightning struck and they clapped their hands over their abused ears. The rumble abruptly died.

"I think that might be the end of Seismic Stan," Peter said.

"Time to go, babe, like you said, we can't fight her." Keepsie grabbed his arm and pulled and they ran on, ducking into the trees and leaving the blinding battle behind them.

"You know," Peter said, starting to pant a little. "I didn't see Ian with the villains. Did you?"

"No, I was hoping you had," Keepsie said, looking around. As they increased the distance between themselves and the park, the darkness became more of the norm.

"I figured he'd be there with the fight," Keepsie said.

"Actually, I didn't see Clever Jack when we came out of the hill, either. This is not promising."

"Peter, none of this is promising. Come on, let's try to catch up," she said and increased her pace.

Time slowed. Michelle, Barry and Alex were far ahead. Logic had won a battle with The Librarian and she now sprinted in bare feet a couple of paces ahead of Tomas, who ran in fits of speed followed by a slow jog, using his brief super-strength to power himself forward. Colette trailed behind them.

After Colette, there was Clever Jack. He had stepped out from an awning and faced them, the pleasant smile plastered on his face. He pointed a gun at them.

Superpowered luck. That meant instant sharpshooter, even in the dark, even with his eyes closed, even behind his back, tied up and hanging upside down. Peter's legs carried him forward in slow motion, and he heard a low, slow curse from Keepsie beside him.

For a small woman, Keepsie seemed quite dense as she slammed into Peter, shoving him aside so that he fell just as the gun emanated a puff of smoke and a very loud noise. He fell, hard, his head pounding.

Then, everything sped up to double time. Keepsie lay on her back, a hole in her shirt right where her heart was. Her eyes were wide and her mouth opened and closed as if she were a drowning fish.

Peter scrambled over to her and held her hand tightly. "Keepsie, listen to me, you can't die, hold on, you can't die."

She looked at him and he saw brief outrage in her eyes. She tried to speak but failed.

"You *can't* die. That's the part of your power I was going to tell you about. If someone tries to kill you, that would be stealing your life, and it won't work."

Peter felt the hot barrel of the handgun against the base of his neck. "That's really neat," Clever Jack said. "But I bet I can still kill you."

21

Keepsie's chest burned. She fought for every breath and tried to will her heart to beat regularly again. She could barely comprehend what Peter had just said. Then Clever Jack was above them both.

"No—" she managed to say, but even she couldn't hear herself above the shouts.

A foul jet of excrement shot over the three of them missing Clever Jack's head by inches, as Ian yelled, "You lying son of a bitch!"

A second later, Michelle's car door, no longer bearing Barry, whizzed towards them, clipping the back of Clever Jack's head. He crumpled, falling over Keepsie's outstretched legs.

Ian whooped. "How's that luck now, you bastard?"

Peter, his hands visibly shaking, took the gun out of Clever Jack's lax grip and pulled him off of Keepsie.

Keepsie relaxed back on the pavement and concentrated on breathing, even though the air was filled with the stench of Ian's attack.

Hands lifted her and she opened her eyes without realizing she had closed them. She lay on the car door while Michelle ran down the sidewalk. She looked for Peter and found him talking to Ian, talking over Clever Jack's body.

"Peter," she croaked, but no one responded. She blacked out.

#

"Damn, Peter, you were right. It didn't even break the skin," Alex said.

"Yes, but the bludgeoning effect of the bullet to her heart still could have killed her," Peter said.

"Except she couldn't die that way," Alex said.

"Well. Yes."

Her breath came easier. Her heart beat loudly in her ears, a frightened yet steady rhythm. She felt uncomfortably exposed, and realized they'd removed her shirt and covered her breasts with it in order to better see what the bullet had done to her. *Thank God I decided to wear a bra today.*

She raised her head and saw Michelle, Alex and Peter with her. Michelle held her hand. She squeezed it and smiled.

"No offense, guys, but sometime I'd like to wake up and not have the two of you arguing about my health," she said to them.

"Welcome back," Alex said. There were dark circles under his eyes and he staggered back a bit. Peter helped him to a booth where he lay down.

They were in her bar; Keepsie lay on the floor. Tomas, Barry and the Librarian sat at the bar, eating. Ian sat alone in a booth, watching them. Doodad stood, outrage gleaming in his frozen eyes, a couple of feet from her. There was a definite scent of cheeseburgers on the air. Colette had been busy.

The door to the kitchen opened with a bang and the short, stocky cook stormed out. Her face was red and eyes wide, but bore with her a plastic basket of a cheeseburger and cheese fries. Keepsie already knew they were for her; Colette knew exactly how she liked her burgers. Employing a Third Wave cook had its advantages.

The basket landed beside Keepsie. "Eat. When you're done, think about what we're going to about the heroes and villains. This is going to kill our business."

Keepsie sat up, the ache in her chest subsiding. "I'm not sure, Colette. I think business was hurt when the heroes shut us down, actually."

Colette shook her head. "Bureaucracy I can fight. My dad is a lawyer. But the Good Lord did not give me superpowers to fight heroes and villains; he gave me powers to feed people."

"We'll think of something, Colette," Keepsie said.

Colette shook her head and went back to the kitchen. "Now if we could just get that nuclear girl on our side, we'd save a bundle on electric bills to heat this place and power the goddamned stove."

"Is she going to be all right?" Peter asked.

"Oh sure," Keepsie said, picking a cheese fry from the basket. "She deals with most any kind of stress by stomping around and cooking. She couldn't do that outside, but here she's in her element."

Keepsie levered herself off the floor, waving off Peter's offered hand. She picked up her lunch—or was it dinner?—and put it on a table at the nearest empty booth. She left her friends, dragging the supervillain behind her and entered the Men's room. She exited without Doodad.

"Everyone uses the women's room from now on."

"You got it," Colette said.

Keepsie returned to her food and motioned her friends to sit. "All right. Peter, what the hell were you talking about after I got shot, and why aren't I dead?"

Peter and Michelle exchanged looks. "I... have to go check on the bar trays. I think if I sharpen the edges they'll be very Xena-like," Michelle said, and went behind the bar.

Peter sat down slowly, as if he wanted to do anything but.

"What's wrong? You said I was invulnerable or something, which is wrong cause that sure as hell hurt," she said.

Peter didn't meet her eyes. He sighed. "During the last couple of days, I've used my powers more often than I've ever consciously used them in my life. I've never wanted to find out secrets about people, because what I find out is usually something I didn't want to know. But, well, in the past couple of days I've discovered that I can do more than the Academy, my father, and even I knew I could."

"Wow, really? Like what?"

Peter picked up a napkin from the table and fiddled with it. "I can track people if I can get a good enough scent. That's how we found The Librarian. I also found out that I can learn the extent of someone's powers. I discovered that your life is one of your possessions. You can't be killed. I assume that you can grow old and die, and you can sicken and die, or die in an accident, but no one else can take your life from you."

There was something he wasn't telling her. She studied him for a moment. "You're serious?"

He finally met her eyes. "Well don't take my word for it—you survived a lightning strike, a spear to the chest, deadly fire and a gunshot to the heart. What do you think?"

Keepsie sat back. Her first thought was an incoherent desire to never let the Academy know this information, if they hadn't figured it out already. Not that there was much of an Academy left. But she had no idea what Timson would do with this information.

"Man. I'm sort of immortal, you've found out all sorts of powers, and Michelle can lift a grown man on a car door. What other stuff do we know?"

Peter studied his napkin again. "Well. We need to discuss Ian."

Keepsie looked automatically at Ian, who stared at them from his booth with an unsmiling face. "I feel like I don't know him anymore, Peter," she said, not looking away from Ian's gaze. "I don't think we can trust him."

"He saved my life, he and Michelle. Well. After you did, of course." He balled the napkin up in his fist and gave it a tight squeeze before setting it down and pushing it away from him. "Plus, he has given us information about Clever Jack. Information that I confirmed with, ah, my newly discovered talents."

"Oh? What's that?" Keepsie said.

"Clever Jack has a weakness. And it's a big one."

He opened his mouth again and Keepsie held up her hand. "Wait. I want to hear it from Ian."

Peter closed his mouth and nodded. He beckoned Ian over.

Her betrayer, her Judas, her Benedict Arnold. Her friend who worked a cash register at Seventh Sity Surfer. The guy who had gotten himself arrested defending her bar. The guy who had given Alex's info so they could recover from Academy's torture. Clever Jack's ally. And eventual betrayer.

He didn't sit at the booth but stood next to it. Keepsie looked up at him. "So what's Clever Jack's weakness, Ian?"

He looked as if he expected the question. "Clever Jack's luck is innate, like a cloud or something around him. But he can focus it. While he's focusing it, there is still enough luck protecting him from one, maybe two attackers. But more than that and someone will have a pretty good chance of hitting him.

"Like when he was trying to shoot Peter, you missed but Michelle hit," Keepsie said.

Ian nodded. "He pretty much said it to me, without actually saying it. I think he thinks I'm dumber than I am. I've got to start carrying my night school diploma with me, I guess. Anyway, I thought the double attack could get him off Peter. And then Pete checked out my story with his shiny new skills, and said I could come back here and talk to you. You know, when you were back up and running."

Running. Keepsie felt like she could never run again. If she had a chance to just lie down in a bed—provided her bed wasn't cinders by now—just for a moment, she would be able to cope so much better.

"So now what?" she asked Ian.

He shifted his weight and looked at Peter. "Uh, what do you mean?"

"Now what for you?" Keepsie felt mean all of a sudden, and wasn't willing to let him back in so easily. "You've been on our side, the villains' side, what's next? Joining the Academy?"

Ian looked hurt, and Keepsie felt both vindicated and guilty. He looked at the floor. "I fucked up. That's all. I wanted to give the heroes as much shit as they'd given us, and I felt like you guys were just rolling over. I didn't know Clever Jack was going to hurt innocent people."

"Conveniently forgetting his past, I suppose," Peter said.

Ian shrugged. "It's like, when you see him in the papers, he's bigger than life. The past couple of days, he seemed a lot more like us, pissed off at getting the shaft from the Academy. And you have to admit they're pretty twisted themselves."

"I guess I did forget what he'd done in the past, and just wanted to be with the winning team for once."

He took a deep breath. Keepsie and Peter didn't say anything. Peter relaxed back into the booth as if he'd heard this before.

"And?" prompted Keepsie.

"Well, after you guys started going against him, he got mad and started talking about killing you. He sent me on recon to find out who was left at the bar. I headed there with the intention of warning you, but I saw you guys coming back to the park, so I doubled back and followed you. By the time I got there, Clever Jack was telling that glowing chick to kill the heroes and then he grabbed me and said we were going to rule the city as soon as we got rid of you guys. That's when I started sticking really close to see if I could stop him. So when you guys escaped the hill, he left Light of Mornings to do her thing and fry the heroes while he went running after you. We slipped past you when you stopped to watch the fight. Clever Jack was so focused on you guys that he didn't see me run ahead to catch Michelle and Barry. I'm sorry we didn't catch him in time to stop his first shot."

Keepsie ran her hands through her hair and sighed. "Ian, how can we trust you?"

"Tell me what you want me to do and I'll do it. I'm back, dude, I'm on your side!" he said.

Keepsie looked at Peter. "So does your new super power let you see if someone is telling the truth?"

Peter shook his head. "I don't think so. I can test emotions and track people, but not truth. I think being a human lie detector would put me in the hero range, frankly."

"But you said yourself that you didn't know about this talent till today," Keepsie said. "So you may be able to, you just don't know."

Peter looked from her to the table, and then to Ian. "I—well, I'll see what I can do."

"Hey, Keepsie, can you leave us alone for the test?" Ian asked. "What? Why?"

"Oh, I just want privacy, I guess. Everyone's been staring at me since I got here. Can we go into the storage room?" he said.

Keepsie narrowed her eyes. What were they hiding? Her heartbeat sped up as she entertained the notion that he had courted Peter to the villains' side and that they were both going to double—or triple, at this point—cross her.

But Peter wouldn't do that. He was one of the few left she could trust. She looked at Peter, who returned her gaze with an intensity that made her uncomfortable.

She threw up her hands. "Fine. Whatever. Get Tomas to stand outside the door in case you need anything, Peter. I'm going to eat for the first time in—" she couldn't remember her last meal, so she just stuffed some fries into her mouth.

"Right. We'll be back soon," Ian said.

"You going to be OK?" she asked through her mouthful of fries as Peter slid out of the booth.

"I'll be fine. I don't think he's lying, for what it's worth. And remember, he never betrayed us. He was honest with us since the beginning. It was Clever Jack he betrayed. Get some food into you; you are going to need the energy, I'm afraid."

Keepsie allowed herself a moment to appreciate the meal; Colette was her best find at the bar, making it the best bar food in town through her superpower. The burger was a perfect medium, with a slice of cheddar on the bottom of the burger and a slice of provolone on the top. She liked her burgers with only mustard and onions, something no cook alive had ever understood or respected, but Colette knew it without asking. She knew the best thing to cook for anyone, and could prepare anything to be the best.

During one drunken night back at her apartment, Keepsie and Michelle had challenged Colette to an Iron Chef kind of competition where she had to prepare both spam and haggis to perfection. Her Spam mincemeat pie was phenomenal, and her traditional haggis made Keepsie wonder what all the fuss was about.

Collette had considered a career in culinary arts, but very few people would hire a Third Waver. It was an unfortunate rumor that their untrained powers would end up being more of a liability in the end than a boon, so Colette wasn't able to work in the best restaurants in the world, as she deserved to. Neither was Vincent, Keepsie's janitor, hired by the cleaning services of the United Nations or the CIA. His hands were actual dirt magnets; all he had to do to leave an area spotless was to pass his hand over it.

Lost in thought, Keepsie realized she had polished off her burger and still wanted more. The door to the kitchen slammed open and she jerked around.

Colette stamped toward her, carrying two small round cakes on a plate.

"Here, thought you'd still be hungry," she said.

"Thanks. Are the guys still in the closet?" She took one of the cakes and bit into it: chocolate with a caramel center. Perfect.

Colette snagged the other cake for herself. "Yeah. I don't know what they're doing in there, but Tomas said he can only hear them talking."

"I wish I knew what they were talking about."

"You, I suspect," Colette said.

"Huh?"

"Do you want to know a secret?" Colette said.

"Please. There have been too many these days," Keepsie said, getting annoyed.

"One thing that science has never studied, so no one knows this but me, but when someone is falling in love, they start to unconsciously prefer food that their beloved does. Now, this doesn't mean that a blue steak kind of man will suddenly start ordering salad to impress his lady, but very subtle things will change. The temperature that they like their fries. The amount of salt. Suddenly ordering strawberry when vanilla used to do just fine. The number of olives in—"

Keepsie finally interrupted her. "How is this important now?"

Colette paused. "What do you mean?"

"We're on the run from the heroes and the villains. We have a friend who we can't trust, half of us are in need of a hospital, so where does love fit into all this?"

Colette smiled at her, a very small smile. "Nowhere, I suppose. Everyone else is discovering new and exciting uses for their powers. I figured I'd tell you about one of mine."

Keepsie felt bad. "I'm sorry, Colette, I didn't mean to discount it. I'm just not thinking straight, that's all."

Colette slid out of the booth and walked towards the kitchen and nearly bumped into Peter and Ian coming out. She said something to Peter in a low voice and Ian laughed. Peter looked startled and watched her go into the kitchen, color rising in his face.

While Ian did not have his usual swagger, he looked considerably more relaxed. Peter fiddled with his sleeves of his t-shirt—Keepsie's sleeves—as he reached the table.

"He's loyal, Keepsie. I am as sure as I can be without actually reading his mind," he said.

Keepsie nodded, staring at Ian. He grinned at her. She fought the urge to grin back; she was still unsure. Half of her wanted to laugh, the other half wanted to kick him out.

She looked at the bar where Michelle was pouring herself a beer from the tap. Keepsie caught her eye and, seeing the look of anguish on Michelle's face, sighed.

"All right. You stay. But—"

He interrupted her. "I know, I know. Fuck up again and I'm toast, I know. I won't let you down again, Keepsie."

"Make yourself useful, then," she said. "We need watches at both doors. You take one, choose someone to join you, and put two more on the other."

He gave a quick nod and turned from her.

Keepsie stared at the table. Her eyes felt very dry. She knew Peter was still there. "Are you sure about him?"

"I'm sure," he said. His voice sounded strained.

"Good." She cradled her head on her arms.

"Pete—come on. I need you to watch with me," Ian said.

You were supposed to choose Michelle, you ass. One thing was supposed to have gone right, Keepsie thought. The bar was very quiet around her as she let the exhaustion carry her away.

22

Ian perched on the steps near the street and took a cigarette pack out of his jeans pocket. Peter raised his eyebrow.

"You smoke now?"

Ian lit it, fumbling with a lighter's child lock. He pulled some smoke into his mouth, held his breath, and coughed. Peter fought the urge to laugh.

"Fits my new persona as a bad boy," Ian said, waving the cigarette.

Peter remained silent.

"Fine. My sister says it calms her. I thought it might work for me. All this crazy shit going on, I figured if these little security blankets can help my sis, they might help me, you know?"

Peter shook his head slowly. "It's really not a good time to get yourself addicted to something. And why would you pick up such a filthy habit? It makes you smell."

Ian started laughing. "No, I wouldn't want to be considered filthy or smelly, no, that would be bad!" He dropped the cigarette and held his stomach, gasping for breath.

Peter chuckled. "All right, point taken. But that's a pretty flimsy reason."

"Oh, so peer pressure is a better reason?" Ian said, wiping tears from his eyes. "Why do you do what you do, Peter? Why are you addicted to being so uptight? That t-shirt is the most laid back

144

thing I've ever seen you in, and it's not even yours. Do you even own a t-shirt, Pete?"

Peter looked at the shirt—*her* t-shirt. He'd forgotten he was wearing it. "It's just me. Why do you do the things you do?"

Ian grinned. "I'm a slob and not afraid to admit it. Don't dodge the question. What's behind the jacket and starched shirt?"

Peter reached over and took Ian's pack of cigarettes from him. He knocked one out and lit it with ease. "Someone who doesn't like carrying others' secrets, especially when they don't tell them to him. Someone who doesn't like seeing the world falling out of control all around him. An ex-smoker who hates to see a non-smoker butcher the fine art of slowly killing yourself. Is that sufficient?" He inhaled deeply and reveled in the brief high that overtook his head.

"Dude. You were a smoker?"

"You zero in on the least important part of that, don't you?"

"No, seriously. You?"

Peter looked down at the cigarette. "It does an excellent job of dulling the sense of smell."

Ian scanned the deserted street. "So why'd you quit?"

"Filthy habit. The only thing I could smell was myself."

"So did you find out all your own dirty secrets at that point?"

Peter snorted. "Yes, I discovered I was a smoker who was slowly killing myself and denying a skill I had."

"But you never really did use that part of yourself, did you?"

Peter didn't answer. He looked over the dark street, and couldn't decide whether he preferred the daytime when he could be depressed about all the obstacles in his way that he could see: heroes, villains, thermonuclear women, and the like, or the night when he could be terrified that one of more of those things would be lurking in the shadows.

Light of Mornings' glow still shone over the buildings, and Peter assumed the fight still raged. The Academy was deserted, dust still lingering from the destruction of the previous battle. Even Doodad's drones had deserted the place.

"What are we doing out here?" he asked.

"Fantasizing about naked Winona Ryder?" Ian asked.

Peter laughed. "Like the dangerous shoplifters, do you?"

"Nah, I am thinking of her in 'Heathers.'"

"Hm. So teenaged murderer in love."

"Yeah," Ian said.

"So what else are we doing out here?"

"Waiting for something to happen, I suppose."

"And what are we supposed to do when it does?"

Ian rolled up his sleeves, his grinning face heavily shadowed from the light inside the bar. "I'm all set."

Peter shook his head and stared at the door. "I'm not. I can't—"

Ian interrupted him. "Hey, what's Clever Jack up to?"

Peter looked at him blankly. "How should I know?"

Ian handed him a bloody handkerchief. "Got it off him after you told me your new and improved powers."

Peter took it distastefully, holding it by the corner. "Thanks, I'll treasure it always."

"So where is he? Is he dead from concussion?"

Peter waved him silent. After they'd agreed to leave him to follow and make sure Keepsie was all right, Peter had seen Ian staunch the blood from Clever Jack's head but hadn't thought of why. Now, holding the wet handkerchief in front of him, he wished for the millionth time that he had been born with another power. Or better, none.

He didn't need to bring the gore-splattered rag close to get a good whiff of the coppery scent. He closed his eyes and nearly went blind with the light.

He reflexively threw the bloody handkerchief at Ian, and Ian made a disgusted noise. "What the fuck, dude? What did you see?" he asked.

Peter rubbed his eyes, the stairwell looking pitch-black to his contracted pupils. "He's conscious. He's with her."

Ian looked towards the park, which had finally gone dark. "That is not good news."

Peter winced at the memory. "Yes. They're... being rather intimate."

Ian whistled. "With a concussion? If he weren't pure evil, I'd salute him."

"I'm surprised he survived," Peter said.

Ian grimaced. "Luck."

Peter nodded.

"Should we tell someone?" Ian asked.

Peter looked down the stairwell to the door of the bar, about the only thing his still hazy eyes could make out. "Who could we tell? What would they do?"

"Right," Ian said.

They lapsed into silence.

After another half hour, Peter got up. "I'm going to check on the other group. See what's going on in the alley."

"And look in on Keepsie on the way, of course," Ian said in a stuffy Peter imitation.

Peter stared blankly at Ian without the familiar squirm of embarrassment in his chest.

"Of course."

#

Looking in on Keepsie proved to be a pointless venture. She was sleeping on the table. Peter took two steps towards her when a hiss stopped him.

Colette stood in the kitchen door, frowning. He flushed and shoved his hands into his pockets. She raised her eyebrows at him and beckoned him to her.

They went into the empty kitchen. Peter avoided her gaze, but swore when he saw the feast she'd prepared.

"Great Christ, Colette, you really do cook when you're stressed!" he said. The prep counter was filled with cheeseburgers, hot dogs, steaks, baskets of cheese fries, chicken fingers, nachos— both with jalapenos and without—and salmon patties.

Peter hadn't even known that the bar served salmon patties.

Colette crossed her arms. "You need to let her sleep."

Peter looked up and met her eyes. "I know. I just wanted to check—"

"I know what you wanted to do," she said. "Let her sleep. She doesn't need you clucking around her like a mother hen. She's tougher than that."

Peter bristled. "I really don't think I'm a mother hen. She needs support."

"Give it a rest, Peter. You're not as secret as you think you are."

Peter shook his head slowly. "We are not doing a good job at this hero thing. Or villain thing. I'm not sure. Whatever it is, with half our team drunk and the other half passed out already... "

Colette pulled up a folding chair and motioned for him to sit. She grabbed a stool for herself and looked at him pointedly.

"Why are we all sitting here hiding in a bar while the heroes are dying? We should be leaving town."

Peter eyed her coolly. "We don't have a car. Public transport shuts down when there's a big battle. But the bigger thing is that Keepsie feels responsible for all of this, and she doesn't want to leave. She wants to fix it. I have no idea how she plans on doing this, but..." He trailed off.

Colette stood and began folding filthy kitchen dishcloths. "So now what?"

"Ian and I keep watch, I suppose. If there's a direct threat to us, then we, uh, deal with it." Peter stood, folded the chair and sat it against the wall.

Colette stacked the cloths, ketchup and grease stains visible on the neat pile, and moved back to the grill. She turned the gas on and began forming more hamburgers from a bowl on the counter. "Well, it sounds like the heroes and villains have enough to deal with. They shouldn't bother with us anymore."

Peter felt the breath leave his lungs. He looked at Colette with wide eyes.

"That would be the case, yes. Except that Keepsie has their drug. So they'll be looking for it."

23

Peter left a white-faced Colette and went out the back door. The concrete steps rose at a sharp angle to the alley behind the bar, and he wondered how Keepsie got any deliveries without the deliverymen breaking their necks. Michelle sat on the back steps alone, silhouetted by a streetlight. She looked around when he closed the back door.

A siren screamed past them. "I guess the normals are doing more than just hiding in their houses," Michelle said.

"The emergency crews are usually out in times of crisis, even if the Academy says to stay inside," Peter said. "I guess we're all rebelling from the heroes today."

"Yeah, that was a super-great idea."

"In hindsight, perhaps it wasn't," Peter said.

Michelle nodded. "How's it going in there?"

"Colette is cooking a feast in absence of anything else to do. Ian is on watch. Everyone else is either drunk or resting."

"So we're all prepared for another attack." Her sarcastic remark wasn't a question.

Peter felt inexplicably angry. "What do you suggest we do, then? Go back out there? Fight the Light of Mornings with my nose and your bar tray and Ian's feculent powers?"

Michelle didn't flinch. She waved her hand at him and shushed him.

Peter listened. He didn't hear anything, but his ears were still ringing from Clever Jack's point-blank gunshot. Michelle stood up and trotted to the top of the steps. She faced the street and then dashed out of Peter's view.

"Michelle!" he said as loudly as he dared, which ended up being a hoarse whisper.

She returned in an instant, breathing heavily.

"Get inside. We need to get Ian inside. This does not look good."

#

Ian was bellowing when they got inside the kitchen. "Where the hell is Peter?"

"Here," Peter said, emerging with Michelle from the kitchen.

"It got worse," Ian said.

Keepsie stirred from her nap and looked up. Her face was creased from sleeping on her arm and her eyes were half-slitted. "God, what now?"

"You still have Doodad under control, right?" Michelle said.

Keepsie rubbed her face. "Of course. Why?"

"Mechs," Ian said.

"Huge," Michelle said.

Keepsie jumped to her feet and ran to the men's room, took a peek inside, and returned, frowning. "How is that possible? He can't use his powers under my control."

The Librarian, previously unnoticed, stood. "You have to tell me everything you know about the drug Jack took."

"Why should we tell you?" Ian asked.

"This shouldn't be happening. None of this should be happening."

"Will you tell us what you know about it?" Keepsie asked.

The Librarian held her gaze for some time before dropping her eyes and nodding.

"The drug is a stronger version of Zupra, designed to make stronger humans in utero."

"Well, it certainly helped Jack out in the Academy," Keepsie said. "And he's not in utero."

The Librarian nodded. "I believe Jack knows something about that drug that even I do not know. Possibly something Dr. Timson had planned without telling me."

Ian laughed. "Something's going on in the Academy that you don't know? That must really burn."

She didn't acknowledge him. "I need to get inside the Academy."

Keepsie choked. "You want to go into the building that just got blown apart by the nuclear girl? How do you know there's anything there to salvage?"

The Librarian sniffed, but a red flush came to her cheeks. "I know."

Keepsie rolled her eyes and threw her hands up in the air. "Heroes."

"The more I know about this drug that Jack and, we now assume, Doodad took, the better we can fight his latest invention."

Alex got out of his booth, his hair rumpled from sleep. "I'll go with her."

"Are you fucking insane? Haven't you been through enough today?" Ian said.

"If she gets hurt, I can heal her. We get Tomas to come with us, and we'll have defense. Shouldn't take more than twenty minutes or so."

Everyone looked at Keepsie, who blanched. Peter smiled to himself; she still hadn't realized she was the leader.

"Hey, I can't stop you. Tomas, are you cool—and sober enough—to be an escort?" she asked.

"I am."

Peter cleared his throat. "You'd better hurry. I don't doubt that mech is coming to collect Doodad."

"Then what are the rest of us going to do?" Barry asked.

"Get ready for a battle, I guess," Michelle said.

Peter's chest tightened as they left, The Librarian walked resolutely up the stairs with Alex and Tomas following her more slowly.

"Alex doesn't look good," Keepsie said, echoing Peter's thoughts.

Ian made a face. "Good? He looks like day old shit."

"We may still need him before this is over," Peter said. "He needs to rest. He's all we have that passes for a doctor."

Keepsie walked to the door and tried to look out the window and up the stairs. Ian followed her. "See anything?" he asked.

"Nope. They're gone."

"They didn't need to go far; what is she up to?" Peter asked, joining them.

Now they could hear the clanging thumps of the mechs striding down the street toward them. One pair of thumps came faster, then, and Tomas yelled. Keepsie wrenched the door open and ran up the stairs, Peter and Ian stumbling after her.

The three massive mechs, one silver, one black and one red, had closed the distance quicker than Peter guessed they would. One was clearly made for transport; an empty black seat and some levers were visible through a glass dome that sat atop a metal chassis and two nimble legs. The other two were armed: the black fitted with countless blades, saws, and drills, and the red one looking to have ranged weapons—one hose connected to a tank that Peter feared was gasoline.

The one with the blades lay on its back, floundering to fold its many joints to get its legs under itself again. Tomas panted next to it, standing anguished over the prone body of Alex.

The red mech raised a hose.

"Ian!" yelled Keepsie.

"On it," he said, raising his arms.

"No, Ian, wait—" Peter blurted, but it was too late. He covered his nose as Ian's stench filled the air, the torrent hitting the red mech as flame spewed from the hose. Ian's feculent spray doused the flame, but the smell of burning shit made Peter retch. He stumbled down the stairs to get Michelle, knowing he would be useless if he were retching.

Michelle came out of the bar when she saw Peter. He gestured to her helplessly and she ran up to the street, carrying several bar trays.

Peter didn't have long to wait for something to happen. He had gotten a wet towel from Colette to wrap around his face and go back out to help, but the group burst back into the bar.

Tomas carried the prone Alex, staggering every few seconds as his strength ran out and then was summoned again. He laid Alex on the floor. Peter winced when he saw the bloody rip in Alex's shirt.

"Dude, is he dead?" Ian asked, kneeling at his side.

Colette touched Alex's neck and withdrew her hand, bowing her head. She nodded.

Peter looked at Tomas with anguish. "What happened?"

Tomas's eyes were wide with shock. "The machines spotted us. I could not stop them all, and the black one stabbed him. It just stabbed him. I was not able to help."

The thumping began outside as the mechs moved again. Ian ran to the window. "Dude, this is way over our fucking heads. He's dead. What do we do now? It's not just dangerous anymore, and there's dead people, and—"

Peter's shock subsided into a tangible fear. "Ian."

"What?"

"Where are Keepsie and The Librarian?"

Ian's mouth fell open. "I didn't see…"

Tomas didn't raise his head. "The Librarian ran away when the mechs attacked. After Ian stopped the red mech from attacking, Keepsie ran after her. They ran into the Academy."

Peter collapsed into a chair. "And I did nothing. We're pretty amazing heroes."

The mechanical legs appeared on the steps outside as the black mech descended.

24

The Librarian had a large head start on Keepsie, but Keepsie was wearing sneakers and the Librarian still wore her sensible pumps. Keepsie started gaining on her almost immediately, and barely paused when she saw her quarry enter the smoking ruins of the Academy.

Guttering fluorescent lights illuminated the corridors. The building had been proudly sculpted mostly of stone and metal, which meant little fire damage—that seemed to come from the lower levels of the Academy—but contributed to a lot of rubble in the halls. Chunks of cracked marble and crumbling concrete made the way through the hall slow going.

Offices lining the outer wall smelled of acrid smoke and ozone, and one open door revealed a desktop computer that still sparked feebly, a chunk of concrete imbedded in the top of its case. The monitor, also a victim of pieces of the ceiling breaking free, had blown outward, showering the room with glass.

Keepsie dodged a piece of falling debris and entertained the thought that she might die here after all, no matter what Peter said about her immortality. He had said nothing about whether she could survive concrete caving in her skull.

The Librarian picked her way towards a red EXIT sign at the end of the left hall. She opened a door with a key and tried to slam it behind her, but Keepsie caught it. The Librarian ran then, clattering down the stairs. Keepsie swore and picked up her pace.

The stairwell went up for only three floors, but down for an indeterminate number. Keepsie jumped the stairs three at a time to catch her. After two flights the Librarian paused for breath and Keepsie tackled her and they fell heavily on the landing.

"You bitch," Keepsie said, panting. "Unbelievable bitch."

The Librarian struggled underneath her, but Keepsie sat on her. The woman wilted, fighting no more, her hair coming free from its immaculate bun.

Keepsie found her exhaustion creeping up on her too. What was she planning on doing? Beat up the Librarian until she, Keepsie, felt better about Alex's death, the hell she and her friends had been through, the destruction to the city, the very small fact that most of this was her fault?

"Alex is dead, you know," she finally said.

"I know," the Librarian said. "That's why I ran."

"Nice," Keepsie said. "Why is it really so important that you come back to this dump?"

The Librarian met her eyes. "Research."

#

Keepsie had no weapon, but she trusted the fact that she had youth and speed on her side, and the Librarian seemed much the worse for wear than Keepsie. The hero kicked off her shoes and padded down the hallway—this one much darker than the ones above. Sometime along the way she had suffered a cut to her foot and she left unfortunate bloody footprints in the dust. She coughed and squirmed against the iron grip Keepsie had on her upper arm.

"Dr. Timson's private records are kept here, the trick will be getting in," The Librarian said.

"I thought you remembered everything, why do you have to go back to old records?" Keepsie asked as the Librarian stopped at a plain brown wooden door.

"She doesn't let me read everything. But I see some things. And sometimes it takes me some time to connect things," she said, running her hand over the smooth wood, ignoring entirely the doorknob.

"Like?" Keepsie prompted.

"Like a folder entitled 'Contingency Plans.' One entitled, 'Eric Timson's Training.' Mixing those with what I know about the Zupra testing and this is not a good combination."

"Ohhhkay..." Keepsie said, watching her touch the door. "You do know the door has a doorknob, right?"

"Timson had Doodad create her a mechanical door to protect her office. This was, of course, when she still had control of him. It has a pressure-sensitive tab somewhere... ah." She pressed her thumb into the wood next to the uppermost hinge. Keepsie didn't see the door change in any visual way, but it swung silently inward.

The dark office was largely unaffected by the damage done by the exodus of Light of Mornings. Large file cabinets lurked along the walls. It was immaculate, entirely unpolluted by trash or even a desk. The tightly packed file cabinets and bookshelves were full to bursting.

"Has Timson ever heard of computers?"

"Yes," The Librarian said, entering the dark room. "And since Doodad came around, she has also heard of hackers. She's somewhat old fashioned."

"How are we going to find the files in the dark?" Keepsie asked as they stepped into the office.

The Librarian turned to face Keepsie, and the light from the sole emergency light flashed off her glasses. "I am a hero, Laura. This is what I do."

#

Keepsie paced the hall. The Librarian had immersed herself in Timson's files and was not surfacing for air. Keepsie had tried to watch, help, and ask questions, but it was clear that The Librarian didn't need her.

A stab of worry pierced Keepsie's chest as she realized she'd abandoned Tomas and Ian and Alex's body on the street with three mechs. They could take care of themselves, she told herself, not quite convincingly.

Her thought process was broken by a curse inside the office. She ran to the door and said, "What? What did you find?"

The Librarian sat on the floor, surrounded by files. Keepsie couldn't make head or tail of her system, if she had one.

The older woman was shaking her head slowly, running her fingers over the documents. "This is unbelievable. I didn't know she was capable of this."

"What?" Keepsie asked.

"The new chemical compound isn't designed to make new heroes in the womb. It's designed to make heroes of normal people. Or enhance the powers of an existing hero."

Comprehension dawned on Keepsie. "Oh! That's how Jack freed Light of Mornings and how Doodad built the mechs that work on their own."

The Librarian nodded. "The compound isn't safe, though. There are still side effects that are not acceptable risks. Doodad stole the compound before it was done."

"So Doodad and Jack could soon have erectile dysfunction or drowsiness or vomiting?"

The Librarian began gathering paper into a folder. "What concerns me is why she kept the information from me. And if she did, who else did she keep it from? I've known for a while that Timson had an inner circle of heroes she could trust. I had thought I was in that circle."

"Who else was in it?"

"White Lightning. Ghostheart. The Crane, Tattoo Devil, Heretic."

Keepsie snorted. "So nearly everyone involved with the Third Wave roundup and torture? What about Pallas?"

"Pallas was sent to New York City last week to liaise with its city government."

"Convenient. She's the only heroic one around here."

The Librarian didn't answer.

"So the heroes really want this," Keepsie pulled the unassuming metal ball from her pocket.

"Let's go, there are better places to talk," The Librarian said. "We need to keep this file safe, and you're the best for that."

As she stretched out her arm to hand Keepsie the file, a bright light flared between them. Keepsie flinched back and shielded her eyes. The file had burst into flame and the Librarian gasped and dropped it. It was already ash by the time it hit the floor.

"Heretic? Are you here?" The Librarian whispered into the silence. Keepsie still felt the heat between them from the fire.

The hallway lit up again, and a figure encased in flames rose slowly out of the floor. It was a female figure, clothed only in fire. Keepsie gasped and staggered back.

The Librarian's cataloging voice took over. "Dr. Elizabeth Timson has no powers."

The figure laughed with a sound like a trees falling during a forest fire.

Keepsie squinted at the bright figure. It was tough to tell without the lab coat or the glasses or the crow's feet around her eyes, but the face did look like Dr. Timson.

The Librarian shook her head. "You've never had powers. The drug is too volatile to take right now. "

"This is why you never made the inner circle," the figure said. "You lack common sense and the ability to keep your mouth shut."

Keepsie heard the malice in the flaming figure's voice, but the Librarian remained stoic. "I am how I was made. Perhaps look at yourself if you see flaws in me. You are what engineered me, after all."

Timson spread her hands wide. She threw back her head and laughed. Rivers of fire ran down her back. "I see no flaws in myself. Elemental control. Teleportation. And lucky enough to catch you with any damning evidence."

"You forget my memory, Doctor," The Librarian said.

"No, I haven't," Timson said.

Keepsie didn't know why the Librarian wasn't crying for mercy. Timson was clearly out of her mind. Keepsie edged her way quietly down the hall, away from Timson and her prey.

The Librarian did not have time to scream. Timson did nothing but sink into the floor and give Keepsie a false sense of relief before she rose again, in the same space as The Librarian. The hero was engulfed immediately, the flames burning white hot.

Keepsie ran down the hall, stumbling frequently, bright spots blossoming in her vision. The flames behind her died along with the Librarian, making the suddenly dark hallway treacherous. Keepsie tripped over a piece of rubble and went sprawling.

She lay gasping, trying to will air into her lungs and strength into her legs. The silent hallway showed no sign of the brief violence that Keepsie had just witnessed.

She had regained her feet and reached the doorway to the stairwell when she hissed in pain. Something that felt like a lit cigarette had jabbed into her shoulder, burning a hole in her shirt. Keepsie ventured a look behind her, squinting in anticipation.

Timson stood there in her normal work attire, only her finger aflame where she had poked Keepsie.

"We need to talk," she said.

Keepsie swallowed her panic back. Timson opened her mouth again, but vomited a great gout of water, splashing over Keepsie's shoes. Keepsie edged back as Timson continued to vomit until she became a gush of water herself, flooding the floor.

The water moved back and forth as if moved by a tide, looking as if it strained to find a form.

Keepsie ran.

25

Peter slipped into the kitchen. Colette stood at the stove, stirring something in a pot. It was a thick, brown liquid and smelled like a fall afternoon. The tension left Peter's shoulders and the breakdown that had threatened since seeing Alex fall and Keepsie run off retreated a bit.

Colette didn't look at him. "Best to get Alex into the freezer."

"The freezer," Peter repeated blankly.

"I'm no coroner, but I know what happens when something dies. You don't know how long we're going to be down here. We owe it to Alex's memory to give him a decent burial or burning, and we owe it to ourselves not to stay here with a rotting corpse. Go get the body, I'll make room in the freezer."

She stopped him before he left. "Wait, what about those robots?"

"They stopped outside the door. They're not doing anything yet. I don't know what they're waiting for."

She grunted and went back to the stove.

Well, he'd wanted her to know what to do.

Barry and Tomas were drinking sodas at the bar, talking quietly. Michelle and Ian kept watch on the door, sitting close together.

Ian looked up when Peter approached. "It's just not moving."

"Where is the other one?"

"Dunno. Back door? Can't watch that one without opening the door, in which case we might as well just slit our wrists ourselves."

Peter squinted at the mech. "What are they waiting for? The door can't hold them back."

Michelle got up. "It's *scanning* us." She pointed to a small red light that danced over the door and window.

Peter watched the red light. "Well, keep alert, I guess."

"I wish Keepsie were here," Ian said. "At least she's immortal. We could throw her at the robots or something."

Peter pursed his lips and sighed. They had forgotten Keepsie's still-human vulnerability to accidents, pain, kidnapping, and the like.

One thing at a time. He touched Tomas on the shoulder. The large man was in the middle of a toast to Alex's memory, and Peter waited till he was done.

"Tomas, I need your help," he said. "We need to move Alex's body into the freezer to keep it—fresh." He stumbled over the last words. Alex—or rather, his body—lay by the door with a jacket over his head. It was hard not to think of him as Alex, not to rail against putting him into the freezer because it was too cold in there.

Tomas nodded solemnly and went to the body. He paused for a moment, then lifted it easily. He walked towards the kitchen, but five seconds later staggered under the weight of the body.

Peter didn't need further reminders that they were no match for heroes and villains. Tomas was incredibly strong, but could not sustain it. And what the hell good was Barry, a middle aged man who could take off his legs?

He chuckled bitterly to himself. Like he was much better.

Colette came stomping out of the kitchen, Tomas following her. He seemed diminished in her presence. Colette stood in the middle of the bar and looked at them all.

"All right. The body is safe. Now. What are we going to do about these robots—and what about Keepsie?" she asked.

Tomas took his seat beside Barry and didn't look at anyone. Ian looked at Peter. Michelle didn't take her focus off the mech standing outside the door.

"Come on. Don't everyone give ideas at once. I can't hear you if you all talk at the same time," Colette said.

"Well, we don't know if she needs rescuing," Ian said.

Colette's nostrils flared and Peter's heart rate quickened. "Sure. Keepsie chased a hero into the Academy. The Academy, that's the heroes' headquarters and training ground. The building that was blown to bits because of a super villain earlier today. Also, two murderous robots are still outside, keeping her from getting in. Yeah. She's perfectly safe. Anyone else?"

"We need to go about this cautiously," Peter said, meeting her hard eyes with difficulty. "We don't know where the heroes have regrouped."

"You know it's not the Academy, Peter. If so, they'd be out fighting those robots!" Colette said.

Peter sighed and sat down. "Fine. What are your ideas, Colette?"

She stared at him, then sat on a bar stool and looked at the floor. "I don't have any. That's why I asked you."

Peter paused, then laughed softly. "Right. So. We need to at least check on Keepsie. Which means we have to go out there."

Michelle still stared at the robots. "Last time we did that, someone died."

Peter nodded. "We need a plan."

"Fuck the plan," Ian said.

Peter looked at him, startled. Ian stood up, frowning. His fists were clenched. "We've been planning all day. And it's gotten us one missing friend, one dead friend, and hell all around our ears. I think we should do things on the fly, it seems to be helping the villains."

"We don't have superpowers that consist of unbelievable luck!" Peter said. "We don't have superpowers of any kind! What the hell makes you think we can do anything without careful planning without getting eviscerated by heroes, villains or demons?"

"Nothing. But the plans don't make it any less likely, dude. I'm going to check on Keepsie. Come with me or not, but dammit, don't just sit here and talk till you run out of food and have to eat Alex."

Color rose in Colette's face and she balled up her fists. She opened her mouth but Peter interrupted her.

"And how do you plan on getting past them?" He pointed at the mechs.

Ian stood. "Keepsie's back steps are too narrow for those mechs. If there's one at the back door, it's in the alley. And since it's the red one, I've jammed it once, I can do it again."

They stared at him as he walked through the kitchen door.

"Damn, damn, damn," Peter said through clenched teeth. "Michelle. Grab some bar trays. The rest of you, stay safe."

"What are you—" Colette said.

Peter interrupted her. "He may be an asshole, but he shouldn't be out there alone." He ran into the kitchen, praying Michelle would be behind him.

Ian stood at the top of the stairs, laughing. The red mech was still covered in shit, but its many hoses were clogged. It pointed a hose at Ian and hummed, but nothing came out. A burning, nasty smell wafted over to them and Peter grabbed Ian's elbow.

"We need to get out of here. That thing doesn't look very safe, even clogged."

Even as he said this, Colette yelled up the stairs. "Peter, get a move on, the other one is heading your way!"

Ian flinched. "That one I can't clog. Let's go."

They dashed across the desolate road as the mech lumbered up the stairs after them. They outdistanced it, and after a pause, it began patrolling the sidewalk between the front and back doors of Keepsies bar.

They stopped at the top of the Academy's steps. Michelle winced. "Let's get inside. This is creepy." She tucked the five bar trays under her arm more tightly and went through the hole that used to hold the front door.

"So where do we go?" asked Ian.

Peter glared at him. "I thought you were doing this on the fly."

Ian looked abashed. "It seemed like a good idea at the time."

"It usually does," Peter replied, looking at the rubble.

"Do you still have anything of Keepsie's?" Michelle asked.

Peter colored and was glad the lights were out. When was he going to think of that himself? Amazingly, her tank top was still in his back pocket. He held it to his face and inhaled, allowing himself one moment to relish her scent before he returned to his friends.

"That way," he said. They made their way down the hall and stopped in front of the locked stairway.

"Now what?" Ian said after tugging on the door.

The door opened then, hitting Ian on the forehead. He bumped into Peter who stumbled against the wall. Michelle yelled in surprise, and the yell was echoed on the other side of the door.

There was a moment of silent as Peter and Ian untangled themselves, and then Michelle screamed happily. "Keepsie!"

Peter grinned, adrenaline making his knees quake. The two women embraced quickly, and Keepsie pulled back.

"What happened? Where's the Librarian?" Michelle asked.

"Dead. Timson killed her," Keepsie said, looking down at the floor. "She's got powers."

Peter swallowed. "Powers?"

"She... killed The Librarian. I ran. She caught up with me, and then, I guess, had some kind of seizure."

"So she's has powers as of when? Is she like us or like them?" Ian asked.

"Them. She's got some kind of elemental control thing, but more than Heretic, she can *become* the element. She killed The Librarian with fire, but apparently can become others, cause she ended up a puddle of water. That's when I ran."

"Western or Eastern elements?" Peter asked. Keepsie stared at him incredulously. "It could be important."

"I have no idea," she said. "I didn't stick around to count her elemental states."

"So she's still down there?" Michelle asked. Keepsie nodded.

Ian took a step down the hall. "Then let's get the hell out of here!"

"Wait," Peter said. "We need to know more about what she took."

They all stopped.

Peter swallowed. "This is an opportunity we've never had before. We have the run of the Academy. The rest of the town is in chaos. We need to know these things if we're going to survive. Now is the best time."

"You're insane," Michelle said.

Ian was nodding. "Yeah, he's totally insane. That's why we need to do it." He clapped Peter on the back. "You're unclenching, dude!"

Peter smiled uncertainly at the backhanded compliment. He looked at Keepsie.

She shrugged. "So much for my daring escape."

"So much for our daring rescue," Peter replied, and she laughed.

Peter looked down. "You knew we were going back down."

Keepsie followed his gaze. He was staring at her foot, which propped the stairway door open.

"Well. Losing an opportunity is a bad thing," she said.

#

Peter pondered those words as they descended the stairs. Ian and Michelle went first, as theirs were the most offensive powers. Keepsie pulled back on Peter's elbow and he slowed.

"Something I didn't tell you," she said. "Before she died, The Librarian found some files. Timson took that drug to get powers. The Academy designed it for normal people, but it enhances regular powers. It's not ready yet, it's too unstable; that's how I could get away."

"That's why Doodad and Jack stole it," Peter said. "They wanted stronger powers. That must be how Doodad made the self-powered mechs."

Keepsie nodded. "I don't like thinking of what the Academy wanted to do with the drug."

Peter was speechless. He didn't know who was good or bad anymore. "We need to tell the others," he said, indicating their friends several steps below.

She looked at him for a moment. "I guess you're the only one I trust anymore."

The kiss was brief, a quick brush of her lips on his, and he could smell her blood, sweat from days of stress and danger, but it made no difference. His mind exploded again with everything about her, things he shouldn't have known, things he'd have preferred she tell him on her own, but he could no more control than he could control his hammering heart.

She squeezed his hand and said, "Let's go."

Mind whirling, he followed her down to the third sub-basement.

#

When they opened the door (Keepsie had propped this one open as well) to the basement level, Peter inhaled and cried out. His mind was aflame with images of The Librarian, her pain, her panic and death. He collapsed and cradled his head in his hands.

He thought he heard retching. Someone said, "Oh dude, that's rank."

Hands landed on his shoulders and helped him up, took him into the cool stairwell away from the flames and the heat.

Keepsie looked at him in concern. "Better?"

He nodded, not wanting to risk speaking.

"I'm sorry, I didn't think. I was so panicked on the way out that I didn't really smell it," she said.

Ian and Michelle came into the stairwell, Michelle looking queasy. "She's just a grease spot," Ian reported. He nudged Peter and grinned. "Guess the Bloodhound has a weakness, huh?"

Peter sat down on the steps and leaned his head against the cool stone wall. "Now what?" he said. "Was Timson there?"

Michelle and Ian exchanged looks. "We didn't see anything except what The Librarian left behind," Michelle said.

"Crap," said Keepsie. "She was in the middle of the hallway when I left."

"Do we think she's gone?" Peter asked. He couldn't help but to look around.

"No idea," Keepsie said, walking to the doorway and peeking into the hall again. The smell of burned flesh wafted back as she opened the door, and Peter's head reeled again.

"Do we still want to look for—wait, what are we looking for, anyway?" Ian asked.

Keepsie threw a furtive glance Peter's way. "Information. Seems a waste if we don't. Peter, are you OK here?"

Peter nodded. "You guys go ahead. I'll serve as lookout."

"OK, then," Keepsie said. "Yell if you need us."

As they left him, he muttered, "You too, that is if you need a completely useless helping hand who will ride up on his white horse and fall off immediately."

He realized he was talking to himself, and stopped.

26

Keepsie glanced once more at Peter as she left him in the stairwell. He stared at the ground, his face slightly green in the emergency lighting, muttering. She sighed and closed the door.

Ian pointed to the open door beyond the greasy husk that was The Librarian's corpse. "This where you found the info?"

Keepsie stepped over The Librarian without comment. Her head felt numb, far too much had happened today. She thought of Alex, who had taken care of her more than once. Her hand trembled for a moment, and she dropped it and clenched the fist at her side.

"You know, it would be really useful if we had some Third Waver who could, I dunno, be a human flashlight or something," Ian said.

"Isn't there someone who does that?" Michelle asked. She picked through papers in a file cabinet The Librarian had left open.

"Letitia," Keepsie said, shifting through some files on the floor. "But she moved a year ago."

"Keepsie, eyes on the prize, check it out," Ian said, pulling a folder out of an open cabinet.

The file said ZUPRA EX. Keepsie stuffed it under her arm.

They searched through the room, which took little time since they were unable to open any of the drawers The Librarian hadn't jimmied open.

"Zupra Ex," Keepsie said softly. She shivered. Was it really going to be this easy? She pulled the ball out of her pocket and twirled it on the floor, experimenting with Jack's technique. It twirled open like a flower, revealing the drugs inside.

She shivered again and realized it wasn't nerves that was causing it. Her breath puffed out in front of her face.

"Oh crap," she said. "Guys, she's here."

"Man, is that why it's so freaking cold in here?" Ian said.

Keepsie nodded. She grabbed the open device, grabbed a pill, and then closed it, slipping both in her pockets.

"We've got enough stuff, let's head out," Michelle said.

Ian got to his feet and promptly slipped, his feet going above his head, which hit the floor with a crack. Michelle swore, going to him.

Keepsie started forward, but she slipped too. Pinwheeling her arms, she regained her balance and look around her. The walls had taken on a sheen that she had not noticed before.

"Is he OK?" Keepsie said.

Michelle knelt beside Ian, softly slapping his cheeks.

The temperature kept dropping. Keepsie looked around but didn't see Timson. "Can he walk?"

Ian groaned in reply, and Keepsie slid to him, trying to walk on the files instead of the solid ice that coated the floor.

With much struggling and complaining, a groggy Ian got to his feet with Keepsie's and Michelle's help. The back of his blond head was matted with blood, but he was conscious, and that was all Keepsie could ask for.

Michelle looked around. "Where is she?"

"I don't know. She just came out of the floor last time," Keepsie said, shuffling forward.

They exited the room into a hall of ice. Keepsie had a fleeting thought of an ice hotel she had once heard of, but the thought was banished when she saw Timson.

Where she had once been a creature of fire, now she seemed to be made of ice—solid, flexible ice—as she grinned at them. Her hand lay on the stairwell door and ice spread from her fingers, creating spidery designs on the door that disappeared as more ice covered it. It looked as if a six-inch sheet of ice stood between them and their exit.

Well, six inches of ice plus a slightly mad woman with elemental powers who was intent on their deaths.

Timson took a step forward, and Keepsie wondered for a moment how she wasn't slipping. Then the woman pushed off with her back foot and went sliding towards them.

Too fast, Keepsie thought, but Timson didn't aim for her. She was on Ian and Michelle, clotheslining them both. They lost their footing on the slippery floor and both went down hard, Ian groaning. There came a pounding on the door, but it held fast in the ice.

Keepsie steeled herself for an attack, but Timson rounded on her friends again. As Ian raised his fist weakly to point it at her, Timson said "No, not this time," and placed her hand on his forehead.

It took a moment. The ice flowed from her hand, coating his face, cutting off a scream.

A disk smashed into Timson's arm with a loud crack, and she cried out. The flow of ice stopped, and Ian lay prone.

Michelle stood up the hall, eyes narrowed and knees bent for stability. She had armed with another bar tray. "Step away from the surfer dude."

Timson cradled her broken wrist against her abdomen. She glared at Michelle with wide eyes, and Keepsie's heart, which had leapt at the thought that they would get out of this alive, sank. Ice flowed down Timson's arm to serve as a cast, and she extended the arm again.

"Bitch, I said step away!" Michelle shifted her left foot, and Timson struck.

A spear made of ice flowed from her hand and struck Michelle in the shoulder. She cried out and slipped, the spear quivering in her shoulder.

Keepsie looked at Ian. The ice sealed his eyes shut, but wasn't blocking his nostrils. He could last a little longer, barring frostbite. Michelle writhed on the floor, groaning.

Timson advanced on Keepsie. "Give me the drugs, Laura. Or I kill them." She fashioned two more spears out of ice. Their tips pointed at the ground.

Keepsie shook her head and backed up. The icy wall made her gasp as she leaned against it.

"One more chance. You've caused enough trouble today, I'm sure you wouldn't want your friends' deaths on your hands."

Keepsie rummaged in her pocket. Timson paused. Just a moment more. She fumbled for a moment with her right hand, and then popped the pill into her mouth, grimacing as she dry-swallowed it.

Timson's eye widened. "No! Those are mine!" She lunged forward, slipping on her own ice and falling. Her ice cast split and she cried out in pain as her wrist fell between her and her body.

Keepsie's ears buzzed. Everything seemed to take on a white aura. No, that wasn't true. Ian glowed. Michelle glowed. Timson didn't glow. Peter's hammering on the door continued, and it sounded much louder. Keepsie smiled. She felt good. Confident.

What is in this?

Keepsie inched over the ice, and Timson growled from her position on the floor. The doctor frowned and engulfed her own body in flames. *Good. That will melt the ice.*

Timson held out her hand and fire shot from it towards Keepsie. It licked around her, feeling like a warm summer day. They soon died away.

Timson now looked like a statue carved from stone. "No, not now." She looked at her stony hands, the right one hanging at an odd angle. She clenched them slowly, grimacing.

A crash sounded from the end of the hall and the walls crumbled. The ceiling fell in and Keepsie shielded her eyes and looked in the direction of the destruction.

There was another hole in the Academy. Light streamed through—or was that Light of Mornings? She hovered slightly above the rapidly melting floor and gazed at them, her blonde hair floating around her head as if she were underwater. Keepsie knew she should be afraid, but she just couldn't bring herself to care.

Timson writhed on the floor, seemingly oblivious to their visitor. "Control, got to control," she said through stone teeth, and then she gasped, taking in air with a great whoop.

"Ice. Fire. Stone. I guess she's going for air," Keepsie said. She made a mental note to tell Peter it was looking like Timson had Western elemental control.

Light of Mornings continued to stare at her. She returned the girl's gaze, interested. The walls dripped as the ice melted from Light of Mornings's heat. The shaft buried in Michelle's shoulder melted, as did Ian's ice mask.

"Hey, thanks," Keepsie called to her. Light of Mornings did not acknowledge her, but floated into Timson's office.

"Best not to bother her," Keepsie said, and went to check on Michelle.

Her friend was unconscious, which was a blessing considering the large wound in her shoulder. As the ice melted, her blood ran freely.

Keepsie turned then to Ian, whose face was bright red from the ice that had recently melted. It looked like first-degree frostbite, as Keepsie had suffered a spot of frostbite on her ear as a child and remembered it vividly. She patted a non-red portion of his cheek.

"Ian, hey, Ian. We need to get Michelle out of here. She's hurt. Well, so are you, but she's worse, I think. Then again, if neither of you can hear me, then I guess you tie at who's worse, and we'll just see which one of you dies first. I suppose I can drag you out one at a time. Hey, maybe Peter can help. Oh, no, wait, the door is sealed shut."

Light of Mornings exited the room and frowned at Timson, who still panted on the floor. The girl raised her hand and her young face became ugly, morphing into a scowl that reminded Keepsie of a child about ready to throw a tantrum.

Timson swelled, and even as the light grew brighter, her form shimmered once, and then she was gone.

Before Keepsie could act, a wave of light and heat burst from Light of Morning's hand, focused on where Timson had been. It lifted Keepsie as if it were a warm hand and pushed her gently through the concrete wall, through the dirt and out through a hill about a quarter of a mile away. Her friends landed gently beside her and she looked up at the smoking remains of the Academy and thought what a nice day it was to be attacked by the strongest super villain there ever was.

27

Peter's shoulder ached from repeated attempts to bust the door down. He had been resting, head in his hands, trying not to breathe the stench of the deceased Librarian too much, and hadn't noticed Timson's sealing of the door until it was too late. When he started hearing cries of pain and yelling, he doubled his efforts, but all he got was a sore shoulder and the promise of a major bruise.

About a minute before, he noticed that he had begun to glow slightly, which was somewhat alarming, but there was no pain associated with it, so he tried to ignore it. The ice had disallowed any scents to seep through, so he felt entirely blind.

Then the door had been blown off, and he only managed to throw his arms up to ward himself before it hit him. Only it didn't hit him; it vaporized.

The shock wave knocked him into the opposite wall, which vaporized as well. He felt little pain—well, new pain, anyway.

He didn't realize he had blacked out until he woke up. He picked himself up out of the rubble. There was no blood or new bruising; he was entirely unharmed. For a guy who bruised when brushing up against a counter, he seemed rather well-off.

He approached the crater that used to be the hallway, sticking his head slightly in and looking up the hall. The gaping hole in the ceiling dribbled fire onto the floor. He didn't see any of his friends, and Dr. Timson didn't seem to be anywhere either, unless she'd taken refuge in one of the rooms. Although none of the rooms looked as if they had survived the blast.

A hole in the wall next to the stairwell led to a crudely- and freshly-dug tunnel. Well, not dug so much as punched out. If this had been from a direct Light of Mornings attack, he assumed Keepsie would be all right, or rather, she wouldn't be dead, but the others...

Peter dove into the tunnel. The going was not as easy as he'd assumed it would be, but the glow that came from his skin gave him sufficient illumination. The floor was anything but smooth and his own breath sounded ragged in his ears as he stumbled along.

He had no plan, which frightened him. If they had come to a stop somewhere in the hill, broken and bleeding in a cave made by their own bodies, there wasn't much he could do about it except for maybe pull them out one at a time. But he couldn't leave them there.

Blood. Some day he would remember to use his power. He inhaled sharply, sucking the cool underground air through his nose, but all he smelled was earth. No strong smell of expired bodies. He stumbled over something—a tree root, it felt like—and lay panting on the uneven floor.

You could just stay here. You'd be safe from the fighting and the heroes and the demons and the villains. Your friends are probably dead. You're far enough underground to be safe. It sounded nice. He was so tired.

He dabbed at his forehead again, keeping the blood out of his left eye, and got up, trying to remember to keep stooped down. He squinted and thought he could see some light. He picked up his pace, breathing in Keepsie's scent from the shirt he still carried. She wasn't far away. He neared the edge of the tunnel, a hole punched into—or rather, out of—the side of a slope that led to a grocery store parking lot.

As he stepped out of the hole, he caught a whiff of something, a something malevolent, frightened, and slightly mad. He staggered back into the hole, falling onto his back, his eyes wide and blind, everything that Dr. Timson had been and was currently overriding his brain.

Peter had never inhaled a super-hero before. Not inhaled some of their body. He convulsed, rolled over to his side and vomited. He blew air out his nose as hard as he could, attempting to remove her. And still, the images ran through his mind.

Young, eager scientist, studying the effects of the super-drug. Offering herself up as a petri dish, wishing for a super-child. Rising through the ranks as her colleagues recognized her brilliance. Taking more time to build the secret Academy than raise her son. Setting up labs to make an even stronger super-drug to give powers to adults.

The images came faster.

Loss, betrayal of her son, imprisonment, grief, rage at the Third Wave, situation spiraling out of control, forming her inner circle, finally, finally, before it was ready, testing the drug. Rush, power, excitement, base elements, power, loss of control, loss of sanity, loss of medicine, the Third Wave, always the Third Wave, they started it, they caused it, it was them, all their fault.

Peter clawed at his nose. This was worse than when he'd kissed Keepsie, he knew everything, and she knew he knew.

Stop it, stop it.

The race of images stopped, replaced with one image, that of Dr. Timson, half of her face fire, half ice, still in her white lab coat. She grinned at him. *Stupid Third Wave. Control is the first thing we teach those with powers. With lesser powers, you'd think you could control yourself.*

Get out.

I like it here. It's quieter than inside my head.

Please.

No.

He screamed then, clutching his head. He could feel nothing, see nothing, *smell* nothing but the woman inside his head. His friends were forgotten.

28

Keepsie sat up and looked around her. Ian and Michelle lay within ten feet of her. Had they lost their glow, or was it simply lost in the daylight? Was it daytime already?

Keepsie shielded her eyes, squinting. Or was it just the glow of Light of Mornings, who outshone the sun, hovering above the Academy? Her back was to the parking lot where Keepsie and her friends lay, and neither Clever Jack nor Timson were in sight.

"I wonder if we're going to start losing teeth." She got up and took stock of her body.

Ill-used, certainly, but there was an odd absence of any indication she had been hit square-on with a blast of nuclear power and blown through a wall and many feet of earth.

Her friends. She felt a stirring of worry. They couldn't have survived it. Wincing, she approached Michelle.

Her wound still bled freely—*need to do something about that*—but otherwise she seemed fine. She stirred, groaning, but did not look to have the crushed bones and shredded skin and other symptoms of death that Keepsie had expected.

Ian, also unconscious, was much the same. Beaten up, sure: they'd had a bad day. But not looking as if he had lost a battle with a nuclear girl and a concrete wall.

Keepsie sighed. She was surprised that she was not more surprised. She leaned over, slipped her arm under Ian's shoulders, and heaved him up. She got her shoulder under his armpit with ease, and went to pick up Michelle. With little effort, she dragged them both behind her, heading for the bar.

#

Keepsie hadn't expected all the commotion. It was nice to walk through the empty streets without being attacked once. She didn't look to see if Light of Mornings was still there; she really didn't care.

The mech patrolled the sidewalk and it stopped when she got near. It ran at her, then, great lumbering steps.

She made a face at it. "Oh please." It reached within ten feet of her and stopped cold, frozen in place.

She shook her head. "They'll never learn," she said to her unconscious friends. She dragged them down the stairs to the bar, then stared at the door. It was closed. She had no hands free. She frowned at it, and it opened. She walked inside, banging Ian's head on the doorjamb before she remembered to sidle in, and the door closed behind her.

"Hey guys, can you help me out here?" she asked. That's when the commotion started.

"Good God, are they dead?" Barry cried, rushing forward to take Michelle from her.

"No, but she'll need a towel, I think."

"What happened?" asked Tomas, helping her lie Ian down.

"There was a fight. A couple of fights, actually."

"Where's Peter?" The voice was the usual matter-of-fact, cut-the-bullshit tone that Colette excelled at. It managed to break through the haze in Keepsie's brain. She rubbed her forehead, frowning. "I'm not really sure. We were separated. He smelled something bad. Then we got blown out of the Academy."

"Was that the blast we heard?" Colette asked.

Keepsie nodded. She felt uncomfortable all of a sudden. Colette motioned her into the kitchen. She followed meekly.

Colette wordlessly handed her kitchen towels from the linen cabinet, a plastic bag of crushed ice, and a first aid kit. Then, with Keepsie's hands full, she crossed her arms.

"How did you open the door?" she asked.

"I —" she paused. How had she opened the door? She didn't know. She just did.

"Does it have something to do with why we're all glowing?"

Now that she focused on Colette in the kitchen's harsh light, she realized that her cook was glowing, like her other friends had been.

"I thought that was just my eyes." She looked down. "Shouldn't we get these in there?"

"Yes, and as we clean up the others, you're going to tell me what happened. The guys are terrified, and how could you leave Peter behind?"

Without waiting for an answer, she banged through the door, which hit Keepsie in the elbow on the backswing.

Her head began to clear. She hurried after Colette and helped wordlessly as the cook directed Tomas on how to clean, dress and ice Ian's head wounds. She and Colette pressed towels on Michelle's wound, which had slowed its bleeding. Michelle groaned as they applied pressure, and Keepsie sighed in pity and relief. She was alive enough to feel pain, at least.

"Jesus fuck," Ian mumbled. "Wha happen?" He rolled over and vomited onto Tomas's lap.

Tomas got up to clean himself and Barry took over tending to Ian. "I feel like someone's hit me several times with a large stick," Ian said.

"Well, that looks to be true," Colette said. "What happened to your face, kiddo?"

Ian passed his hand over his face, and his eyes widened. "That bitch Timson. Now she's got like ice powers or something. She covered me with ice, I couldn't breathe. And I don't remember what happened after that."

Colette looked at Keepsie, but Michelle groaned again. She sat up with difficulty and Keepsie's help. "She's like an elemental or something." She looked around, frowning. "How did we get here?"

"Keepsie carried you. Both of you. And how did Timson get powers?" Colette said, looking again at Keepsie.

"Wow? Is it that drug you took?" Michelle interrupted.

"I guess," Keepsie's words trailed off. Something was important. Something that didn't seem important before.

"Drug?" Colette's voice was very soft. "You took that drug?"

"She was going to kill them," Keepsie said. "I think. I took one of the pills that Timson used to get her powers. Or—I'm not sure what it was."

She pulled on her ear. If only she could think. Colette held out her hand, as formidable as a mother, and Keepsie retrieved a pill for her and handed it to her without comment.

Colette turned her back and stomped into the kitchen.

"What was that all about?" Tomas asked.

"She can figure out what's in it." Keepsie scowled at the floor. "Or rather, she can figure out how to use it to make the tastiest dish with it. From there she makes, um, guesses."

Michelle pulled the towel from her shoulder. The nasty puncture wound had nearly closed. She looked at Ian, who was no longer needing Barry's help to sit upright. "OK, this is not right. We should be seriously injured. What happened?"

"Oh. We got blown through a wall. That's right," Keepsie looked up suddenly. "Light of Mornings came back, looked for files, and blew us through a wall. We ended up in the parking lot of the diner. Oh, and I got a file. Here." She handed the file she had managed to bring with her to Barry.

They stared at her as if she had suggested they form a militant commune in the bar and have lots of love children. The glow around them subsided and her head finally cleared.

"Keepsie, that's—" Barry started, but Keepsie interrupted him.

"Wait, where's Peter?"

#

Into the bar. Out into danger. Back into the bar. Back out into danger, despite the state they were in when they last came to the bar.

Shit. Shit. I can't believe—shit.

Keepsie ran. The moment the thought of Peter had muscled through the noise in her mind, everything had cleared except for her horror and determination, and she dashed from the bar.

Her memory was clear now. Timson's attack. Her last ditch effort. The move of her mind to go on vacation. The shocking, yet painless, travel through the wall and the hill. Her relative ease in transporting her friends. Most of her friends.

God.

She ran. The streets and the skies were still clear. She didn't stop to wonder where her many attackers of the day were, just Peter. Her friend. Her—well, her Peter.

She trotted up the Academy stairs and paused. The hill leading down from the Academy to the diner's parking lot obscured her exit hole. She turned and headed that way.

He lay in the mouth of the hole, on his back, staring at the sky. Blood flowed from his nose in slow but steady stream.

Keepsie dropped to her knees beside him. "Oh no, Peter, no, what happened to you, aw, come on, sweetie, come on." She touched his face lightly. He was warm and his eyes twitched when he felt her touch.

"OK, good, alive, that's a good start." Her monologue continued as she felt him clumsily for broken bones. He seemed intact.

"Now we sit you up, yeah, OK, no, don't worry about me, I can do this just fine, right, oh, crap." She attempted to get her arm underneath his shoulder to lift him, the way she had Ian and Michelle, but he had slumped over and to the side.

"OK, right, guess that super strength or whatever is gone. Wish it had lasted. But I guess if it had lasted, I wouldn't be out here, I'd be all Lucy in the sky with diamonds again. How did you get hurt, anyway? Did you get the bad luck of getting hurt right after it wore off?"

Peter's eyes were disconcerting, and she wondered if they were drying out. Shuddering at the implications, she carefully closed them. Now he seemed unconscious, not completely paralyzed. That was easier to deal with.

She finally went for the undignified route and grabbed his wrists. She grunted and pulled and dragged him down the hill. Gravity helped her a great deal, but once they reached the sidewalk, he wouldn't budge.

"Peter, I thought you were a thin guy. What gives?" She sat next to him on the sidewalk, close to tears.

"Keepsie!" Tomas's Norwegian voice called from around the corner.

"Stay right there," she told Peter's body, and ran to meet Tomas.

"Colette's pretty angry with you," Tomas said.

"Yeah, well, if she can tell me what she would have done in the situation, I'd love to hear her suggestions," Keepsie said.

"Shall we get Peter inside?"

Keepsie shook her head. "Right. Let's go."

"Where is he?" he asked.

Keepsie groaned. "No. No no no no. This isn't happening!"

"What?" said Tomas.

"He's gone."

Two grooves in the hill marked where Keepsie had dragged him to the sidewalk, which was smeared with blood, but Peter was, indeed, gone.

"Crap! He couldn't have gone far. What are we going to do? You head up the street, I'll check inside the Academy."

Tomas laid a large hand on her shoulder. "Keepsie."

"Come on, he's hurt!"

"Keepsie. Look."

She raised her eyes. The Academy was a burning husk, even worse than before. It was little more than a hole in the ground.

Tomas pointed again. Clever Jack stood atop a roof a block away, watching them. Light of Mornings hovered nearby.

"Keepsie, we have to go back to the bar."

29

Peter looked up, groggy and disoriented. He was running through a garbage-strewn alley. A couple of bodies—homeless people, by the look of them—lay in pools of blood. The work of Doodad's robots? Light of Mornings? By-products of hero battles? Random slaying? Peter didn't understand why he had no physical reaction to the grisly deaths. He also didn't understand why the copper smell wasn't filling his head with terrifying images of death.

"Third Wave. None of you could ever control your power," he heard his own voice say. He turned and ran down a street parallel to main. Why wasn't he headed to Keepsie's Bar?

He stopped running and put his hand to his head. Only, his body didn't respond to either of those demands. What?

"Don't fight it. I'm driving now," he said again.

His heart started to race, but only in his perception. His body traveled on, determined, driven by this other power. He began to panic, but forced himself to calm down and think of a way out of this prison.

"You are welcome to try," he said.

No. Not he. She. Timson. He had inhaled her as a gaseous form, she was in his brain.

This is impossible. There is no calm way to deal with this because it is not happening. I should have stayed in the cave.

But his body continued its run. He hadn't even been paying attention to the course it was taking. He found himself face to face with the Crane, looking into the narrow, cold eyes.

181

"It's Timson," he growled at the threatening figure. "Password is elite."

"Oh, ah, ma'am..." said The Crane, backing down. "How—"

"The idiot inhaled me when I was in gaseous phase. His power is one that causes his brain to be profoundly affected by scent. I was able to grab hold."

"Oh. That was, ah, clever, ma'am. But what happens if your body takes on another elemental form? You had said you were having trouble controlling it."

"Well. The change will likely be painful for me, but I should be all right."

There was an inflection to his—her—tone that made Peter shiver. If he could have shivered, that is.

The heroes assembled in an apartment in the good part of town. Peter realized they were in The Crane's secret identity home. The spotless white walls gleamed, as did the plush white carpet and furniture. The Crane served sparkling water—nothing that could stain—to the heroes. But a certain few were missing. Pallas, namely. Every hero, save White Lightning and Samantha—Ghostheart—who had been involved with the torture at the Academy was there, as well as some younger recruits who he didn't recognize.

The Crane sat on a spare spot on the couch, looking frightened and uncertain. Peter saw with some satisfaction that the hero's wings were sullied with blood and soot, and he trembled slightly.

"We've finally had some luck," Peter announced to the heroes. "Clever Jack and Light of Mornings are converging in the city again. Ghostheart and White Lightning are working on our backup plan. Doodad has been captured by the Third Wave.

"The bad news is that Doodad has clearly taken the Zupra-Ex and it has increased his abilities so that he can now make machines that power themselves. There is some question as to what else he might have made. Further bad news is that Laura Branson is in possession of the only collection of Zupra-Ex that exists, and she possibly has the chemical compound as well."

The heroes looked at each other uncertainly. This news clearly wasn't good.

"I have discovered I can take possession of this Third Wave's body when I am in gaseous form," he answered. "I have some time before I switch again, I believe."

"Why a Third Wave, Doctor?" asked The Crane. *Peter could feel Timson's underlying revulsion for his sycophantic nature.*

"Besides the fact that his power is unique in that it allows me to do this, it's perfect for infiltration, Crane," his voice took on an oily quality he was unaware it could do. "This man is a close friend of Laura Branson. He can get the drugs from her.

"But I need to hurry."

Panic made his ears sing and his vision blur. He tried everything he could to wrest control from her, but as he had no idea how to fight this kind of threat, he felt as if he were trying to move a glacier with a frozen chicken. He didn't even know where to start.

As Timson talked to her flock, he tried to gain control of something he figured she wouldn't notice. First he tried to twitch a calf muscle. He had never thought about the effort it took, the synapses that had to run through his body, the exquisite concentration. No go. He moved to something smaller. Timson had grasped the side of the armchair and he tried to grasp it just a little tighter, make her think the emphasis was her own. Nothing responded.

Hell. He tried to cry, to weep, to beat hysterically against her iron control, and his prison did not crack. All he was able to do was watch out his own eyes and listen through his own ears.

The most frightening thing was that he could not smell anything at all.

#

"All right. Heretic and Devil, come with me, the rest flank us and stall Clever Jack. If I need aid, Tattoo Devil will send word."

Heretic was at Peter's side at once. "Doctor, what will Pallas say about our new, ah, plans?"

"I have arranged for her to be in New York for the duration. She won't interrupt her trip unless I call her. Our PR people are working on a plausible spin for it. It will all work out."

Peter barely paid attention to her. He was out of ideas. She carried him out the apartment door and down the road several blocks. People peeked out of windows and smiled at them, giving thumbs-up signs.

They reached Main Street too quickly. Timson's heroes and Clever Jack and Light of Mornings had engaged and the battle was bloody. Timson guided Peter's eye briefly to where White Lighting and Ghostheart were conducting the battle from their vantage point, high in the sky, safe from attack. Ghostheart called down to the streets below, egging on—*oh Jesus.*

The city's destitute, the homeless, the hoboes and bums, those that cities tried to keep care of but secretly wished would go and plague another city, had formed an army. Ghostheart's army, guided by her power of lies and suggestion. They marched forward toward Jack and Light of Mornings.

How are bums going to fight a nuclear child?

Light of Mornings appeared beside Clever Jack on the roof. Peter's question was answered as the army began throwing things at her, causing no damage but clearly distracting her. She flew down to the street and raised her hand.

No...

Her blast blew their forces back, the limp bodies tumbled like dice, stopping only when hitting something larger than themselves. They did not get up.

The heroes' grisly plan was working, however, as White Lightning was able to get through the girl's defenses and strike her with a lightning bolt. She looked up, however, and glared at him.

"Idiot," Timson said with Peter's mouth. "If she's made of energy he can't hurt her that way."

Peter felt something as Timson stared at the girl: rage. He hadn't been able to notice her emotions before, was it because he was getting more attuned to her, or his own panic was fading enough for him to notice her?

The hobo battle seemed to be focused on the street right in front of the bar, but Samantha's forces had retreated just enough to where Timson could carry Peter and his body to Keepsie's front door. She turned and nodded to Tattoo Devil and Heretic, and entered the bar.

Peter felt Timson's surprise as his arms were suddenly full of Keepsie. "Where the hell did you go? What happened?" she demanded after hugging him.

Peter sat back—metaphorically—to watch. There was nothing he could do. He could watch, and wait for Timson to mess up, or change from her gaseous form... and then what?

Well, he would see.

30

Peter looked positively startled when Keepsie hugged him, something she attributed to the stress. A small part of her mind wondered if she had been reading him, or Colette's clues, incorrectly, and she was making an ass of herself. Another part of her was angry at his response. But mostly she was monumentally relieved to have him back.

"I don't really remember what happened," he said, hugging her back tightly. "I woke up in an alley and made my way back here."

"How did you get past the ruckus outside?" asked Barry.

"They didn't even notice me," Peter said confidently.

"So what happened to you after we got blown out of the building?" Michelle asked, still holding her injured arm awkwardly.

"I, uh, don't remember that part either. I was in the stairwell, and then I was in the alley. No clue."

"Well, we're just glad to have you back. We've pretty much decided to hole up here and let them duke it out," Keepsie said, leading him to the bar.

Ian sat in front of six painkillers, all lined up in a neat row. He methodically popped one into his mouth, chased it with a gulp of beer, and moved onto the next one.

He shot Peter a look. "Dude."

Peter stared at him for a moment, and then took his seat.

"So, after someone wins out there, then what?" Peter asked, jabbing his thumb toward the door.

Keepsie shrugged. "I don't know. There aren't any good guys left. Timson is insane, Clever Jack has a nuclear bomb… I can't keep these drugs forever, but I—shit, we've been over this. Let's worry about it when the dust clears."

Peter nodded. "Where is everyone else?"

"Who do you mean? Everyone is here. No one else has made it out since the initial attack, and anyone we've called said they didn't want to come down. Not that I can blame them."

"So, just us, huh?"

"Yes, just us, like it's been all day. Minus Alex, of course," she added sadly.

"And where is Alex?"

Ian whipped his head around and winced. "Dude, they must have hit you harder than they hit me. What do you mean 'where is Alex?'"

Peter looked around, blushing slightly, "I'm really not following today very well."

"Maybe your blood sugar is low," Keepsie said. "You want Colette to make you some food?"

Peter nodded. "Cheeseburger and fries, please."

Keepsie reached out and squeezed his hand. He smiled at her and squeezed back.

In the kitchen, Colette fussed around the stove.

"You know, you can come join us," Keepsie told her.

Colette turned, murder on her flushed, round face. "Something is wrong."

"You mean besides the fact that we're trapped in a bar with death and chaos right outside the door?" Keepsie laughed, able to relax a bit now that Peter was back.

Colette didn't answer. Keepsie sighed and said, "Peter is back, he's OK. He wants a cheeseburger and fries."

Colette raised her head slowly. "He wants what?"

"Cheeseburger and fries," Keepsie said.

Colette reached out and grasped the butcher knife on the counter.

Keepsie threw out her arms to placate Colette. "Whoa, what's going on? What's wrong?"

"Peter doesn't eat well-done burgers." Colette's voice was cold.

"So? He's been through a lot today."

"But he doesn't eat them like that. He doesn't have mayo on his burger. And the man is a cheddar man, not American cheese."

"And that's what he wants?"

Her cook nodded slowly. "That's what whoever ordered this burger wants."

"So you're saying what?"

"Dammit, Keepsie, are you still addled?" She waved the knife around as she gestured, and Keepsie stepped back. "Heroes are torturing citizens, you saw a woman with no power turn into a pillar of fire, and you're saying that one of them can't take on Peter's shape and try to get the drugs from you, or worse?"

All of the hair on Keepsie's arms stood straight up and she shivered.

"Make the burger. I'm going to see what I can find out."

"Try to be quicker out there than you are in here," Colette said, turning back to her stove. Keepsie ground her teeth but didn't reply.

She paused in the door and said, "Colette, what was in that drug?"

"Zupra. Pumped up, jacked up, enhanced, and the good Lord knows what else. But definitely Zupra. Everything you told me about what it will do to Third Wave and a super is true. But it's unstable and will screw you up if you take too much."

"And where is it?"

Colette stopped cutting tomatoes.

"Colette. We don't know what we're up against. It's better for one of us to get fucked up rather than we all die."

Colette pointed with the butcher knife, dripping tomato juice down the blade and onto the floor, at the Lost and Found box. Keepsie relaxed. "Good. Leave it there."

"Like I could move it if I wanted to," Colette said coldly.

Keepsie took a deep breath and put on the face she would have liked to wear if Peter really were back.

Dammit Peter, where are you?

#

"What the hell took you so long?" asked Ian. "Peter's starving."

"Colette had to tell me about the drugs," Keepsie said, "so that took some time."

Peter looked up from the glass of red wine he held. "Oh? What did she say?"

"She doesn't know what it does, only that it's pretty powerful stuff." Keepsie kept her head down as she slipped behind the bar and pulled a pint of beer. "We have no idea what it does."

"But didn't it enhance your powers?" Peter asked.

"Did it?" Keepsie looked as if she were trying to remember. "I can't remember much. And I thought you didn't remember anything anyway."

"Ian told me," he said.

Keepsie glared at Ian for an instant and moved to sit beside Peter. She sipped her beer. "Damn, I'm so tired of all of this. I wish it could just be over."

"We need to think of another plan," Peter said decisively.

"Oh? What do you have in mind?" she said.

"We need to make a deal with someone. We're surrounded; it's clear that we can't beat all of them."

"Dude, what are you saying? Surrender?" Ian asked, choking on his beer.

"Not surrender," Peter said, backpedaling. "I just think we need to pick a side to go with and support them. Then the conflict should sort itself out, right?"

Keepsie began nodding, thinking fast. "Let me think about this." She got up.

"Dude, you're fucking kidding," Ian said. "Clever Jack and Doodad tried to kill us enough today to be off the list. Heroes, torture and kidnapping, also not cool. Who has the least suck value? 'Cause I'm thinking they're all in a tie."

"Let me think," Keepsie repeated, putting Ian back in his seat with a look. "I'm going to check on Peter's food."

"And I need to use the bathroom, if you'll excuse me," Peter said. He walked across the bar and into the women's room, and then came right back out, blushing madly. Then he went into the men's room and yelled when he saw Doodad's body.

"Colette was right," Michelle said. "That's not Peter."

He came back out. Ian laughed at him. "Dude, you forgot pretty much everything, didn't you?"

Peter nodded and attempted to smile, but he glared at them all for a moment. "So how long are we going to keep… that villain in the men's room?"

"I am going to hand him over to the authorities when all of this is done," Keepsie said. "Probably the police."

"Not the Academy?"

"Peter, honey, there is no Academy anymore," she said.

"You both have lost your mind," Ian said, and headed to the women's room.

Keepsie relaxed a fraction; Ian almost blew it. Not that he knew there was something to blow.

She met Colette just inside the doorway, chatting with Michelle. The cheeseburger sat in its basket, perfectly grilled, with a garnish of an orange slice.

Colette grinned at Keepsie's raised eyebrow. "Just trust me. And be ready." She pressed a pill into Keepsie's hand. "We'll find out right now for sure if it's him."

She slipped the knife into her apron strings and led them out of the kitchen. Keepsie and Michelle shared a tense look, and Michelle said, "I'm going to check and see if the guys need any beer." She looked at Tomas and Barry, sitting quietly in their usual booth.

"Your shoulder up to it?"

Michelle nodded, flexing. "Not sure how, but I'm healed."

Keepsie palmed the pill and followed Colette.

The cook put the burger right under Peter's nose. He rubbed his forehead and inhaled gratefully. "That smells amazing, my compliments to the chef."

"Smells good, does it?" she asked without smiling.

"Very. I'm famished."

"Doesn't remind you of anything?"

Peter look alarmed and glanced around. Michelle was setting drinks on a bar tray, watching them. Keepsie waited in the doorway, wondering what Colette was up to.

He forced a laugh. "I'm sorry, my memory is not what it used to be."

"So nothing smells odd about it?" Colette said.

"Aaaaahhhh…" Peter sounded as if he remembered something. "Right. Let me see." He stuck his nose right up to the basket and inhaled deeply.

"Colette," he said, a teasing tone to his voice. "Did you leave a hair in here for me to find?"

"No," she said. "But I did figure you'd find the present underneath the orange slice. I left it just for you."

Peter lifted the orange slice and recoiled back, falling off the barstool. "What the hell is wrong with you?"

Keepsie squashed her final doubts and tossed the pill into her mouth, gulping it down with her beer.

Colette grinned and held her knife tightly. "Nothing at all, Peter. Or whoever you are."

Peter's eyes widened and he threw his head back, slamming it against the floor. He screamed and screamed, hands pulling at his hair. Blood began pouring out of his nose.

Colette strode forward with the knife. She raised it, but Keepsie chased after her and caught her wrist.

"No. Wait."

Her ears were beginning to buzz again. "Just. Wait."

Keepsie tried to keep her wits about her but the world began to glow with a fuzzy white light. She shook her head. Peter's screams seemed far away, and she struggled to focus on them.

She still held Colette's hand, which was glowing as well. Michelle glowed too, with her tray of beer held ready to fling at the convulsing figure on the floor.

Colette's hand relaxed and she stepped back. Keepsie knelt by Peter, who began vomiting. She held his head to the side and looked up at her friends who had surrounded them.

"It's Peter," she said.

"What? How do you know?" Colette asked.

"Look. You all are glowing again. So is he. I doubt he'd be glowing it if weren't him. Hey, that thing coming out of his nose isn't glowing. Do you think that's the problem?"

Peter continued to choke and vomit while a long rope of fire, hissing in the blood, streamed from Peter's nose. It coiled on the floor beside his head, coalescing in the shape of a woman.

It seemed to last a long time. Keepsie watched in detached interest, still holding Peter's head. When all of the fire was out and the woman lay, sizzling in the blood and vomit, Keepsie turned her attention to Peter.

His nose continued to bleed but he had stopped vomiting. He looked up at her with heavily lidded eyes.

"Keepsie," he managed to choke out before he went unconscious.

Keepsie smiled at her friends. "There. All better."

They stared at her.

#

Timson continued to burn on Keepsie's floor, which, strangely, did not smolder. The heat wafting off of her kept them away, but Colette dumped some ice water on her to keep the temperature down. The woman lay there, eyes open, staring at the ceiling, captured by Keepsie's power.

"What happened?" Michelle said, shaking her head in disbelief.

Keepsie stroked Peter's hair. "He had a Timson in his nose, I think. I could feel her in there. She was hurting him. She was trying to take what's mine."

"What do we do with her?" Tomas nudged her with his work boot.

"We could put her in the freezer with Alex, but then that would negate the purpose of putting Alex in there."

"No. We're not putting something on fire in my freezer," Colette said.

"Why not just throw her out the door?" Michelle asked.

Keepsie shook her head. "She tried to kill Peter. Well, she's tried to kill lots of us. But this one is pretty gross. She's gone off the deep end, I'm sad to say. We need to hold her here."

"Now we're back to where." Colette said.

"Put her in the bathroom with Doodad," Barry said. "She'll be out of our hair then."

Keepsie clapped her hands. "And they'll be reunited!"

"Keepsie, have you tried to figure out what that drug does to you?" Colette said.

Keepsie held her arm out, admiring the glow. She reminded herself of a unicorn. "Well, I'm clearly high."

"Your powers, Keepsie. What about your powers?"

"We can't be hurt," Michelle shrugged her shoulder without wincing. "Or rather, we heal quickly."

Keepsie peered at Peter's face. The ropy burns that had streaked his face as he had labored and delivered Timson were rapidly losing their angry red color.

Colette nodded. "What else?"

Keepsie looked around at all of them, with everything in the bar glowing brightly with a white aura. "I can feel everything that I own, my things, my friends, my assets." Keepsie snapped her head up. "Hey, let's go out and see the battle!"

Colette looked at Michelle. "Looks like you're in charge until she comes back to us."

"Jumping Jesus! What the fuck happened here?"

Ian had returned from the bathroom.

#

Keepsie continued to stroke Peter's hair. He had such nice hair. Dark brown, almost black. Sure, there was blood in it, and some of the ends were curled and melted from getting too close to some fire or another, and it could stand to be washed, but it was nice because it belonged to Peter.

Michelle and Colette whispered behind the bar. Ian sat with Tomas and Barry with a stunned look on his face as they tried to explain what had happened. Ian had explained that he'd heard the screaming, but he had been on the john, and sometimes there were higher priorities.

Keepsie realized the feeling of forgetting something important was getting familiar, and she struggled to grasp it.

With a sigh, she lowered Peter's head the floor, careful to keep it out of the vomit, kissed his forehead, and wandered over to Colette and Michelle.

"So what's the next plan?" she asked.

"Keepsie, you saved Peter's life by taking that drug. Probably all of our lives. But you're, well—" Michelle trailed off.

"—too high to help right now," Colette finished.

"But you gave me the drug."

She nodded. "I know. And I don't regret it. But that doesn't hide the fact that you're no good to us right now."

Keepsie watched them retreat into the kitchen, still whispering. She frowned and crossed her arms. It wasn't fair. Here she was with all this power...

She turned and wandered into the ladies room. No one paid her any attention. They'd propped the immobile Timson up against the wall (Keepsie had been outvoted when she asked to put Timson's feet in the toilet to keep her cool). The doctor had taken on her stone form and looked very much like a statue.

Keepsie hefted Timson easily. "I know how to prove I'm useful."

She walked out into the bar and kept going nonchalantly when the three men looked up at her.

"Keepsie," Ian asked warily, "what are you doing?"

"Figured I'd let the heroes know we had her," Keepsie said. They scrambled to their feet.

Typical. She continued to the door. Ian lunged forward and caught Keepsie's shoulder. He was very pretty when he glowed like that. "Wait wait, you shouldn't do that, we shouldn't be attracting attention right now. Let them fight it out."

"Ian, they want her. They want me. I'm all über-powered on that Timson drug right now, let's see what I can do!"

"You're also fucked up, Keepsie." She was surprised at his gentle tone. "You really shouldn't go out there till you start to come down. We're rather have you as sensible Keepsie with your lame Third Wave power than über-Keepsie with no sense at all."

Grinning at his compliments, she bristled at the end. "I do too have sense! I'm only going out there *because* I'm strong now."

"Let's just wait till we have a plan, OK? Lots of bad stuff happens when we don't have a plan, remember?"

Keepsie sighed, defeated. Her head didn't seem to be buzzing so much anymore. She put Timson down and leaned on her. "Doesn't matter much. They already know." She jerked her head towards the door.

Tattoo Devil and Heretic stood in the doorway, jaws slack and eyes wide. Keepsie waved at them. "Yeah, they know we have her."

31

Peter opened his eyes. He winced. Had he been snorting cayenne pepper? Crusty foulness cracked when he moved his mouth and he groaned. He passed a hand over his face and blinked. He could move his hand. He sat up suddenly and looked around.

Keepsie, Tomas and Barry stood at the front door, looking out with frowns creasing their foreheads. Well, Tomas and Barry looked concerned. Keepsie's eyes were wide and she was grinning. They all glowed with a soft white light.

The light again. He held out his hand: it glowed too.

He sneezed once, stifling it with his hand. Jesus that hurt.

Tomas turned around. "Peter! You are awake! Are you well?" He turned from Keepsie and came to kneel by his side.

Peter saw what Tomas had been hiding with his bulk— Timson, in a stone statue, stood by Keepsie. He sighed raggedly, feeling suddenly weaker with relief. He hadn't felt any presence of her, but he hadn't known if she was gone for good.

Keepsie looked over at him and waved. "Peter! Come here! It's looking exciting!"

"What's going on?" Peter asked.

"Keepsie is high on the drug she stole from the Academy. But it looks like she saved you. Something about the drug seems to make her and her friends heal. I do not pretend to understand it.

194

But she took it, and that doctor came out of your nose. It was strange."

Peter had never heard Tomas talk so much. "I remember everything up until the toe."

Tomas stared at him.

"The toe? The one Colette hid in my food?" Peter said.

Tomas got to his feet and went to the forgotten basket of food. He lifted the orange and made a disgusted sound. "Colette!"

She came out of the kitchen, saw Peter, and smiled. "Doing better?"

Peter nodded. "I think I have you to thank."

Tomas shook the basket at Colette. A frozen human toe, the big one, was nestled next to the fries. "What the hell do you think you're doing?"

Colette didn't blink. "If it really was Peter, he would have been able to realize it was Alex's toe in there, and he wouldn't have eaten. It proved his identity to us, didn't it?" Her focus shifted to the door where heroes conferred. "Shit, why didn't anyone call me?"

"You don't cut up your dead friends!"

"We have to get out of here."

Tomas slammed the basket on the counter. The toe bounced out and onto the bar. He shivered back in revulsion. Keepsie left her post by the door and went to the bar. She bent down and peered at the toe from eye-level.

She straightened abruptly. "Did he complain at all when you cut it off?"

Colette looked as if Keepsie had asked her to fix her a corn and squirrel sandwich. "Uh, no."

"And he didn't tell you to stop or anything?"

"Keepsie, he's dead."

Keepsie rounded on Tomas, who still stared at the toe. "So if Alex doesn't mind, why should you mind?"

"It is not done," Tomas said.

Keepsie shrugged. "It worked pretty well. Let's forget about it right now. Colette, take the toe back to its rightful owner, and please clean off the bar. With bleach. And then let's look out the window. It's like watching TV!"

And indeed, it was, if TV consisted of two angry superheroes staring through the TV set looking as if they were trying to decide whether they were going to leap through the set at you or just blast you from where they were.

Peter tried to rise and failed. He was already feeling better, but he was still amazingly weak. Keepsie came over to him and grabbed his arms.

Peter grunted in alarm when she heaved him easily to his feet.

Keepsie dragged him to the door. "So Peter. You're the smart one. What should we do?"

Peter shot a desperate glance at Colette and Michelle, who conferred in hissing tones near the bar.

He left Keepsie's side and went to them. "We have to get out of here."

They nodded. "There are lots of things we have to do." Michelle said. "I guess we'll have Ian and Tomas point, the rest of us following. And someone has to be in charge of making sure Keepsie doesn't do anything stupid." They both looked at him. He sighed.

"I can't lift a bar stool right now. What makes you think I can control her?"

"You're the only one she'll listen to," Colette said. "Back door, then?"

Peter nodded.

"We'll go check it out. You get Keepsie."

He approached her, heart hammering in his chest. She was liable to do something immensely stupid, this drug was pretty intense. He tried not to think about the long-term effects.

Tomas stood at her shoulder, looking ready to grab her if he needed to. She leaned against Timson's stone form and watched the heroes outside the door.

"Why aren't they doing anything?" Peter asked.

"I do not know," Tomas said. "They keep whispering. They have had several opportunities to attack, but they do not."

"They're scared of me." The men stared at Keepsie. She nodded at them. "Yeah, they know I took their little drug. They don't know what I can do."

Tomas met Peter's eyes and he shrugged. It made sense. They didn't stare at Peter or Tomas, they watched Keepsie wave at them.

"We're going out the back door, Keepsie, we're going to try to get out of here. You can leave Timson here."

"What? Leave? I'm having so much fun!"

"Keepsie." Peter took her shoulders and turned her to look defiantly into his face. "This is not fun. We've been attacked, tortured, betrayed, and one of us has died. I nearly died. You nearly died. We need to get the hell out of here while we still can. Leave the city and let the big guys fight it out. We can't beat them; we've tried and failed numerous times."

She set her jaw. Peter's heart sank. He lowered his voice. "Please. I just found you, Keepsie. I really don't like the thought of losing you this soon."

She dropped her eyes and took a long shuddering breath. "All right. Fine. But you owe me some fun." She leaned up and kissed him quickly on the lips. "Let's go. But first, you get cleaned up so I can kiss your proper. You taste awful."

Michelle ran into the bar, her face set. "No can do. The alley is full of bums. We're trapped in here."

Ian laughed. "Bums? We're afraid of bums now?"

Peter's eyes widened as he remembered. "That's right. They're using homeless people as an army."

"The villains?" Michelle asked.

Peter shook his head. "The heroes. Samantha is using her lying power to control them. They're dying by the scores."

They paused in shocked silence.

Something else nagged at Peter, but he pushed it aside as he tried to think of another solution. His mind was blank. He took the wet bar towel Keepsie handed him and wiped his face absently. She went back into the kitchen.

It was only when Heretic reared back and punched through the glass window of the front door that Peter's mind went into full action. And it did so only to remind him that when had kissed Keepsie, he had sensed nothing.

32

Everyone jumped back, Ian swearing loudly.

Heretic's arm stretched into the room, losing momentum from her punch as her fist got further in. The last few inches looked like she had moved through molasses to get there, where her fist remained, frozen in space. Heretic's eyes widened and she strained backwards. Nothing happened.

Everyone was silent for a moment.

Ian snickered. "Well goddamn."

"What is going on?" Michelle asked, taking a hesitant step forward.

Colette stomped into the bar from the kitchen. "I couldn't stop her, she just winked at me and ran out the door!"

"What?" Peter asked, his voice low and steady.

"Keepsie's gone. She just ran off."

"How could you let her go?"

Colette glared at him. "What did you want me to do?"

Michelle turned her back on Colette and focused on Peter. "Why aren't you more upset?"

"Of all the things the past couple of days have showed us, the most obvious one is that Keepsie is capable of taking care of herself. And if she's not, her power certainly is."

Heretic continued to strain backwards, pulling on her arm. Tattoo Devil had grabbed her shoulders.

"If I'm not mistaken, this is Keepsie's power at work," Peter said.

"Whoa, deep statement, dude," Ian said. "The deal is, Keepsie isn't here. How is this working?"

"She protects us when we're on her property. Everything in the bar is hers, and is protected by her. We're her friends. We're protected by her."

Colette frowned. "That drug she took. It's protecting all of us."

Barry snorted. "How do you know all this, Peter?"

"My—my power allows me to know this. You know that."

"Yeah, if you smell them, you're 'the Bloodhound', but I didn't know you could do that."

Peter looked up, and Barry actually stepped back at the look on Peter's face. "If I taste them, like in a kiss, I can learn a lot more. I kissed Keepsie. I learned more about her powers. That's how I know she can't be killed."

"Dude, what's wrong?" Ian asked, flinching at the look on Peter's face. He looked at Colette. "You guys make sure that fist doesn't go anywhere. I'll be right back."

Colette stepped forward, butcher knife in hand.

Ian pushed Peter willingly into a booth.

"You know she'll be OK. She can't be killed, you said it yourself."

"I'm not worried about Keepsie."

"Then what the hell is the matter?"

"I can't smell, Ian. I can't smell anything. Not even you."

"What, you mean you've lost your power?"

Peter nodded. "Timson must have... I don't know. I don't know how she did what she did, or what she did in the first place. I didn't notice until Keepsie kissed me again. I didn't feel anything. And then when I tried to use it, I got nothing."

Ian sputtered. "OK, when were you and Keepsie kissing? Where the hell have I been?" Peter glared at him. "Right. Not the topic at hand. Go on."

"There's nothing more to say. I'm of no use to you guys. Keepsie's apparently keeping us safe, since nothing looks like it can get in here to hurt us. We know she can't be killed. We're at a stalemate. So I guess this time is as good as any to go impotent."

"Aw dude," Ian gave Peter's forearm an awkward pat. "You're more than a power to us. That's the point of us. We've all felt useless until the past couple of days, but we still stuck together. Without your and Keepsie's brains, we all would be dead about three or four times over. That St. Peter dude would get sick of seeing us parade by. You're like the smartest person in the room, and with Keepsie gone, we really need you. Colette is trying, sure, but she's going to fall apart any minute now. Christ, she was cutting up Alex's dead foot. Tell me that's rational behavior."

Peter chuckled. "It worked, but I suppose there could have been a better way."

"So, please, to keep Colette from chopping any of us up, get up there and do some leading. Hell, no one will listen to me, which is probably for the best."

Peter stared at his hands. "I've felt like my power was pointless my whole life, and now I realize how much I used it, if unconsciously. I don't know if I can do this."

Ian sighed, deflating after his "go-get-em-tiger" speech had failed. "I don't know what to tell you, dude. All I know is we've got bigger problems. And I'm always here for you, but not right now. I got a hero's arm to deal with." He got up and left the table. Peter followed him after a moment, very much not wishing to be alone.

"Are you OK?" Michelle asked Peter.

Ian shook his head. "That Timson bitch scrambled his brains or something. He lost his power. He's a little freaked out."

Michelle gasped and looked at Peter. "Is that all she did?"

"I don't know," Peter said. "Right now we have more important things to worry about," He pointed to the heroes outside the door as Ian slapped him on the back.

Heretic was still stuck, and was conferring quietly with Tattoo Devil.

"What now?" Michelle said.

Tattoo Devil concentrated and threw his head back, eyes closed in concentration. From his abdomen leapt a bobcat, small and compact, not as deadly as a cougar but much more powerful than a housecat. The cat shook itself and then leapt for Keepsie's window. It crashed through another pane and fell on the floor, motionless.

"Dude. That was cool," Ian said. He went to examine the cat. It looked like all of Keepsie's victims, frozen entirely. He poked it; it was stiff as if dead.

"Does Colette know how to cook bobcat? And hey, what happens to the Devil if we eat one of his tattoos?"

Michelle looked out the door, grinning. Ian stood and peered out of the broken pane.

In a world with bizarre superpowers, they should not have been surprised at what they saw. But Peter grinned and Ian laughed out loud when he saw Tattoo Devil struggling, panic scribbled over his face. His arms flailed and his head lolled, his feet scrabbled over the concrete steps, but he didn't move at all. His abdomen had been captured by Keepsie's power, and wasn't going anywhere.

"Keepsie's power rocks more and more," Ian said. "I could watch this all day."

"So we've caught two superheroes. Now what?" Michelle said.

"Now we fight back," Peter said over her shoulder.

#

In Peter's horror at his own loss, he hadn't noticed that when he and Ian had gone to deal with Heretic, Colette had returned to the kitchen. Now he realized what she had been up to.

"That," she said, pointing to a deep fat fryer, "is safflower oil. Nearly the highest smoke point of any oil. It can get upwards of 510 degrees without catching fire. You know how they showed you horrific movies in driver's ed to scare you into wearing a seat belt? Well, in culinary school they showed us movies of oil burn victims. It's not pretty."

She moved to the stove where something bubbled in a large stockpot. "This is sugar. Mixed with a little corn syrup. This can't get as hot as the oil can, but will work like napalm as it will stick to skin and continue to burn."

"That's great, but, uh, why?" Ian asked.

"Weapons. Think dark ages wars with the boiling oil pots."

"But how in the hell are we going to pour the stuff up the wall? We're in a basement!"

Colette snorted. "Use your imagination. That's what we have to do to get by. If you'd prefer something more mainstream, the knives are over there. But careful, they're sharp." She gestured to a neat row of five knife blocks.

Ian eyed the concoctions, and then took Colette's challenge and pulled a chef's knife from the block. "I was burned by hot water as a kid. Then in college I set an oven mitt on fire. While I was wearing it. I'll stay clear of the hot stuff."

"Suit yourself," she said, and pulled out another pan.

"More weapons?"

"No, dinner. I'm hungry."

Peter remembered the scraggly, dazed people following Ghostheart. "Colette. Who is this meant for?"

"Anyone who gets in our way."

"But those men and women in the alley are victims of Ghostheart's lies. It's not their fault. We can't fight them."

Colette frowned. She looked at Peter and he thought he saw tears in her eyes. "Was Dave up there?"

Peter winced. He'd forgotten Drinky Drunky Dave, the Drunk, a Third Wave homeless man whose power went right up against Keepsie's: he had the power to get any alcohol without paying for it. Peter knew she took pity on him and allowed him in the bar, but he never knew if Dave's power would work if Keepsie didn't want him to take the beer.

When Dave had met Keepsie and learned of her adopted hero name, he proudly called himself Drinky Drunky Dave, the Drunk. He'd been a favorite of Colette's as he had a sense of humor and always tipped the waitress for his free beer.

"I—I didn't see him. But we can't fight them."

She stirred a pot on the stove and nodded. "If you can pour this down Clever Jack's pants, though, I'd appreciate it."

Peter opened his mouth to answer, but shouting and laughter from inside the bar stopped him. He ran through the doors to see Tomas doubled over laughing at the heroes outside.

"What's happening?"

Michelle grinned at him. "He decided to try pulling on Heretic's arm to see what would happen."

Heretic was now up to her shoulder in Keepsie's Bar, the arm inside immobile but the body writhing like a fish on a line.

"Can you push her out?" Peter asked.

Tomas gave the fist a little push, then harder. It didn't budge. "I suppose she cannot leave until Keepsie lets her."

How is it going to be when all of this is over? If we survive, will we all go to jail? Peter thought as he watched his friends tease the hero. Although he did not recall anything on the law books about teasing a hero, there was probably something there about hindering a hero in his duties.

"Dude." Ian poked him in the shoulder. "Are you listening?"

"What?" Peter hadn't noticed Ian and Michelle were behind him. Then he realized he hadn't smelled them.

"I said we need to start thinking of a plan of attack."

"Right. Um. Tomas and Barry and Colette in the back door, dealing with Ghostheart's army. You, me, and Michelle here to deal with this door."

"What about them?" Ian poked Heretic's arm.

"We could pull them inside and hold them. That might be safest. For all involved.

Heretic swore, her face mashed against the glass pane above the one she'd punched out.

"Don't worry, it doesn't hurt," Peter said. Tomas gave another heave, and the glass gave way and Heretic slid effortlessly into the room, not even cutting herself on the broken panes.

"Remind me to kiss Keepsie," Tomas said, laughing, as he placed the immobile Heretic on the floor next to Timson.

Tattoo Devil looked at them with wide eyes. "Stay away from me!"

"I apologize, but we need to clear the stairway. You understand, I'm sure," Peter said. "We won't hold you here forever."

"Just let me go and I'll clear out, no problem!"

Peter raised an eyebrow. "Mr. Devil, I'm sure we've had enough encounters in the past several hours to show that neither of us can trust the other. So, with the upper hand, we're going to neutralize you. You will not be hurt, and who knows, you might make it out of this fight better than we will."

Peter hefted the frozen bobcat and experimented with carrying it further inside the bar. The cry of alarm outside satisfied his curiosity, and he instructed Tomas to bring Tattoo Devil inside.

Tomas stacked him with the rest. Michelle and Ian went over to the door, Michelle to crouch by the bodies and Ian to look out.

"You know, I've always wanted to look at his tattoos," Michelle said. She coughed and pulled back his lapel of his vest. "Guys. This is sick."

Ian bent down. "So what? Lots of guys have tattoos of naked chicks."

Michelle stared him. Peter looked at the anatomically correct tattoo and said mildly, "That must come in handy on lonely nights."

Michelle stood and punched him playfully in the arm. Ian choked and said, "Oh. I get it. Dude. That's a lucky power, right there. But, oh..." Ian pulled back Tattoo Devil's lapel some more and revealed a naked man tattooed into his armpit.

Michelle laughed. "Well, he covers all bases."

"I did not need to see that," Ian said, hiding his face in Michelle's shoulder.

"So the coast is clear, boss," Tomas said. "Now what?"

"Now what indeed," Peter said, sticking his head out the window and looking up. The heroes and villains and hoboes still fought above the bar, and there was no clear winner.

And were they actually thinking of taking on the entirety of the hobo army, heroes and villains if it came to it? Armed with candy and fry oil and Ian's foul weapon?

It was all they had. It would have to do.

He turned and looked at his troops. "Get ready. It's time."

33

Keepsie's sense of relief mixed with loss as the drug began to wear off. She was happy to have the high wear off so she could think clearly, but the added power had been a bonus. The ability to protect her friends had apparently been the key to expelling the horrific Timson out of Peter's head. Now she was just plain old Keepsie, outside for what was beginning to seem like a very stupid reason.

The homeless had attempted to attack her as she emerged from the bar, and now a good twenty frozen trailed helplessly behind her as she ran.

What the hell am I out here for? The drug must have been wearing off, since Keepsie realized she was clearly questioning her actions when two minutes before she had completely sure of herself. She ducked into a side street and flattened herself against a wall to watch the carnage.

The fight, however, had slowed. All she could see were heroes and hoboes. Clever Jack and Light of Mornings were nowhere to be found.

Seismic Stan hadn't been seen since the scuffle at the park. Keepsie guessed that White Lightning had taken care of him, finally. He and Light of Mornings could probably tear up this battle in an instant. But then what would Clever Jack rule if the city fell into a great fault, with a nuclear winter settling over them all?

Psychological studies had been done on the villains ever since Seismic Stan had broken free of the Academy and attacked the city. There was the age-old question when it came to bad comic books—why does the bad guy want to destroy the earth? Why did he want to kill himself, not to mention all of his cool secret lair and stuff?

If his nemesis had been as insufferable as the heroes, Keepsie could see the point behind total annihilation. Is it that easy? Can simple bitterness drive you to evil?

She ran a few steps and then released the men and women under her control; it was hard to be stealthy with 20 corpse-like people floating behind her. She ran down the side street and marveled at how quiet the city was just one block over.

The Weaver River, renamed for Pallas's acts of bravery twenty years prior, usually had ducks and swans paddling in its slow current. People would rent boats a couple of miles up and spend the day canoeing up and down the river. It was a popular pleasure spot, and Keepsie enjoyed hanging out there on days off. The birds often made considerable noise when they saw someone walking the banks, as it usually meant free food.

Today the birds floated, their long necks splayed across the water, their open eyes staring into the sky. They circled lazily and bumped into each other, shedding feathers and drifting farther downstream with the current.

Keepsie's mind was returning to her swiftly, and although going back to the bar might seem the best idea, she had to check out the lone figure sitting on the riverbank, dangling her dainty bare toes in the water.

Light of Mornings had apparently gotten enough of her powers back to control the glowing, and now actually resembled a regular girl. She stared out at the dead ducks as they floated by. Tears leaked from her eyes, trailed down her face, and evaporated with a *pop*.

Can her radiation hurt me if it's not a conscious attack? Do I want to find out? Keepsie hadn't wanted to find out a lot of the things she had discovered recently. But the most powerful super villain ever sat before her, crying on the riverbank, and Keepsie, wonder of wonders, felt sorry for her.

"Hey, what's up?" she asked.

"It's not fair," Light of Morning said. She was more coherent than Keepsie had seen her.

"Um, what's not fair?"

"Him. When I went to sleep, he promised me he'd get me out. And he did. But it's been years. It's been so long."

Keepsie tried to do that math. She looked to be fifteen or so. Clever Jack was in his late twenties, so she couldn't have been asleep longer than ten or fifteen years. She said as much, inching closer in what she hoped was a concerned way.

Light of Mornings whipped her head around and glared at Keepsie. The air between them heated up, and Keepsie swallowed and sat down about ten feet away.

"Not so long? Eleven years isn't a long time? What has he been doing in that time? Who has he been with?" She stared back at the water, and Keepsie fancied she saw a squirrel fall from a tree on the far side of the river.

"In school I thought he liked me for me. Now I've been back less than a day and all he's wanted me to do is go here and fight this and steal this, and kill that hero and piss that person off, and then, hey, let's fuck for old time's sake, and then go fight some more!"

Keepsie's heart quickened. She felt this way when playing poker with her friends and she was dealt a good hand and prayed she wouldn't screw it up.

She's still a kid inside.

Keepsie looked out over the river too and hugged her knees to her chest. Her cheek felt as if she were getting sunburned.

"Yeah. That really sucks. So you're feeling used?"

Light of Mornings looked up to the sky, looking as if she were trying to hold back more tears. She failed; they sizzled on her cheeks as they spilled over. She nodded, her lips trembling.

"I felt used," Keepsie said. "By the same guys. Doodad used me just the other day."

"Really?"

"Yeah. Such a jerk." Keepsie tried to remember what was important to her when she had been fifteen, what she talked about. Boys. Overwhelming crushes on boys.

Clever Jack would be the key.

"So wha'd he do to you?" Light of Mornings asked.

207

"Tricked me into using my powers for him. I really didn't have any say in it."

"Asshole."

"Totally." Keepsie's heart was thundering away, and she held her knees tightly.

"I mean, it's not like I wanna marry him or anything," Light of Mornings blurted. "I just thought they were my friends. They rescued me, and they're all like, 'Oh we're so glad you're back, now can you blast those assholes?' And I wasn't even awake yet."

"So, uh, where are they now?"

Light of Mornings waved towards the battle. "I wanted to talk to him about all this shit that's going on, and the other shit, but he wanted to fight." Her voice grew deep and mocking. "'Come on, just nuke their asses!' So I left."

Keepsie watched another duck float by. "So, uh, can you tone that down? Cause you're not helping the local wildlife."

Light of Mornings threw a rock into the water. "What do I care? I don't give a shit. I don't care about anyone or anything." The light increased, and Keepsie winced. "I mean, how would you like it if the guy you loved woke you up from sleeping, like, a billion years and said, 'go nuke those people!' instead of, 'hey babe, how are you feeling after being asleep for a billion years? Here's what's going on in the world, here's the latest Celtics' score, and by the way the president is Tom Cruise?'"

"The president isn't Tom Cruise, if that helps," Keepsie offered. Light of Mornings snorted.

The light intensified. Keepsie finally looked away, which was a good thing that Light of Mornings couldn't see her face when the girl spoke next.

"And if Clever Jack thinks he's going to have visitation rights on the baby, he can suck my dick."

#

In a world of superheroes, Keepsie rarely got frightened. For obvious reasons, she wasn't scared of most criminal acts. Until the incidents of a couple of days ago, she didn't fear villains, for she knew the reprehensible heroes would save her. There hadn't been a civilian death at the hands of a villain in eight years; asshole or not, the heroes saved people. That's what they did.

Keepsie nearly wet herself at the thought of Light of Mornings' baby.

She cleared her throat, ignoring the screaming voice inside her head telling her to run, run far, run long, become a hermit in Tibet. She'd always considered shaving her head at least once. Run away from this little girl with the big girl power, run away from her baby. There had been a wave of children of the first people with powers. But there had been no public record of Second Wave with babies. This was new.

With careful prodding, and reassurance that Keepsie wasn't going to "get her into trouble," Light of Mornings revealed how she and Clever Jack had slept together three times before her entrance into stasis. She had exhibited several pregnancy symptoms and had done a web search, but had told no one, not even Clever Jack. She had been too scared.

"She would have taken my baby from me," she whispered. The heat dissipated, and Light of Mornings put her head in her hands and cried.

Keepsie breathed a quiet sigh of relief and leaned in to reassure her.

"She won't take it from you. Don't worry. Timson will not take your child. I promise.

"Listen, why don't we go somewhere and get you some food? Have you eaten much since waking up?"

Light of Mornings shook her head and sniffled loudly. Keepsie got up and pulled her to her feet. "Let's go."

34

Three heroes frozen and stacked in the corner. Check. One villain in the men's bathroom. Check. People with low-grade superpowers stationed at each exit, prepared to fight with a strange concoction of powers and super-heated liquids. Check. A nosebleed that wouldn't stop. Check.

Peter waved off Colette's concerned arm as he nabbed one of her dishtowels and held it to his face. The bleeding had started soon after Keepsie had left and hadn't stopped. Her drug must have worn off. He gave a fleeting thought for Alex's powers and then felt guilty.

Colette had every burner on the stove covered with her largest pots, full of oil, sugar, and other concoctions Peter didn't want to ask about. Michelle had stacked all of the bar's trays beside the kitchen door. She stared at the stack, her dark face a few shades lighter than normal.

Peter pinched his nostrils and went back into the bar. Ian, Tomas and Barry clustered around the front door beside the captured heroes. Timson had a bar towel over her head. Peter poked Ian in the back and pointed to her.

"Oh. That. She was creeping me out. And who knows if she can see anything in there."

"So what about the others? Why didn't you cover their heads?"

"Well they're not the brains of the organization, are they? The homicidal, insane leader of superheroes should probably be in the dark. Toadies, not so much."

Peter suppressed an exasperated sigh. "Don't you think Heretic and Tattoo Devil could tell Timson what they saw?"

"Oh. Then I guess it was just because she creeped me out. Does it matter?"

Peter looked out the hole in the door. "I suppose not."

"Ah, Peter, are you all right?" Tomas asked.

Peter looked at him. "No, Tomas, I don't think I am. But since we're under siege in a bar with the most powerful beings in the world outside our door, all of whom want us dead or captured, I don't think any of us are all right."

Tomas coughed. "I meant your nose."

"I know what you meant. Now, are we ready?"

"Honestly, no," Barry said. His red, heavy face sagged and Peter was forcibly reminded that he was much older than the rest of them.

Peter smiled. "I suppose that's a good thing. Because if you were ready for something like this, I would worry."

"Where are you going to be through all this, dude?" Ian asked, rolling up his filthy sleeves.

"I'll be where I am needed, I suppose. Once the fighting starts, I won't be much help. I'm sure Colette can use a hand. Call me if you need me."

Ian caught up with him at the door to the kitchen. "Hey, Pete, quick question. What are we working for here? I'm fairly sure we're not trying to defeat everyone and save the day."

"Well. We're trying to confuse them. Split their numbers. But essentially, we're trying to punch a hole through and get the hell out of here."

Ian nodded and grinned. "Or just sow chaos?"

"You can do that too."

Michelle had opened the door and stood in the doorway. She carried a bar tray on her shoulder loaded with empty glass mugs. Colette balanced one more mug on top of the others, pyramid style.

"Now remember, try to get the glass to break as well. It's tough glass, but you can probably throw it hard enough, right?"

Michelle gulped. "I've never tried."

"Always time to learn new things."

Peter dropped the gore-soaked towel into the trashcan and grabbed a new one. Colette glared at him. "Pick that up. Vincent can clean it."

"You're concerned about that now?"

"We've destroyed Keepsie's front window, now we're going to be throwing her mugs at the homeless. Don't make her buy new towels too."

Keepsie was going to have a lot more to worry about than linen replacement when all of this was over, but Peter didn't want to argue with her. He plucked the bloody towel from the trash and put it on the floor. The health inspector was unlikely to visit during the battle, and even if she did, she would be a little more upset at the nine-toed dead body in storage rather than the bloody towel on the floor.

Blood dripped down his chin, and he remembered to put the towel to his nose tighter. How much blood could someone lose through his nose before passing out?

He forced the thought from his mind and stood by Michelle. The hoboes in the alley had not yet noticed her. They sat against the walls, resting.

Peter leaned in close to Michelle. "Can you control it to knock them out instead of kill them?"

Michelle took a deep breath and set her jaw. "I can try. Untested skill here. Going for the one on the right."

As easily as if she were throwing a discus, Michelle threw the bar tray and it left her hands, spinning. She watched it, her lips pursed and her eyes slit. She relaxed with a sigh as the tray hit the man in the belly. The glasses, free from her will, flew off, slamming into the wall on one side and his companion on the other.

He grunted and fell heavily. His friend fell as well, the mug to the head knocking him out.

"Two down," she said, hefting another loaded tray to her shoulder.

Response was nearly instantaneous. The other three ran toward them, yelling.

Peter loaded her tray again. He winced as the heavy mugs found their homes, knocking the pathetic men down. All five were knocked out or moaning, and on a whim, Peter dashed outside.

"What the hell are you doing?" Michelle said, loading her own tray.

"We forgot about Ghostheart!" Peter yelled back. He knelt beside one man who moaned as he clutched his bleeding head. "Ghostheart lied to you."

The man's eyes flew open. "Well fry me up with a dumpling. So she did. That little whore."

Peter fought to keep from smiling. "Are you all right?"

The man winced but sat up. "Hell, boy, I've had hangovers worse than this."

"Do you think you can pass the word on? Once you know her secret, she can't control you."

The man nodded and staggered to his feet. He and Peter spoke to the remaining felled warriors of the hobo army, and all of them except for the one knocked out were angry and fully ready to spread the word through the rest of the army that the heroes had used them as cannon fodder.

The hoboes walked purposefully toward the street but then stopped as one, their mouths open. They turned around and ran back toward Peter, picking up their friend and heading down into the bar.

"What the hell?" asked Michelle, who had joined Peter. They ventured out into the street and stared.

Peter swallowed. "I honestly thought I couldn't be surprised any more."

Michelle's voice was level. "I guess that's another one of Doodad's enhanced machines."

"Guess so."

Jack stood atop the stairs of the ruins of the Academy, holding a metallic hoop. The air inside the hoop swirled and shimmered, and a leathery winged creature emerged from it, twisted rabbit-from-the-hat trick.

Michelle cleared her throat. "Dimensional portal?"

"Looks like it."

"Back inside?"

"Definitely."

#

Peter and Michelle dashed down the stairs and into the kitchen just in time to save the five hoboes from Colette's wrath.

Peter panted. "OK, Colette, we can use your napalm now."

Colette frowned at him. "Why?"

"Doodad made another machine when he was enhanced by Zupra-Ex. A sort of dimensional portal."

"What does that mean?"

Michelle peered back outside. "I think it means he's building a demon army."

Colette threw her hands into the air. "Demon army! Hobo army! Can this day get any weirder?"

Ian ran into the kitchen. "Hey guys, the heroes and homeless ran off, the coast is clear, let's get out of here!"

Peter shook his head and explained why that would be bad. The color drained from Ian's face.

The first man Peter had freed from Ghostheart's influence stepped forward. "Our friends are still out there."

Pater wiped at his nose again. "Fine. Ian, you're with me. Michelle and Tomas, you hold the fort. Everyone else, do what Colette tells you."

He sighed and ran back into the alley, Ian following him.

"Cover me while I spread the word," Peter said, running into the street at trying to ignore the screeching above their heads.

"Cover what?" Ian said. "There's monsters above us and a zombie hobo army below!"

Peter dodged a stick thrown by a dirty older woman. "They're not zombies. Or hobos. They're just tricked." He got closer to the woman who looked for something else to throw. "Ghostheart lies. She's controlling you."

The woman snapped out of her fury immediately.

"Please tell others. The more we have telling, the faster we can get people to safety."

She nodded and turned to a man next to her. Peter sighed as he backed down and turned to others.

That immediate threat stifled for the moment, he ventured a look upward.

Three—monsters? Demons? What were they?—flew on wide, black wings above them, attacking the heroes, who fought in confused terror.

"They're pretty much focusing on the heroes now," Ian said. He paused to hit an attacking man in the face with a finely-focused stream of filth, and Peter gingerly approached the man to deliver the information.

"I feel like a missionary," he said.

Ian pointed to where Ghostheart was watching them, her face contorted with fury. "Uh oh, dude, we need to head back."

Ghostheart's army was turning for sure, now, some of the people melting back into the shadows from where they had come, but others advancing angrily on Ghostheart. Her fury turned to fear, and she looked up at where White Lightning fought the circling demons.

"He can't help her now," Peter said. "Should we?"

For once there was no sense of irony or humor in Ian's voice. "No."

#

Clever Jack's portal continued to give birth to more monstrous creatures. Peter and Ian watched them with a wary eye as they ran back to the alley.

Peter was heading down the stairs first, relieved at everything going right for once, when Ian gave a garbled cry of pain behind him.

A creature had swooped down and grabbed Ian's shoulders, sinking in its claws. He screamed, and Peter reached out and grabbed his arms as the creature began flapping its wings, trying to carry Ian off. Tomas ran from the kitchen and grabbed Peter. He heaved and they all fell backwards, Ian tumbling in over everyone, bringing the creature with him. It froze the moment it passed through the doorway.

The creature's sharp claws were deep into his arms. He groaned and closed his eyes as Tomas managed to pry its claws apart. He flung it aside and Michelle pressed towels on the bleeding gouges.

"How was it going out front?" Colette asked.

Peter watched Ian, worried. "I think we're clear, Ghostheart's army is broken up. But Clever Jack keeps pulling out those... things." The homeless men sighed with relief.

Colette began wrapping tape around Ian's towels to hold them in place. "Any sign of Keepsie?"

"None," Ian said.

Peter rubbed his face. "We have to believe she'll be all right. She can take care of herself."

"And if she can't, well, she's got the strongest power of us all," Barry said. "It's not like I can throw my legs at those things or anything."

No, he couldn't. Peter stared at the immobile monster on the floor. He thought about the heroes, immobile ones pulled into the bar. He thought of the demons lurking in the alley. And then he smiled.

"I've got an idea. I'll need Barry and Tomas for the next round."

#

He told them his plan. They stared at him. Tomas laughed. Barry turned white and scowled at his friend. "Sure, laugh, it's not like it's you out there."

Tomas continued to chuckle. "What is wrong? It is a perfect plan. Peter, you are the king of plans. We live with insignificant powers our entire lives, and we cannot think of ways to use them until we meet you!"

Barry glared at them. "I'll try it. Once. And if I can't handle it, we stop, all right?"

"What, you want a safe word, Barry?" Ian asked, pale from blood loss.

"A what?"

He grinned and Michelle snickered. "Never mind."

Tomas put his hand on Barry's shoulder. "Of course, Barry. If you do not think this will work, we try something else."

"It should be fine, Barry," Peter said, hoping he was telling the truth.

The two men got into position, Barry in front and Tomas behind him, their arms linked.

"Are you ready?" Tomas asked.

"I'm going to die, you know that, right? This is not going to work and I'm going to die."

"Are you ready?"

216

Barry took a deep breath and nodded. He walked outside and put his leg on the step as if he planned to ascend.

Immediately a creature swooped down, grabbing for him. He kicked up, making his leg the first thing the demon could grab. It sank its teeth in and tried to carry him away, but Tomas heaved backwards, easily pulling the two of them into the kitchen.

Barry overbalanced with the creature attached to him. He toppled back into Tomas, whose strength gave out and they landed in a heap. Barry made a disgusted noise at the immobile thing on top of him and pulled himself free from his leg. Peter dragged the creature, still clutching Barry's leg, off to the side.

Barry lay on the floor panting until his leg grew back. He winced and moved his legs around. "I think I pulled a groin muscle."

"Sucks to be you," Ian said as Colette secured his makeshift bandage on his right arm.

"Can you go again? There are more out there," Tomas said, peeking outside.

Barry slowly got to his feet. He didn't say anything, but got in front of the door again.

"I just hope someone notices that we're doing everyone's jobs tonight," he said.

35

"What in the hell?" Keepsie said as she saw Clever Jack bringing the creatures through the portal.

Light of Mornings sniffled—she'd been crying since she told Keepsie about the pregnancy—and waved her hand. "Oh, Doodad took that super drug shit and built a bunch of stuff that could work without him. I think they're seriously scared of you. That's a portal thing that can tap into some demon dimension or something."

"Great."

Keepsie watched the fighting on Main Street and decided to try to sneak Light of Mornings in through the alley. Knowing that she could use some nuclear backup to get into the bar safely, Keepsie was trying to figure out how to ask for help without sounding like she was using the woman as Clever Jack had. Then again, would the baby be immune to the mother's radiation? Well, the damage from the earlier fight would have destroyed it already, so there's probably nothing more it could do.

"Can I count on you to defend yourself if you have to? Are you up to that?" Keepsie asked, watching the heroes and demons battle. They hid behind a dumpster so that Keepsie could collect her thoughts.

Light of Mornings nodded, sniffling. She wiped her eyes with her sleeve.

"OK, run when I say run."

Keepsie took off, hugging the buildings and willing herself invisible. If only that had been her power, but then with that she'd likely have been able to enter the Academy. And none of this would be happening.

But it wasn't her power. A demon flew at her, screeching. *Oh, now you attack me, when the drug's worn off.*

There was a bright light and the demon evaporated, covering Keepsie in a shower of ash. She coughed and wiped her eyes. "Thanks."

"Let's go."

They ran again.

The alley had one or two demons in it, not nearly as many as Keepsie had expected. Light of Mornings raised her hand, but Keepsie stopped her.

"Wait." She wanted to see what was going to happen, but she was also worried about whether her power was protecting her against this radiation. She was not impervious to damage, and Light of Morning's radiation was no longer hostile against her. Fairly certain she could be killed by an accident, she didn't want to experience any more friendly fire from Light of Mornings than she had to.

One demon swooped down and shouting filled the alley, then some swearing. The creature did not come back up.

The last demon, a winged snake, attacked, and this time instead of shouting, there was screaming.

Keepsie nearly retched when she got to the top of the stairs. Barry lay at the bottom of the stairs, struggling with a python-like demon that had swallowed his arm to the shoulder. He screamed and fought, not with the demon, but with Tomas.

"God, don't pull me inside, you'll never get it off!"

"Well he sure as hell can't leave it on!" Ian yelled.

The demon inched up Barry's arm and he groaned.

"Can you rip it in half, Tomas?" asked Colette.

Barry was hysterical. "Someone kill it, just kill it!"

They hadn't yet noticed Keepsie and Light of Mornings. In the corner of her eye, Keepsie saw Light of Mornings begin to glow.

"No, wait—"

Two narrow, bright yellow beams shone from the girl's eyes, bisecting the demon. She misjudged the distance, however, and the bottom half of the demon—and Barry's hand with it—fell onto the steps cleanly.

The wound, cauterized immediately, smoked slightly. Barry's screaming intensified and he flailed against Tomas' grasp. The top half of the dead creature slithered off his arm, and Barry fell against Tomas in a faint.

Peter and Ian yelled in surprise and ran out the door. Colette followed them, wielding a cleaver.

Keepsie held up her shaking hand. "Stop, guys. She's with me."

#

"You're still high."

"She cut off his fucking hand."

"We can't trust her."

"What happened?"

Keepsie sat at the bar sipping a glass of water. Colette, Peter, Michelle and Ian surrounded her. Light of Mornings and Tomas sat in the kitchen, Tomas watching her and the still-unconscious Barry at the same time.

Keepsie quietly told the story of finding Light of Mornings. She explained she was not high. She mentioned how Light of Mornings' companions had betrayed her and how she needed friends. She reminded them about how it was to their benefit that the most powerful person, either villain or hero, was on their side now.

She did not tell them about her pregnancy.

"How do you know she's on our side?" Colette demanded. "She took off Barry's hand like it was butter!"

"She *saved* him. She just made a mistake in the distance. If we're going to persecute for mistakes, then I suppose all of us need to line up for the next stone's throw. I'll be first. Who's behind me?" She looked at Ian. He had the grace to avoid her gaze.

Keepsie shifted her gaze to Peter. "Look. We're safe in here. She can't hurt us. We know that much."

He looked at her with a crease in his forehead that he hadn't had before. "I suppose we can see how things go."

His blasé manner angered Keepsie. "It's not like you have a choice. You don't want her around, you're free to leave. The back alley is clear for the moment."

She got off her stool and slid between Colette and Peter.

"Keepsie—" Michelle said.

Keepsie tromped into the kitchen. Light of Mornings had given Barry a pillow of a bar towel and she was crying again. She held his one hand to her chest and sobbed.

Tomas came up to Keepsie, his face fixed in his typical "you Americans confuse me" expression. "She killed a hero. Incinerated him. Attacked you. These things did not concern her. She cut off a man's hand and cannot be consoled."

"Cutting off his hand was an accident. That's what's different. When you try to save someone and end up hurting them, that can be somewhat upsetting."

"Barry will be all right, yes? His power, I mean."

"I would guess so. It's a strange power. We don't know if it applies to his whole body or just his legs or what. But he still feels the pain of having his hand cut off, and that can't be fun to experience. He looks like shit, by the way. We need to get him to the hospital."

"Him. Michelle. Ian. Peter. You." Tomas ticked them off on his fingers. Keepsie smiled slightly.

"Course, I could always take another one of those pills, that should cure him."

"No," Colette said harshly. Keepsie jumped; she hadn't heard her enter.

"You saw what that drug did to Timson. We have had enough of you out of your mind as well. Look what you bring back when you're high," she indicated the wailing woman on the floor.

"I'm not high! And I wasn't when I found her. Do you really want an all-powerful fifteen-year-old roaming the streets? She needs someone to watch her. If Clever Jack finds her, he'll use her. If the heroes find her, they'll provoke her. She's safest here."

"But are we?" Peter asked.

Keepsie gritted her teeth. "You're safest in the bar. Don't want to be here? Fine."

Peter crouched down beside her. "I was not freed from Timson's control until you took the pill. We don't know how safe we are. What if she is controlled in the same way?

"In all honesty, Keepsie, we don't know exactly how your power works."

"But I thought you had us all figured out, Peter," Keepsie said. "You found out you were all knowing with your power, just walk up and kiss someone and know everything about them!"

Peter flushed. He opened his mouth, then closed it. He stood and left the kitchen.

"Great. Now's the time to start alienating each other. Way to go," Ian said. He followed Peter.

Keepsie stared at Light of Mornings, who still sobbed next to Barry. "No one can help her. No one wants to. She's fifteen."

Michelle put her hand on Keepsie's shoulder. "Keepsie," she began.

"Just leave me alone, Michelle. Go have another little talk with the others about how I'm losing it, and leave me alone for a little bit."

The hand withdrew, and Keepsie sat on the floor, knees pulled up to her chin, and watched the weeping child.

36

"She's losing it," said Colette.

Peter stared at the kitchen door and shook his head slowly. "I don't think so. Not really. I think she's just doing what she should have done since the beginning."

"What, bring in an unstable nuclear reactor into our kitchen?" Ian asked.

"No. Leading us. She is the one who is protecting all of us. We'd be dead now, several times over, if it hadn't been for Keepsie.

"And Ian, it's *her* kitchen. Never forget that. She can make us thieves with a thought, you know."

Ian paused, a pint of beer to his lips. He took a cautious sip, and when nothing happened, a longer gulp. "She must not hate me yet."

"OK, so she's our leader by default that she's the strongest of us all. That doesn't mean she's making good decisions," Colette said.

"Again, I'm not sure of that. Aside from the rather violent entrance and the shock of, well, everything, she has excellent points regarding Light of Mornings. If the girl is truly needing guidance from someone who will not use her, Keepsie is the only one she can trust."

"Your feelings are getting in the way of common sense," Colette said.

"He has a point," Michelle said. "She doesn't normally have outrageous plans. She's pretty conservative, when you come down to it."

"Yeah, but she's been high on that superdrug today. Twice, in fact," Ian said. "What if it's eating her mind like old Catharine the Great over there?" He jabbed his finger at the stone statue of Timson.

Peter closed his eyes briefly. "Then I don't know what we do. If she's unstable, then we're truly in a great deal of danger. Our safety lies with her. If she chooses to remove it…" he didn't finish.

"How do we find out if she has lost it?" Michelle asked.

"Peter can find out, right?" Ian asked.

Peter shook his head and dabbed at his still dribbling nose. "Not right now. I can't smell a thing."

"Would she want different food if she was losing her mind?" Michelle asked.

Colette shook her head. "I don't think so. I cooked for my grandfather while he had Alzheimer's disease, and the bastard always wanted fried chicken and giblet gravy." Michelle stared at her. Colette laughed. "Oh, yeah, it was sad that he died, but he was a bastard when he was in his right mind. Losing his mind did the best thing for his demeanor that you could have asked for."

Ian shifted from one foot to the other and winced at the blood blossoming through the thick towels on his shoulers. "I could use Keepsie's drugged up power now. Then again, if she runs out again, I have no idea what she'll bring back for us to be friends with."

"We need to end this soon. Too many people need medical attention. And there's Alex to think about," Peter said.

"So do you have any bright ideas?" Colette asked.

"Dude. We kinda forgot something," Ian said, eyes growing wide. They looked at him. "Well, the demon attacked Barry, Keepsie and the nuke chick ran in and sowed themselves some chaos, but we didn't really check and see if the back alley was clear now."

They stared at one another. Michelle grinned and Colette swore. Together they tumbled through the door.

Tomas perched on a stool with a look of disbelief on his face. Light of Mornings had curled up beside Barry's body and had gone to sleep. Keepsie was gone.

"You let her go? Again?" Ian said. "What the hell good are you?"

Tomas got off the stool, thunderclouds forming on his face.

Peter put up a hasty hand. "When did she go?"

Without taking his eyes from Ian, Tomas said, "She said she was going to step right outside. She has been there maybe one minute." He leaned forward into Ian's face. "I think this one should go look for her."

Ian laughed. "Sure!" Before Tomas could say anything else he bounded up the stairs.

Tomas snorted. "Insufferable." Peter patted Tomas's beefy shoulder and then followed Ian.

There was a lack of something in the air as Peter exited. The mid-morning light did nothing to lessen the impact of the horrific carnage of the day. Of course, since Timson had messed up his power (he refused to think of it as "lost") there was a lack of something everywhere he went, but this time it was auditory in nature. Keepsie stood in the middle of the alley, looking into the sky.

"I think it's over."

"Do you think we'll be safe to go get help?"

She paused. "I don't know."

Ian walked to the end of the alley and took a peek outside. He withdrew his head quickly as something slammed into the pavement. He ran towards them. "Not safe, not by a long shot!"

#

"First demons attack. Now heroes." Ian raged, pacing the bar.

Peter had had the foresight to close the kitchen door on the way in to keep anyone following from seeing Light of Mornings. They'd gathered in the bar, except for Tomas who was to watch the former villain, and Ghostheart's released soldiers, who dozed in booths. Apparently mind control was tiring.

Keepsie sat in a booth, tracing the outline of the wood grain with her finger. She appeared not to pay attention to them.

225

"I'm so tired of this," Michelle said. Her voice had a defeated quality to it.

"Well, let's look at our arsenal," Colette said. "We have more oil and sugar."

"Hey, we could get Keepsie to free the demons and sic them on the heroes," Ian said.

Peter shook his head. "I think we need to stop fighting the heroes. We're already heading down a path that will likely lead to prison or becoming villains by association. We have to stop fighting them at some point."

Ian stopped pacing and stared at him. "Are you saying we should surrender?"

"Well no. Not exactly. We need to meet them on equal ground."

"Peter, they're super heroes! We have never been equal to them. We never will be equal to them!"

"There's something we haven't tried," Keepsie said. Peter thought he was the only one to hear her, but they all stopped.

"I haven't tried, really tried, to use my powers since I was a kid. It's been pretty much assumed that it was passive."

She didn't look at them, but kept tracing the wood grain. "But those drugs were pretty intense. I feel... different."

"Different? Like what?" Michelle asked.

"Powerful. Like I have a little bit of control over this power. A little, anyway." She stopped running her fingers along the table and looked up at them. "We can test it."

"How—" Peter began, but stopped short. Everyone around them had frozen. They were only that way for a moment—long enough for him to register—before they all relaxed. Ian took a step back.

"Whoa." Ian held up his hands. "What the hell happened?"

Keepsie's face was white, but she smiled slightly. "You were all breathing my air."

They glanced uneasily at each other. Michelle cleared her throat. "So whatever you own is yours. And now your friends and the very air in this bar are yours."

"If I want it to be, yes, I think so," Keepsie said. "But I'm not sure how far it travels. What if the air outside could be mine? Or my personal space?"

No one spoke. Peter tried not to look as if someone had poured cold water down his back, despite the shivers he felt.

Ever pragmatic, Colette spoke up. "So how can we use this against the heroes?"

"I don't want them to know I have this ability. Not if I can help it. But these statues here," she waved her hand towards the direction of the heroes in the corner, "are mine. And if a hero tries to take them back, then, well, you know what will happen."

"Then what?" Michelle asked. "Make our getaway?"

"No. We ask to talk to Pallas."

"Yes. She's always seemed the most rational," Peter said.

"The most heroic, too," Michelle said.

"And if it doesn't work?" Ian asked.

"I freeze anyone who gets in our way and we leave Seventh City."

"Then let's go." Ian walked over and started to pull the heroes out of their corner.

Peter snapped his head up and he grabbed Keepsie's hand. He pulled it to his mouth and kissed it, not even minding the lack of information the kiss didn't bring. "No, that's not what we're going to do. It's a good plan. It's an amazing plan. We'll keep it as Plan B. I think I have one better. One that will expose everything Timson has done, and possibly get us out of here alive and out of prison."

"Huh. Really?"

"Really."

37

"Pallas. No one else," Keepsie said. She stood at the kitchen door, facing The Crane who stood at the top of the stairs in the alley. His face was streaked with blood, ichor, and distress. *He must be going mad with this mess.*

Peter smacked his forehead. "Oh, no, I forgot, Pallas is out of town."

The Crane's wings dropped. "She'll be in town soon."

"I thought you were trying to keep her away so Timson could put her plan in action?"

The Crane looked at Peter with obvious dislike, but the malice was gone from his blue eyes. "That was before Ghostheart started using citizens. That was before the demons. But before I talk to Pallas, how can we trust you?"

Keepsie snorted. "You're just going to have to. You really haven't given us a reason to trust you today, so we're pretty much on equal footing. You send your strongest hero in here alone, among a bunch of Third Wavers, and you know she's not going to be harmed unless she attempts to harm us first."

The Crane looked to his left and muttered something. He sighed. "We don't negotiate with terrorists."

Keepsie felt her stomach drop. There was usually no argument against that statement. It was like trying to defend against being an alcoholic. "That's ridiculous, Crane. The past few days have been nothing but constant misunderstandings. Third Wavers getting stuck in the middle of something they weren't prepared for. We're not asking for press. We're not asking for sanctuary, money, ransom, anything. We just want to talk to Pallas. She won't be hurt as long as she doesn't hurt us. She will leave here, very likely with all your heroes that we have. And then the proper actions can be taken."

"Like putting you wastes of DNA into jail," The Crane said, but his voice lacked the threat of previous encounters. He looked as if all he wanted was to go home.

"Don't do the comic book language, Crane, it doesn't suit you," Keepsie said, hoping her voice stayed strong.

The Crane retreated, glaring at her. She stepped back and blew out a huge sigh.

"I don't think this is going to work," she said.

"It will. Pallas is the only one with common sense. And if The Crane has come to his senses, that's even better," Peter said, putting his hands on Keepsie's shoulders and keeping an eye on the stairs. "He's coming back. Go on, you're doing fine."

She stepped forward as she saw the telltale leather sandals laced up the well-muscled calves. Pallas. The first hero. The best hero.

That was fast.

Pallas stood, impassive on the top step. "How can I be sure your word is true?" Her voice sounded goddess-like: rich and deep and comforting, even when annoyed.

"I am prepared to release one of the heroes here as assurance of my goodwill."

"Two."

"That's fine, as long as Timson stays here until we've had our talk."

She stepped down another step, her gray eyes sharp. "Done."

Keepsie waved her hand, feeling ridiculous. Peter had suggested she act like a decisive leader, so it was very odd to have Tomas and Colette drag Tattoo Devil, his bobcat, and Heretic forward at her command. Barry and Light of Mornings still slumbered in the safety of the storage closet.

They placed the heroes outside the door, making sure to keep inside the bar. Keepsie released them with a thought, and they stumbled briefly. Without looking at her, they ascended the steps and whispered to Pallas. She nodded and came downstairs to face Keepsie.

"Thank you for keeping your word. I would like to speak with only you."

Keepsie tried not to grimace, but nodded. "Done."

#

Peter, Michelle, Colette, and Ian lurked behind the bar, watching Keepsie and Pallas chat secluded in a booth. Keepsie tried not to look at them. Pallas had only grudgingly allowed them in the room to assure Keepsie's safety, even though they knew she didn't need it. They were there for moral support, and to keep their curiosity from bursting their brains while Keepsie spoke with the most powerful hero known.

To her credit, Pallas fulfilled all their expectations. After determining that Timson was as unharmed as she could have been, with Keepsie's assurances that she was stone because of her power and not because of anything the Third Wavers did, she sat down and allowed Keepsie to tell the story of their end of the past couple of days. Keepsie did not leave anything out except for the part about Light of Mornings.

Although Keepsie's comments must have agreed with much of what The Crane said, Pallas was hesitant to blame Timson, preferring to chalk things up to "a misunderstanding." Keepsie let that sit for a moment.

Then she outlined their plan.

Pallas's stony face broke at this point and disbelief replaced her impassive exterior. "You can't be serious."

"I am totally serious. Look, we're giving you everything. We're giving you Timson. We're giving you the drug and the files. We're only asking that if our plan works, we get a pardon for our crimes the past couple of days. If our plan fails, and we're wrong, we will surrender with no issues."

Pallas stared at her.

"We need you to stay with us. And you'll want to, anyway, to make sure we don't leave town."

"Why do I need to stay with you?"

"Because we trust you. Because we know you'll do the right thing if you see someone doing the wrong thing. Because Timson won't do what I think she's going to do in front of you. Because we may need protection."

"I think you're wrong."

"On what part? I said a lot of stuff."

"About Dr. Timson and the heroes. They may have made bad decisions, but they are on the right side. You have no proof."

"You are entirely entitled to your opinion. But I have a differing one. And I am offering proof. Will you take it?" Keepsie bit her lower lip and then stuck her hand into her pocket. The ball was cool in her hands as she gripped it, and then she placed it on the table between them.

"So this is what's causing all the fuss." Pallas paused for a moment, eyeing Keepsie. Then she picked it up and peered at it. "How does it work?"

Keepsie spun it on the table, causing it to open. "It's just a cute drug bottle—it's what's inside that's important."

"And I can take this?"

"Will you trust me?"

Pallas slipped the ball into her tunic. She stared at the immobile Timson leaning against the wall by the door and then nodded.

"I hope you understand that for our safety, I'm going to make sure Timson is a good distance away before I release her."

Pallas nodded again. "I need to talk to my colleagues."

"I understand. Just please keep our plan between us. I think more heroes are involved in this than we think. And don't tell Timson I have given up the drugs."

Her gray eyes didn't waver. "Agreed."

#

"So can we trust her?" Ian asked, watching Pallas carry with ease the stone Timson up the stairs.

"I think so. I don't know, honestly," Keepsie said. "She seemed receptive. Said that if I released Timson in five minutes, she'd return to stay with us."

"She's always been the only one I could stomach," Michelle said. "Maybe it's because she was always the one who did more work than publicity."

"She was the first one. She started fighting crime before there were any heroes. There was no hero adoration when she came on the scene, so she didn't have expectations," Peter said.

"Or maybe she's just a decent person while the others are assholes," Keepsie said.

"If the demons are gone, that means that they either caught Clever Jack or he ran off." Michelle peered out the window.

Peter grimaced. "He doesn't have Doodad or Light of Mornings anymore. Stan is dead."

Keepsie stared after Pallas. "He's going to want her back."

"Did Pallas guess about Light of Mornings?" Peter asked.

"She didn't even ask. But about the girl, I need to tell you guys something.

"She's pregnant."

Pause.

"Finally. A good reason for you to bring her here," Colette said, and went to the stove.

"What are you doing?" Keepsie said, startled.

"She is going to be hungry when she wakes up."

38

It was as if Peter's spine had electrified. Excitement soaked his bones and he couldn't keep still.

Keepsie had released Timson and Pallas had returned.

Sirens sounded in the distance. "Damn I missed that sound. Where the hell have they been?" Ian asked.

"Emergency systems are instructed to shut down when a super villain attack occurs. We take care of everything," Pallas said.

"Good job, too," Ian muttered, grimacing at a dead homeless woman lying on the sidewalk.

"What happened to Ghostheart?" Keepsie asked.

"She's missing," Pallas said, not looking at her. "We think Clever Jack may have done something with her."

Michelle stayed back at the bar with Colette and Light of Mornings and Barry. The latter two still slept, and Colette kept watch over them with a cleaver in her good hand, but with a plate of meatloaf and orange slices within reach.

"I'm prepared for whatever mood she wakes up in," she had said.

Peter hadn't wanted to leave them, but he didn't have a choice. They couldn't leave Barry and someone had to watch Light of Mornings. They didn't want Pallas to know about her yet. They had called an ambulance for Barry, but were told by a tired dispatcher that unless his life was at risk, he'd be on a waiting list.

"So how do you know they'll be at the park?" Pallas asked.

"I don't know," Keepsie said. "But it's where Clever Jack and Doodad have their lair."

"What did Timson say when she was free?"

"She demanded you be captured. But she forgot about it when I told her about Doodad's new portal. She said White Lightning and Heretic would meet with her regarding it, and sent the rest of us away."

"What form did she take? Did she talk about her powers?"

Pallas said nothing.

"You knew she was working on that drug." Peter did not ask a question.

"You wouldn't understand."

"Oh, I'm sure I wouldn't. She's losing her mind and leading the most powerful humans alive. There is something wrong with that."

Pallas stared ahead.

Some people leaned out of their windows and waved at her, and she smiled and waved back.

"So how do you do it? Like, you're up there fighting crime, and then your groupies fawn all over you and you can just smile about it?" Ian asked.

"I have to. It's the face of the Academy. It's what they really treasure over being saved."

"Most of them, anyway," Ian said.

Keepsie looked around nervously. "Should we be walking in the street? What if a hero sees us?"

Pallas gave her a withering look. Keepsie sighed.

"All right, you're so mighty you can take care of all of us if we started getting uppity. I get it."

Pallas stopped. "Do you want me to help you or not?"

Keepsie walked past her. "You're going to want to help us. Trust me."

"So what happened when Clever Jack got away?" Ian asked.

"We decimated the last of his army, but Clever Jack got away while we were distracted with demons."

"You let him get away," Tomas grumbled.

"When you're fighting a hundred demons that you have no experience with, you're likely to put the villains you do know on the back burner. We know how to fight Clever Jack. We do it all the time."

"And yet he is still out there," Tomas said.

Pallas did not answer.

"I'm thinking we should stop baiting the superhero who is helping us," Peter whispered to Tomas and Ian. Tomas glared at Pallas' back. "We can go back to hating them tomorrow, but we need her right now." They nodded, a bit grudgingly.

Keepsie was talking to Pallas. "I just want you to see, that's all. If she doesn't show, then you can take us in."

"She's going to surprise you."

"If she were in her right mind, Pallas, maybe. But that drug has made her go bugshit crazy."

They arrived at the park. An electrical crew worked on a sub station two blocks away, otherwise the area was deserted. The hill where Doodad and Clever Jack had imprisoned Peter still had a jagged hole in the side, reminding Peter forcefully of the movie Alien.

"They're not here," Pallas said.

"Give them a little time." Keepsie looked into the sky.

"We've given them three hours. I'm going up for a look, then we're going." Pallas bent her mighty legs and leapt away from them, soaring upward and landing on the apartment building next to Keepsie's, which seemed damaged by fire but still there. Colette's car stuck out of her living room. Her power did not keep her possessions from being destroyed, sadly enough.

"Show off."

"Ian, I told you—" Peter began.

"Hey, she's not here to hear me!"

"Super hearing, you dolt," Peter said through clenched teeth.

Ian muttered something, but Peter didn't pursue.

Pallas jumped off the building, five stories down, and landed lightly next to them, smiling slightly at Ian.

"I see nothing. Are you ready to give yourselves up?"

Keepsie bit her bottom lip. She looked at Peter. One eyebrow rose slightly. Peter shook his head barely. Not yet.

"I guess so. Just do me a favor and watch Timson, all right?" Keepsie said.

"Good. Let's go," Pallas said, and started to walk back toward the Academy.

Peter still felt the excitement in him. Something behind him *pulled*. He forgot the plan to have Keepsie freeze Pallas in front of the bar and then make their getaway. He wanted to return to the park.

"Wait. Go back. Just one second."

Pallas began to protest, but the look on his face convinced her. They turned around.

Pallas sniffed once and paled. "Oh no—" she said, and leapt away from them, toward the park.

"So is that super-leaping or flying?" Ian asked.

"Shut up, Ian. Let's go," Keepsie said, and ran.

#

Pallas hadn't gone far. She had stopped outside the park and battled the fires that raged in the trees—fires that hadn't been there a moment before.

"Looks like the work of an elemental," Keepsie said conversationally as they caught up with her.

"I thought you were wrong," Pallas said, taking a deep breath and smothering another blaze.

Peter put his hand on her strong shoulder and pointed. Clever Jack held the portal open again.

"He's alone! She's not here." Pallas's voice was full of denial.

"Look at the trees, Pallas! Timson has lost her mind," Peter said. "Nothing she does is rational now. She kept her wits to try to hide her intentions from you, but now she has all the power she wants—and it looks like Clever Jack will welcome her strength. He has little choice."

He leaned in and kissed Keepsie's earlobe. "Good guess."

Instead of a bunch of smaller demons, only one seemed to be forcing itself through this time. Jack grasped the portal and attempted to stretch it farther apart as one tentacle, longer than a bus and just as thick, waved lazily in the air, groping.

"Holy fuck, what's on the other end of that?" Ian asked.

"Timson's not with them," Pallas repeated.

"The hell she's not," Peter said. He knew why he had been so restless. Timson was there; she was just in her gaseous form. He launched himself forward and ran into the park.

Keepsie yelled something after him, and he heard a whoosh as Pallas jumped over him. Was she trying to stop him?

No. She launched herself at the tentacle and wrestled with it. It wrapped itself around her, shocked into action at last. She struggled with it, punching it in its suckers. Peter refused to allow the struggle to distract him—Pallas had accepted him as an ally in this battle, and he wasn't going to let her down.

She was here. He knew it. He could feel her. He could *smell* her. His head still buzzed from where she had crawled around in there like a bee in a hive. He had no chance in catching her until she solidified, though, but he couldn't lose her again. Not until he got back what she had taken.

His logical mind paused a moment to wonder how he was going to get her to give it back, but he figured he would get to that later.

"Keepsie! Do it!" he yelled. Then Timson appeared in front of him, flames dripping from her mouth like she had been drinking from a volcano. The madness of her eyes frightened him more than her elemental power, and he took a step back.

She punched him with surprising strength, but the burn hurt worse than the hit. He stumbled and fell on the soft ground.

Ghostheart appeared from inside Clever Jack's lair, yelling something. She froze. Keepsie had started her work.

Timson kicked him, igniting his sweatshirt and cracking a rib. He rolled away from her, smothering the flames and gasping to regain his breath. She kicked him again and he curled into a ball, trying to yell for help, but not sure if he got anything out. Had Keepsie reached them? Was she helping Pallas instead of him? Was she aware that Timson had just breathed in a great intake of air and aiming her lips at him?

The flames gushed from her mouth. Peter covered his head with his hands and waited for the end.

39

Keepsie hadn't expected Peter to run headlong into a fight against heroes and a giant tentacle thing. She stared as he and Pallas charged as if they had been partners in crime fighting for years. The tentacle she put out of her mind; that was someone with super strength's problem.

Of course, Tomas ran in to join Pallas, and that wasn't good.

She looked at Ian. He shrugged. "Peter'll be really pissed if I try to help him. I'll hang here and guard you."

"I think he'd rather be covered in shit than dead, Ian."

"Dude, do you even know Peter?"

Keepsie choked out a laugh and tried to focus on the fight. Peter ran around the park, clearly looking for something. "What is he doing?"

"Shit, Keepsie, there's Samantha. She'll try to control that thing. Get her." Ian pointed, his face scrawled with dislike.

Keepsie thought of all of the food she had eaten in her bar, and Ghostheart froze in place.

The tentacle continued to squirm and inch further into their world. Pallas still struggled in its grip, and Tomas ran around, punching it and running out of the way as his strength failed.

Ian shouted and ran into the park. Keepsie would have followed except that something hit her in the back of the head. Black blossoms appeared in her vision as she tried to struggle to her feet.

But Clever Jack perched on top of her, pressing her face into the dirt. She hadn't even seen him leave his spot at the portal. Bad luck, she figured.

"Where is she, bitch?" Clever Jack screamed.

Keepsie couldn't answer even if she had wanted to. Clever Jack pushed her face into the ground, splitting her lips and breaking her nose. She grunted and struggled against him.

"Oh, you will pay, you will pay for that and for Light of Mornings and for everything you've done. You've ruined it all. I can't kill you but I can make you hurt. I can make you hurt a lot. And there's nothing you can do to me." He punched her in the kidney and she grunted again.

Clever Jack. Clever Jack. Charming Clever Jack. Clever Jack. Always getting out of scrapes, never getting caught, always so very careful. She tried to think of everything Clever Jack had done to them, but his attacks made it impossible to think clearly for even a moment.

He grabbed her shirt collar and yanked back violently. The tag ripped and separated from the shirt.

One tiny rip was all it took. She finally held him.

She rolled away from him, panting, blood pouring from her mouth and nose. "Hell."

Even beyond the pain and blood in her nose, Keepsie realized a new foulness clouded the air. What had Ian done? She stumbled upstairs to follow him.

Peter lay on the steps, singed but otherwise seeming fine. Ian panted, filth covering his hands. Powerful fumes burned Keepsie's eyes and she coughed.

"Holy shit, are you OK?" Ian asked.

Keepsie nodded. "Got Clever Jack and Samantha. What happened?"

"Timson was here. She tried to fry him. I put out the fire in time, but she disappeared."

Keepsie tried to think beyond the pain on her face. She walked forward and checked on Peter.

At her touch, he uncurled and looked up at her, eyes wide. "So who won your fight?"

She managed to smile. "I did, I think, but I look at lot worse than he does. Are you all right?"

"I'm covered in excrement and burned in several places. Never been better." He accepted her hand up and they embraced briefly. "I think my nosebleed stopped, though." One of his sleeves dangled, nearly burnt off. He pulled it free and handed it to her.

"This was one of my favorite sweatshirts," she said ruefully.

"Well, it's been well-loved lately."

Ian rolled up his filthy sleeves. "Guys, we need to help them out. I think our team is losing."

Pallas still lay in the clutches of the tentacle, struggling with it. She looked very small. Tomas lay on the ground, motionless.

Ian ran forward. "Oh man, it must have hit him when he wasn't so strong."

"Ian, look out!" Peter yelled, but the tentacle caught Ian in a backswing, knocking him through the air.

Keepsie and Peter ran forward, Keepsie knowing that they couldn't reach him in time to catch him or break his inevitable fall into the still-flaming trees. He seemed to sail forever, and she squeezed her eyes shut. Then Keepsie remembered all the food and beer he'd taken since the siege began in the bar. It was all hers. He had taken her food, her drink, her trust, her friendship, her hospitality, her—

"Keepsie?" Peter's voice was soft.

She cracked her eyes open. Ian lay at the edge of the trees like a toppled statue. He was frozen in a comical position, arms flailing, eyes bugging out, looking as if he was trying to swim through the woods. He seemed unharmed, and Keepsie let out a sobbing sigh of relief.

"What are we going to do about that?" Peter asked, pointing to the tentacle. It flexed and released, flexed and released, and Pallas looked to be getting weaker.

"Where are all the other heroes?" Keepsie asked.

"Timson must have sent them away so they couldn't stop her. Anyway, are there any left?"

"Peter, she's batshit. She probably doesn't remember why she's summoning the demons, just that she needs to control the city. To control the city, she has to have them scared. Dr. Timson is the one-woman mafia of Seventh City."

"Fine, but she's gone and everyone else is incapacitated. What can we do?"

Keepsie remembered Ian, and he ran up to them soon after she released him. "Dude, that was fast thinking. I owe you, Keepsie."

"What are we going to do about that?" Keepsie pointed to the tentacle, still waving.

"Well. I could shoot it."

Keepsie stared at him.

"It's all we have," Peter said.

"Fine. Go. I can't smell anything anyway," Keepsie said through the torn fabric held against her throbbing face.

Ian raised his fists again and pointed them at the tentacle.

"No, go for the portal," Keepsie said, pointing his upper body to the portal.

"You got it, boss." Ian shot his fetid stream at the portal, covering the tentacle.

The tentacle jerked and dropped Pallas. It started questing around. Pallas lay still.

"It's interesting," Ian said. "No one likes to be covered in shit. Even hell demons from another dimension. And the Academy said I wasn't worthy. Ha!" He inched forward to get a better angle at the portal, shit streaming from his hands at pressures to rival a fire hose.

"Ian, be careful," Keepsie warned as the tentacle grew near. Ian was still laughing, coating the length of the tentacle before pointing it again at the portal. Once he hit the tip of it, it jerked again and wrapped around him with frightening speed. He uttered a surprised squawk, and then the tentacle squeezed. He screamed.

The air temperature increased noticeably as a golden beam shot through the air and bore a hole through the tentacle. Light of Mornings stood at the edge of the park, fully awake. She grinned and ran up to them.

Instead of dropping Ian, the tentacle squeezed again and withdrew, dragging Ian with it.

"Ian!" Keepsie ran forward and stopped at the portal. Peter caught up with her.

The world through the portal nauseated her. The landscape moved and writhed. The creature that held Ian was gargantuan, making Ian look like a doll in its clutches. Part octopus, part quadruped, the tentacles reached from its chest out closer to their world. The one that held Ian drew it closer to an orifice that looked to be a mouth. He screamed.

"Close it! Close the portal!" he cried.

"No!" Keepsie took a step into the portal. The searing wind of the other world baked her bare ankle. Peter pulled her back.

"We have to close it. Look," he pointed. More creatures ambled closer, their tentacles reaching towards Keepsie and Peter.

Ian struggled against the beast that the most powerful hero in the city couldn't defeat, and it brought him closer.

"He's my friend," Keepsie said through clenched teeth.

The beast froze. The others paused and stared at it. One howled something, and began lumbering towards Keepsie in the portal.

Ian slithered out of the tentacle's grasp and looked at them. He had something like an eighth of a mile to travel, and the large monstrous creatures could cover the ground more quickly.

"Close it!" he yelled, waving his arms. "I'll be OK! Close it!"

"I've got him!" Light of Mornings flew past Keepsie and Peter into the portal.

"Oh no," Keepsie said. Some of the creatures swiped at the girl, and she eradicated them easily. Others continued to run toward the portal.

Peter pulled Keepsie back and she fell to the ground, sobbing. She didn't see him close the portal, only heard a whoosh of air.

40

Keepsie had remembered the bar in much worse shape than it turned out to be. But aside from the broken glass in the front room, the several dishes from the meals they had eaten, and the broken pint glasses in the kitchen, the cleanup was remarkably similar to cleaning up after a rowdy Saturday night.

Pallas had helped out with smoothing some of the hairier questions out, from the vigilante groups to the missing toe on the frozen body in her bar. The meeting with Pallas had gone better than she had hoped, as everything she had promised had been true. Timson had been trying to work with a handful of the heroes to make the Academy stronger in the city, to thus increase tax revenue. Her hero cronies as well as Clever Jack and Doodad were in a hero jail in New York awaiting trial. Ghostheart and Timson were still missing, and The Crane was under house arrest under Pallas, pardoned because of his full agreement to testify against Timson.

A main issue of contention was Light of Mornings. Since she had caused so much damage after waking up, Pallas was ready to condemn, but Keepsie tried to explain how Clever Jack manipulated her. Without the actual accused, Pallas decided to reserve judgment until she sent some heroes to the demon dimension to see if Ian and Light of Mornings survived.

Pallas and The Crane and the younger teens of the Academy worked out of a warehouse as they fought for revenue to rebuild. Keepsie had offered some of her friends' unique talents to help clean up and rebuild the Academy, and Pallas offered their hero with healing powers to patch up Keepsie's friends. Their meetings had been frequent; some of them tense, some friendly.

Keepsie's Bar stayed closed for a week, mourning Ian and Alex. They held a wake the next Saturday night.

Keepsie's black dress was modest, but she covered it with her leather jacket.

When Peter had seen her, he frowned. She scowled at him. "Do you really think Ian wants me to be dowdy at his wake?"

"I see your point," he said. He bent to kiss her.

He had told her of his loss a couple of nights before. They had been in bed, exploring each other as new lovers do, when she asked him why their intimate contact wasn't shutting him down. He admitted what had happened to him. She comforted him, trying to focus on the positive, but it had felt hollow. The look in his eyes when he told her hurt her, and she didn't know how to fix that hurt.

He wore a dark suit. His tie, however, was a Hawaiian print. She tugged at it and grinned. "Yeah. You're all proper."

Colette had outdone herself for the wake. She and Keepsie had had a very long argument about the food for the wake, and finally capitulated when Colette had pulled the superpower card. Keepsie couldn't argue with Colette's superpower.

So when Colette served demon canapés, demon soup, and demon pie during the wake, everyone remarked on how delicious it was. Peter knew, and Keepsie noticed how he kept to the veggie platter and punch bowl.

Everyone wore something brightly colored along with their black clothing, and the brightest of all was Michelle. Dressed in a bright red dress, she chatted and laughed at the wake with Barry and Tomas. Although she easily swapped stories with them, she refused to speak of him as if he were dead. She had accepted Ian's disappearance with a stoic determination that Keepsie feared was denial.

"Was he alive when you saw him?"

"Yes, but—"

"And did you tell him he was your friend, your friend, before the portal went down?"

"Yes, but—"

"And Pallas is working to understand how to work it?"

"Yes, but—"

"And if she can't, Doodad is still alive to work on another one?"

"Yes, but—"

"And the most powerful human alive is in there with him, and she's on our side?"

"Well, yes—"

"Then he'll be back."

She would talk no more about it.

Keepsie was chatting with Pallas about the new direction of the Academy when Peter came up to talk to her.

"I appreciate the offer to enroll us, but I don't think we're ready. There's too much bitterness, I'm sorry to say."

Pallas nodded. "The offer remains. Please let your friends know."

"Keepsie, may I interrupt?"

Keepsie smiled at Pallas and followed Peter to an unoccupied corner of the bar.

"This is hard for me, Keepsie," he began.

"Shit. You're dumping me," Keepsie blurted, her stomach sinking.

His put an arm around her. "No, not at all. Keepsie, I've been in love with you for longer than even I know. I could no more leave you than step out of my own skin."

"Then what?"

"Well. I have to leave you."

She blinked at him.

"Timson is still at large. No one can find her except me, and I know she's not in Seventh City anymore. She's mad, volatile, harmful, and, on a selfish note, she may have the answer to why my powers are gone. She took them, after all."

Keepsie swallowed. "So, where are you going?"

"Wherever my nose takes me. I can sense her pretty well, it's all I can sense now."

"When are you coming back?"

"I… don't know that part. I am sorry. But I will be back. I promise."

He took her hand and kissed it. She clung to his hand for a moment, then withdrew it. "Leave tonight. The sooner you leave, the sooner you'll be back." She turned her back on him, gritting her teeth against the tears that sprang to her eyes, and bumped into someone rather unexpected.

"Ah, Mr. Mayor, I didn't expect to see you here," she said, wiping her eyes. Pallas stood at Mayor Bell's elbow, her creased face in an unfamiliar smile.

"Ms. Branson, I wanted to come and offer my condolences about the loss of two heroes who helped the city during a very dark time," Mayor Bell said. He was a tall, African American man with gray eyes and a politician's smile. Keepsie was suddenly very aware of her splinted nose.

"Yes, they did a lot for us. Alex kept us alive, and Ian got rid of that thing."

Mayor Bell frowned and took her hand, half-intimately, half-shaking. "I understand you were close to both men. I am so sorry for your loss. We are giving both of them posthumous medals in their honor, to be granted in a ceremony two weeks from tomorrow. Will you honor us by attending?"

"Oh, uh, sure, I'd be glad to. They deserve some recognition."

"I wanted to include you in the ceremony, but Pallas has recommended I do this sooner than later. You will be honored as well, but I wanted to give you this now."

He handed her a leather case about as long as her forearm.

She clicked the case open and saw a large, brass key sitting in a velvet bed. "To Keepsie Branson," it said along the length. "For service to Seventh City."

"The key to the city. Huh." Keepsie hefted it into her hands and then turned and grinned at the mayor.

"My city. Mayor Bell, I accept. Thank you."

EPILOGUE

"Thanks for seeing me on short notice."

"What's on your mind, Keepsie?"

"I've been doing a lot of thinking lately. So much has changed."

"Ian and Peter are gone, most of Seventh City's heroes are gone and you're a hero now—in reality if not in name. Saying a lot has changed is an understatement."

"I know that, Pallas, but I mean within me. The drugs changed me. It terrifies me."

"Do you want training?"

"No. I don't know. Maybe. Oh come on, don't look at me like that."

"Training would give you control and teach you ethics."

"Like it did Heretic and Tattoo Devil and White Lightning?"

"That was uncalled for."

"I'm sorry. It's just, my powers scare me. I don't want to be associated with the Academy, even now. Not yet. But I don't want to scare myself."

"Every hero goes through this. It's frightening knowing you can kill someone with a thought or break into a house by walking through walls or stop time. Or cripple everyone who breathes your air. Think about the training."

"That's twice you've called me a hero."

"It fits."

"I still won't join."

"I know."

"See you tonight at the bar?"

"You couldn't keep me away."

"Actually, I could. Quite easily."

Pause.

"You know, Pallas, maybe I will take some training. Off the books."

"I thought you might."

ABOUT THE AUTHOR

Mur Lafferty is a podcaster and writer. She has produced award-winning audio content to over 20,000 listeners since 2004, and has written for over 15 RPGs. Her work has appeared in Suicide Girls, Knights of the Dinner Table magazine, PC Gamer, Computer Games, Scrye, and SciFi magazine. Her short fiction has appeared in Hub, Escape Pod, and Scrybe. She is the co-author of the Amazon.com 2006 #3 Research Book, *Tricks of the Podcasting Masters*. She lives in Durham, NC with her husband and daughter.

ACKNOWLEDGMENTS

This book would not exist if not for the incredible support of J.C. Hutchins, Matt Wallace, Angi Shearstone, Evan Goer, Scott Sigler, Cory Doctorow, James Patrick Kelly, Teresa Nielsen Hayden, Matthew Wayne Selznick, Joe Magid, Richard Dansky, and my parents, Will Lafferty and Donna Smith. You've all taught me that writing is not something we do in a vacuum and that I'm never alone.

This book was originally released via audio and PDF podcast at playingforkeepsnovel.com. That podcast could not have been if not for the hard work of producer Jamie Jordan, artist Jared Axelrod, photographer J.R. Blackwell, graphic designer J.C. Hutchins, web designer Podcasting's Rich Sigfrit, PDF layout ninja Paul Fischer, artist Natalie Metzger, and podcaster Chris Miller. The original theme song "Playing For Keeps" was written and performed by Beatnik Turtle and is available at thesongoftheday.com.

BRAVE MEN RUN

April 18, 1985—Into a world already wound tight with the desperate tensions of the Cold War comes Dr. William Donner with a startling declaration: superhumans exist, they demand autonomy, and he has the reality-bending power to enforce their status. The traditional balance of power is thrown askew by the addition of not one super powered human, but *six thousand.*

Before the Donner Declaration, high school sophomore Nate Charters was just an outsider and self-proclaimed freak. His unusual appearance, hair-trigger reflexes, and overactive metabolism should have made him something special, but his differences and low self-esteem have long since marked him as a target for the jocks and popular kids.

Now, just as his unique nature brings him the attention of a self-assured older girl, Nate must find his place in the world. Why is he the way he is? Where did he come from? Is he part of a remarkable, powerful new minority... or just a misfit among misfits?

Nate must discover the answers to these questions quickly, because others want the truth, and they're closing in...

A MODERN SUPERHERO TALE BY
MATHEW WAYNE SELZNICK

THE BEST FICTION FROM ALL GENRES...

WWW.SWARMPRESS.COM

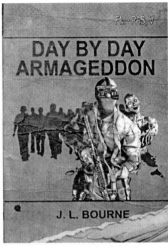
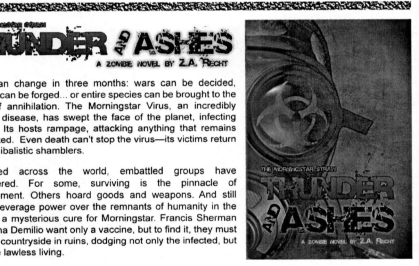

Printed in the United States
203613BV00003B/43-69/P

9 781934 861165